THE SONG OF
MIDDLE-EARTH

THE SONG OF
MIDDLE-EARTH

*J.R.R. Tolkien's Themes, Symbols
and Myths*

D A V I D   H A R V E Y

HarperCollins*Publishers*

HarperCollins*Publishers*
1 London Bridge Street,
London SE1 9GF
www.tolkien.co.uk

This paperback edition 2016
3

First published in Great Britain by George Allen & Unwin 1985

ISBN 978 0 00 818481 0

Set in OpenType Adobe Garamond Pro

Printed and bound in Great Britain by Clays Ltd, St Ives plc

To my Father and my Wife
with love and thanks

CONTENTS

PREFACE

When I was approached about re-releasing *The Song of Middle-earth* I wondered if it would present an opportunity, if not to rewrite the text, to revise it in light of the extraordinary amount of material that has been published since 1985 under the collective title of *The History of Middle-earth*.

The Song was written in 1985 and shortly after the manuscript was finished *The Book of Lost Tales I* was published. I referred to it in the Foreword to the 1985 printing. I observed that the themes that I discussed in *The Song* were present and what was different was the tale-telling. As further volumes in *The History of Middle-earth* were published the enormous scope of Tolkien's creation became apparent. What those volumes presented was the way in which the various tales and deep background that Tolkien developed was published in *The Hobbit*, *The Lord of the Rings* and, posthumously, *The Silmarillion*.

Had I decided to recast *The Song* it would have turned out to be substantively the same book but with a vast array of cross references to the various volumes in *The History* which would interrupt and distract from the narrative of the various arguments that I had developed. Certainly, such an approach would appeal to a completist – and I confess that I am such – but it would produce an book of unwieldy size and unnecessary complexity. Those analytical studies have been produced in the many compendia that have been published about Tolkien's work and I single out for mention the excellent and extraordinary work of Wayne Hammond and Christina Scull – *The J.R.R. Tolkien Companion and Guide* in two volumes: the *Chronology* and *Reader's Guide*.

In addition there has been an extraordinary amount of other scholarship that has been published since 1985, and a proper recasting of *The Song* would necessarily require a consideration of these subsequent works. The result would be a completely different work from that which is before you.

My conclusion was to let the text stand as it was originally written. Its approach was a thematic one and Tolkien's texts – *The Hobbit, The Lord of the Rings, The Silmarillion* – formed a 'canon'. *Unfinished Tales* shed a little extra light on the nature of the creation and some different tale-telling. External published sources such as Tolkien's *Letters* and Humphrey Carpenter's *Biography* provided some added assistance. But I thought that the best approach was to use the published canon – a discrete set of material that provided a defined compass for an examination not so much of tale-telling – to which I will return – but of the way in which the various themes within a mythos were developed and realised.

I have noted above that *The History* provides us with an insight into the creative process. It is also an example of the way in which story-telling develops. Many mythological structures derive from oral tale-telling. What survives as Homer's *Iliad* and *Odyssey* was originally an oral tale with frequent use of mnemonic structures to assist the tale teller. Inevitably there are shifts in the tale as the story is taken up and recounted by other tale tellers. The fundamental tale may remain the same in terms of major plot development and the themes that underlie it. But the telling of the tale itself may shift either subtly or significantly. In some respects *The History* reflects this tale-telling method and the way in which shifts may occur. What is interesting is that the one author has fulfilled the role of different tale tellers.

There are those who will say, correctly, that Tolkien's creative style and his desire for perfection is the reason why we have alternative versions of the same story. I cannot dispute that. But I suggest that in the same sense that there are variations on the stories that comprise a mythos[1] so Tolkien's retellings can be viewed in the same light. But even with a variety of story-telling approaches, the essential thematic elements are still present. These do not change substantively.

For these reasons I have decided to let the original text speak for itself, using the canon as the essential sources for Tolkien's subcreation, although at the same time acknowledging that variations of some of the stories appear elsewhere.

This book was first published in 1985 and has been out of print for some time. I have had enquiries from a number of readers who had tried to locate it and found the prices for secondhand copies to be rather high. Given that over 30 years have elapsed since the first publication, there is a new generation of readers for whom this analysis may present a refreshing and informative study of Tolkien's creation, and it is a joy for me that the book is finally available again at a more affordable price for them to enjoy.

FOREWORD

This book was written for two reasons: curiosity and dissatisfaction.

The curiosity has been present for the last twenty-three years, and began when I first read *The Hobbit* and *The Lord of the Rings*. The same question that was raised then continued as, each year, I read and re-read the books. I felt that there was something greater, more significant, more meaningful than was immediately apparent upon the printed page. A cause of the curiosity, of course, lay in the method of Tolkien's writing. He had an incredible depth to his tale, a great sense of time and a deep and rich historical background. The action in *The Lord of the Rings*, although set in a mythical past, takes place at the end of the historical cycle. Preceding the story is a vast tapestry of history, extending over many thousands of years, and to which frequent allusions are made, and, of course, the characters are inextricably a part of that tapestry. The question that flows from this is, 'What are the details of this historical background?'

My attempts to answer this were hampered by the lack of detail and clues that appeared in the Appendices to *The Lord of the Rings* which gave tantalising glimpses only of fragments of the overall design. A part of the problem was that the Appendices to the first edition did not contain many of the clues that Tolkien included in the revised Appendices to the second edition, and it was only when I came to this latter publication that I perceived the first hints of the existence of *The Silmarillion*.

In 1977 *The Silmarillion* was published and for me it was a matter of great expectation. But the book raised even more questions whilst at the same time it answered many others. The answers began to filter through from other sources. Humphrey Carpenter's *Biography*, with its hints of *The Book of Lost Tales*, *Unfinished Tales* itself, and Tolkien's *Letters* began to provide the wind that dispersed the clouds from the face of the sun of understanding. It was rapidly becoming clear that Tolkien had not only woven a tapestry of history, but had also created a mythology. But for what purpose, how successfully, and with what result? It was after my studies for the New Zealand and International Mastermind shows that I determined, once and for all, to try to satisfy my curiosity and answer the questions that had plagued me for so long.

I have also mentioned dissatisfaction. My dissatisfaction is with much of the published literature about Tolkien's Middle-earth. With the exception of Carpenter and Shippey, most of the writers and commentators seemed to have missed a vital point. I did not think that Tolkien's work was merely derivative – that he had examined other mythologies and extracted tales, elements and themes and plopped them into his creation. With great respect to the authors who have followed such a course, it is a simplistic one and unflattering to the creator. Nor did I think that mere critical comparisons with the earlier greats of English and European literature were wholly productive. There was something deeper and more meaningful to Middle-earth than that.

I decided to eschew the derivative approach and avoid, as much as I could, comparisons with other works and examine and analyse the Middle-earth works as they stood – alone. And the obvious starting point, and one which has received scant examination in the earlier literature, was myth. Tolkien had left for me, and for others, an abundance of clues – that he was creating a Mythology for England – and I began my examination from the point of view of myth and mythology. Rather than examine the works as derivative from other mythologies, it became clear that the approach should be thematic – study the themes that are common to most, if not all, mythologies and ascertain what elements are present in Tolkien's work. As this book shows, the elements are satisfied.

The starting point must be *The Silmarillion*, a difficult book to read and with which to come to terms. But it is essential to an understanding of the creation and development of the Tolkien cosmos, as well as being a history of the Elves in Middle-earth, and it establishes the framework within which is set the Third Age as portrayed in *The Hobbit* and *The Lord of the Rings*. Yet *The Silmarillion* gives hints of other writings and accounts that deal with the Matter of Middle-earth. Some of these accounts are collected in *Unfinished Tales,* and in this volume we find more detail of the acts of Tuor and of Túrin, a background to the realm of Númenor, the Tale of Aldarion and Erendis, and much information about the Istari, the *palantíri* and the early history of the Third Age. For one interested in the stories, *Unfinished Tales* is essential. For the aficionado it provides a penetrating insight into the manner in which Tolkien worked.

The publication of *The Book of Lost Tales I*, the first volume of an extended 'History of Middle-earth', came shortly after the completion of this manuscript, and whilst it was being prepared for publication. *The Book of Lost Tales I* comprises a part of what may be called a 'proto-Silmarillion'. Most of the ingredients of the tales of *The Silmarillion* are present, although it is obvious, both from the Tales themselves, and the notes by Christopher Tolkien, the editor, that the Tales underwent many fundamental changes before they became *The Silmarillion*. But *Lost Tales I* is, in my opinion, almost as significant as *The Silmarillion* in that it indicates that it was always Tolkien's desire to create a Mythology for England. To give even greater credence to his intention (as if we needed more than the confessed desire of the writer), the manner of the telling of the Tales is significant. Eriol, a traveller from Middle-earth (or The Great Lands), comes to the Isle of Tol Eressëa and in his travels in that land comes to a dwelling which is, in some respects, a forerunner of Imladris in Middle-earth. During his sojourn he requests and is told tales of early Arda. Most of the tales are told in a common-room before a Tale-fire which is 'a magic fire, and greatly aids the teller in his tale'.[1] The tales are told by Lindo, Rúmil and Gilfanon, Elvish inhabitants of Tol Eressëa. Now the significance of the setting is that the Tales are recounted orally, and indeed are so written that they have a lyric and rhythmic quality when read aloud. Thus, in introducing his myth, Tolkien resorts to the oral or bardic tradition of story-telling, a feature of mythological tale-telling that predates Homer. Apart from the themes of the cosmological myths that comprise *Lost Tales I*, the whole cycle is distinctively myth oriented and is a clear indication of Tolkien's desire and intention. Christopher Tolkien gives us tantalising hints of things to come in later publications, but perhaps most interesting is the reference to Ælfwine of England. Ælfwine is another realisation of the character Eriol.

Later, his name changed to *Ælfwine* ('Elf-friend'), the mariner became an Englishman of the 'Anglo-Saxon period' of English history, who sailed west over sea to Tol Eressëa – he sailed from England out into the Atlantic Ocean; and from this later conception comes the very remarkable story of *Ælfwine of England*, which will be given at the end of the *Lost Tales*. But in the earliest conception he was not an Englishman of England: England in the sense of the land of the English did not yet exist; for the cardinal fact (made quite explicit in extant notes) of this conception is that *the Elvish Isle to which Eriol came was England* – that is to say, Tol Eressëa would become England, the land of the English, at the end of the story.[2]

Apart from the very method of tale-telling, the major themes that I have examined in *The Silmarillion* are present, as one would expect, in *Lost Tales*. Certainly some major changes in plot as well as changes in matters of detail have occurred. But this too is consistent with the development of myth. The tales of myth are never constant, and there is no one 'authorised version' (even the Bible has its Apocrypha). Rather, as I note later, the tale-tellers vary, refine and embellish. But the constant ingredient is the basic theme, and certainly the themes that Tolkien propounds and illustrates do not change.

The Silmarillion, Lost Tales and, to a degree, *Unfinished Tales* set the stage for the drama at the end of the Third Age recounted in *The Hobbit* and *The Lord of the Rings*. The mythology is complete and the questions that have been bedevilling readers for the last forty or fifty years may now finally be answered. But I believe that the main inspiration for the questions and the curiosity that readers have for Middle-earth lies deep in the realms of myth. Because the Middle-earth saga was conceived as a mythology the reader, perhaps only subconsciously, recognises myth as the sound of a far-distant trumpet echoing through the mind. Can the reader, perhaps, recognise within his own experience the desire for a subcreated realm of faerie that is as meaningful to him or her as were the great tales that rang through the rafters of the mead halls of early England and the Viking lands, or which were majestically and sonorously intoned by Homer sitting by the tale-fire on an evening in ancient Greece? Perhaps that 'desire for dragons' that we all have is now realised in Tolkien's created mythology for England.

ACKNOWLEDGEMENTS

A number of people have played a part in the realisation of this book. Some of them are not aware of the influence that they have given but it behoves me to take this opportunity to thank them, and acknowledge their support and assistance.

First, I must thank my late father for all things but, more especially as far as this book is concerned, for providing me with the necessary finance to purchase a trilogy of books by a then little-known Oxford don twenty-three years ago – after not a little boyish cajoling – and also for his encouragement, for as long as I can remember, in the study, understanding and love of the glories of English literature and the majesty of the English language. No greater legacy could he have left.

I must also thank former magistri David Canning, Dick Sibson and Den Burton, graduates of Oxford all. One of them, I know, sat at the feet of Tolkien. They provided some of the signposts for the road that I have travelled. Also I must thank Max Cryer for his patience and kind understanding and unflagging assistance at the time of trial by interrogation.

My gratitude must also go to Rayner Unwin, whose advice during the writing of this book and whose encouragement, comments and patience with a new traveller on the road to writing have been of invaluable assistance.

There are many writers whom I have never met who have written reams on the subject of myth and mythology. They helped to clarify the questions and provided leads to the answers. But of all the writers I must acknowledge the one whose works this book examines. J. R. R. Tolkien has provided me with reading enjoyment for the last twenty-three years and his work was the inspiration for this book.

Finally I must pay tribute to the limitless patience, co-operation and understanding of my wife who really must wonder what she started when she suggested I enter Mastermind in 1980. Her help in all phases of this work has been invaluable.

CHAPTER 1

A Question of Mythology

There is a feature common to all human cultures and that is the creation and use of myth. Cultures such as those of Central America and Polynesia did not develop the skill of writing, or the basic technology of the wheel. Yet both these cultures, and many others that lacked similar attributes, had as richly developed a mythology as the civilisations of the Mediterranean, India, Persia and north-western Europe.

C. S. Lewis said to Tolkien that 'myths are lies'. In one respect he may have been right. Certainly the cosmogonic myths cannot be anything but the hypotheses offered by primitive cultures to explain their own presence and purpose. But the development of myths and their use in societies both primitive and modern is of such importance that to dismiss them as the products of an overactive imagination is to denigrate man's curiosity and his quest for the answers to the eternal questions, 'Why am I here?'; 'Where am I going?'; 'Where did I come from?'; 'What lies at the end of the road?'

In our twentieth-century world myths and mythologies seem rather remote. In the technological age they represent a primitive past – a past that goes before recorded history. Myths to the historian are tales that are unsubstantiated by fact or evidence. Yet they may be based on fact. They may have their foundation in some actual historic occurrence that was not (or could not be) recorded. However, the passage of time and the raconteur's ability for embellishment have submerged or even obliterated what historical facts there may have been. It is valid to suppose that at some stage in history the Greeks came into conflict with a civilisation in Asia Minor that had its centre in Troy. The historical detail of that conflict is lost. What remains is Homer's account of it. The historical fact has become myth. The intervention of the deities explains the ebb and flow of the fortunes of the participants. Even so, Homer's account is a mere fragment of the total history of the conflict and really is the tale, as Robert Graves has entitled his retelling, of the anger of Achilles.

The mythologising of historical events, or the explanation of historical events in a mythological context has continued into the age of recorded history. Aeneas becomes the forefather of the Latin races who founded Rome. That there may have been a Romulus is possible. But his origins and activities that led to the founding of the Roman community on the banks of the Tiber have become the subject of myth. A similar situation takes place with the actions of folk heroes. As time passes the hero grows beyond his immediate community and becomes representative of an ethic or attribute of a nation or a country. St Patrick casts snakes out of Ireland. Robin Hood embodies an individualistic nobility of spirit that was not possessed by the nobility of the time, and also serves as the focus for the feelings of frustration on the part of a disenchanted community. Coeur de Lion becomes the embodiment of the noble warrior king to both Englishmen and Saracen and by the latter was named Melech-Ric and was used to frighten the young Islamic children of the day. Arthur and Barbarossa are the founders of nations, who will come again when the land is beset. Even such an historical figure as Richard III has achieved a mythical stature, mainly as a result of the writings of the Tudor apologists Sir Thomas More, Shakespeare and more recently A. L. Rowse, as the embodiment of evil in search of power, and the archetypal wicked uncle, although the latter symbol has been common through myth, folktale and history, to the displeasure, no doubt, of a multitude of benevolent uncles.

As with individuals, so do classes achieve a mythical stature. The cavalier image, no doubt fostered and exploited after the Restoration, has achieved the status of an archetype that would make it mythical for, as we shall see, myth deals with archetypes both in the actual sense and in the sense attributed to that word by Carl Jung. The 'working class' is a myth that had its origins in the revolutionary movements of the late eighteenth and early nineteenth centuries, and which reached its flowering in the works of Marx and Engels. It is a myth to which politicians pay more than lip service.

The European part of the North American culture is in the throes of developing its own mythology. As time progresses the historical figures of Daniel Boone and Davy Crockett become the embodiment of the pioneering spirit. The myth of the American frontier as a boundless new horizon was subtly used by President J. F. Kennedy in the catchphrase for his administration as 'The New Frontier'. Longfellow mythologised the Sioux Indian in *The Song of Hiawatha*, using the image of the noble savage, a rich Plains Indian mythology, and the metre of the Finnish *Kalevala* – a New World mythic tale told in Old World mythic form. Similarly the folk heroes of the American West have been raised to mythic proportions, embodying or having attributed to them traits that they never had or intended, and having attributed to them actions that embody or exemplify a philosophy from which, hopefully, later generations can learn. The historical proximity of such characters to the present means that some demythologising may also take place. Thus, the heroic bad guys such as Billy the Kid, Jesse James, Bonnie and Clyde, Ma Barker and, in Australia, Ned Kelly, are found, historically, to have feet of clay and black hearts. Yet they do not lose their mythic or heroic status, despite the assaults of historians from the groves of academe.

As the mythic heroes grew in the new lands, so a mythology developed about the new lands. The colonial ethic, the movement of peoples from the old homeland to the new, was historically motivated by economics and the need for supplies and wealth for the depleted home territories. As the colonial movement grew, colonies achieved strategic as well as economic significance. Yet the panacea which was used to encourage departure to the new lands was based largely upon the myths of 'ennoblement of inferior races' or 'spreading the benefits of civilisation' or the downright greed of 'there's gold in them thar hills'.

I do not dismiss such factors as poverty at home, bad crops or a general disenchantment with the old system. But the colonial movement used a form of myth which was factually based to a small degree, but which was inflated beyond reality to justify a wholesale system of landgrabbing.

The mythologising process continues as man searches for answers even today in the modern heroes. In a system that is so profoundly materialistic and historically based as Communism, mythical figures arise and some even suffer the fate of demythologisation. Large portraits of Marx and Lenin in Red Square on May Day attest to this fact as does the removal of Stalin's body from its Kremlin tomb. Even the life of Lenin has much in common with that of the classic hero of epic. It is no accident that Soviet historians have seized upon this in the process of virtually deifying the founder of the Russian Soviet State. Yet, even more surprisingly, another Communist leader lived a life in which, from time to time, he engaged in symbolic acts and who was a myth in his own lifetime. Who can forget the 1967 photographs of Mao Zedung having a recreational swim in the torrents of the Yellow River in the midst of the Cultural Revolution. Mao, like Lenin, is a modern epic hero, whose quest is the liberation of a nation from oppression. The mere words 'The Long March' to a student of Chinese history conjure up a symbol which has its parallels in the exile phase of the epic hero in mythic literature.

Because the process of mythologisation continues, it is wrong to relegate myths to the status of children's tales of the past which have their origins beyond the beginning of recorded history. The fact that the process does continue demonstrates the fact that myth is an important aspect in the continuing development of human society. So at this stage I should like to turn to what constitutes a myth, and how mythologies have developed. This is more an overview than a detailed study, and I intend to avoid an anthropological discussion of the signifi- cance of myth in primitive societies. Rather, what I intend to do is to view myths and mythologies as a factor in the development of societies and in a following chapter I shall look at how myths have become a part of the literature of societies.

There is no common definition of the word 'myth' or for the concept that it represents. Myth means one thing to an anthro- pologist, another to the psychologist and yet another to the thematologist. Curiously enough, within all the different views and opinions there is only slight divergence – a shift in empha- sis. Each of the various definitions of myth have a small seed of common agreement and because myth has been so important in the past, and as a motivator in the development of man and of his institutions and as an inspiration for, and indeed a part of, much of his literature, we should understand the basis and meaning of myth.

Myth in its basic form was a vehicle of religious symbolism. It was symbolic in its approach. It was not like ritual which is symbolic or imitative behaviour, or a symbolic object such as an icon or a reliquary. It is a tale told in a symbolic language. A child's definition of a parable is 'an earthly tale with a heavenly meaning'. A parable uses everyday objects and events to symbolise a greater and often divine truth. Not so myth, for frequently the myth uses divine beings either as participants in, or symbols for, a supposed truth. In the main, myths are tales concerning gods or superhuman beings and extraordinary events, or amazing circumstances, in a time that is quite different from normal human experience.

Robert Graves defines true myth as 'the reduction to narrative shorthand of ritual mime performed on public festivals, and in many cases recorded pictorially on temple walls, vases, seals, bowls, mirrors, chests, shields, tapestries, and the like'.[1] He then goes on to distinguish 'true' myth from what could otherwise be described as 'mythlike' accounts. He numbers these as:

1 Philosophical allegory, as in Hesiod's cosmogony.
2 'Aetiological' explanation of myths no longer understood as in Admetus's yoking of a lion and a boar to his chariot.
3 Satire or parody, as in Silenus's account of Atlantis.
4 Sentimental fable, as in the story of Narcissus and Echo.
5 Embroidered history, as in Arion's adventure with the dolphin.
6 Minstrel romance, as in the story of Cephalus and Procris.
7 Political propaganda, as in Theseus's Federalization of Attica.
8 Moral legend, as in the story of Eriphyle's necklace.
9 Humorous anecdote, as in the bedroom farce of Herakles, Omphale and Pan.

10 Theatrical melodrama, as in the story of Thestor and his daughters.
11 Heroic saga, as in the main argument of the *Iliad*.
12 Realistic fiction, as in Odysseus's visit to the Phaecians.

Thus, Graves defines true myth by elimination, and claims that it is a tale embodying a magical ritual, invoking fertility, peace, water, victory at war, long life to the ruler or death to the enemies. He also comments that genuine mythic elements may be found in the least promising sources. In studying mythic writing he says:

When making prose sense of a mythological or pseudo-mythological narrative, one should always pay careful attention to the names, tribal origins, and fates of the characters concerned; and then restore it to the form of dramatic ritual, whereupon its incidental elements will sometimes suggest an analogy with another myth which has been given a wholly different anecdotal twist, and shed light on both.[2]

Graves' study of the Greek myths is as vast as some of the epics that he studies. His examination is not merely of the myths, or their religious background, but their significance within the political and religious systems that existed in Europe before the advent of the Aryan invaders. Yet his sources are the great writers of the classical period: Homer, Herodotus, Plato, Aeschylus, Plutarch, Ovid, Virgil among many others. In effect Graves must go deep into the stories, past the peripheral words of the tales to discover their true meaning, context and significance.

Graves' approach to the Greek myths may lead him to one definition. His subject matter and his mythology are the best documented in existence. In settling upon his particular definition Graves is able to approach his subject from that point of view.

But despite the apparent sophistication of 'true' myth, and the exclusion of those other tales that may be regarded as 'mythic', Graves could not deny that all the mythic tales both of the 'true' or other forms of myth deal with liminal phenomena. They are tales told or conceived at a time or in a location that is apart from the here and now reality. 'Myths relate' by direct language or by symbols how a particular state of affairs came to be, or 'how one state of affairs became another'.[3]

Myths tell how the world came to be out of chaos, and how an unpeopled world became populated. They tell how those who were immortal forsook their immortality or departed the real world for some other region where immortals dwell. Myths tell or explain how the seasons came, the cause of rain, the origin of particular plants and how a united mankind in a Golden Age became a plurality of nations. There is, of course, religious significance in myth. The gods or supernatural beings of myth were the object of worship. If we see myth as being an explanation of natural phenomena under the control of supernatural beings, a myth then embodies a desire to control nature for the advantage of the tribe, group or society.

However, the field of myth and the purpose and the definition of myth has been a battleground for scholars for many years. Mircea Eliade says:

Myth narrates a sacred history; it relates an event that took place in primordial Time, the fabled time of the 'beginnings'. [It] tells how, through the deeds of Supernatural Beings, a reality came into existence, be it the whole of reality, the Cosmos, or only a fragment of reality – an island, a species of plant, a particular kind of human behavior, an institution. Myth, then, is always an account of a 'creation';

it relates how something was produced, began to be ... In short, myths describe the various and sometimes dramatic breakthroughs of the sacred (or the 'supernatural') into the World ... Furthermore, it is as a result of the intervention of Supernatural Beings that man himself is what he is today, a mortal, sexed, and cultural being.[4]

Eliade himself has been the subject of controversy and his views have been subjected to vitriolic academic denigration or paeans of critical praise. The difficulty is that 'there is no agreement as to what the myth and ritual pattern actually is'.[5] Each scholar who has established expertise in the field inevitably comes into conflict with others – Frankfort cannot tolerate the views of Frazer; Rose savagely attacks Graves and Graves gores Carl Jung. And if this academic carnage were not enough, there is no agreement as to the meaning of myth. Whalley describes it as a direct metaphysical statement beyond science; Watts believes that the purpose, source and end of myth is revelation; Wheelwright opines that myth is a set of depth meanings of perduring significance within a widely shared perspective; whereas Frazer says that they are mistaken explanations of phenomena founded on ignorance and misapprehension – they are always false for if they were true they would cease to be myths.[6]

Yet perhaps K. K. Ruthven, although not resolving the problem, casts sufficient light upon it to clarify the difficulty.

We have no direct experience of myth as such, but only of particular myths: and these, we discover, are obscure in origin, protean in form and ambiguous in meaning. Seemingly immune to rational explication, they nevertheless stimulate rational enquiry, which accounts for the diversity of conflicting explanations, none of which is ever comprehensive enough to explain myth away.[7]

Myth and legend have been often equated or compared. They have similarities and differences. Purists would say that myths and legends are quite distinct, because myths have as their purpose the explanation of things and the embodiment of a religious heritage, whereas legends are folk or national tales of the heroes or outstanding persons of a nation, state or tribe.

Legends are stories embedded in some elements of fact and history, however tenuous, concerning heroes and events. In my opinion legends and myths have a point of connection; like overlapping circles they have in common a part of each other, but also may occupy separate areas. Fancy and exaggeration may elevate the hero to a superhuman status; he may have a god for a parent or an ancestor and may, as a result, receive divine aid or suffer divine disfavour. In common with myths, legends were handed down through generations and enriched the lives of their listeners, and their values and lessons were a link with a heroic past and often divine wisdom. Legends became the heroic or traditional stories that were modified or embellished, but although there may have been divergence in the detail of the tales, such modifications were used for the purpose of explanation or clarification. Always the basic theme remained the same. Myths, legends and, to a degree, fable (which was obviously untrue and allegorical only, whereas myth and legend are represented as 'true') all underwent embellishment, addition or modification in the telling process. Yet both myth and legend arise from the nature of man and his desire to know the answers to the same universal questions, demanding to understand the same universal truths. Perhaps it is because myth is so elemental and basic that it is hard to settle upon a fundamental definition that will satisfy all. But if myth cannot be satisfactorily defined, its use, function and purpose merit a study so that we may understand myth within the context of the human experience.

Many views have been put forward to explain the function of myth. These seem to differ in the same way as the attempts at definition. Thus we have Frazer stating that the function of myth is a primitive fumbling attempt to explain the world of nature. According to Müller, myths are the production of poetical fantasy from prehistoric times, misunderstood by succeeding ages, and to Durkheim, a repository of allegorical instruction to shape the individual to his group. Carl Jung advocates the psycho-analytical view that myth is a group dream, symptomatic of archetypal urges within the depths of the human psyche, and the view of the Church or organised religion is that myth is God's revelation to His children.

Whatever differences there may be in the sophistication of the opinions, they all come down to the same function in the end – myths answer the awkward questions that seem to be asked, primarily by children, 'Who made the world?' to 'How will it end?' According to Graves, myths justify an existing social system and account for traditional rites and customs. Thus myth may explain why I am here and where I am going and in addition it may explain why things around me are as they appear to be.

The word 'myth' that we use derives from the Greek *mythos* which means 'word' or 'spoken word' or 'speech'. *Logos* originally had this meaning and the use of both words together meant, and still means, 'stories' although in Greek context such stories included the pantheon of Olympus, the activities of the heroes and the allegorical folktales of Aesop. Even to the Greeks, myths were the subject of debate. In the fifth century BC the word *mythos* is applied to those stories for which the truth is not vouched. Pindar considered *mythos* to be decked out with lies in excess of the true story.[8] Thucydides commented that some historians incorporated material into their work which got to the stage of being *mythodes*.[9] Plato described the *mythoi* as being essentially untrue although there may be elements of truth in them. Thus Thucydides doubts the truth of myths whereas Plato views them as a vehicle for imparting *a* truth, rather like a parable. Plato, in fact, draws upon mythological elements and characters to explain why certain skills may be peculiar to certain members of society, whilst a sense of justice is common to all. Indeed, at the end of the *Georgics*, *Phaedo* and the *Republic*, he recounts what happens to the soul after death. The reason for this account is to evidence a lesson and to lead the reader to a resultant behavioural practice. The story draws on traditional religious symbols and upon traditional religious beliefs. With the passage of time these traditional beliefs became lost, leaving the stories as symbolic vehicles. Thus there is a very strong body of opinion which holds that beneath the apparent meaning of a myth lies a deeper 'real' meaning.[10] Certainly myth has within it the richest of symbols and was the language of the ancient mystery religions with their highly symbolic rites. Indeed, it has been suggested that all the sacred books of the world are written in a symbolic language, and certainly an example must be The Revelation of St John the Divine.

For the anthropologist, myth has a different function or purpose. For example, the controversial Eliade defines 'fables' or 'tales' as false stories. Where myth is still alive, it is a *true* story. Tales dealing with the origin of the world, the adventures of a national hero or of the world of the shaman are true, whereas tales of a profane content, such as those of tricksters, deceivers and rogues, are false. However, caveats must be added to Eliade's theories because for Eliade a myth is always an origin story which functions for existential orientation in the widest sense. They 'transport men ontologically and experientially into the non-temporal "time" of the "beginnings". They originate as expressions of the desire to accomplish this orientation.'[11]

But can it be said that myths and mythologies have any relevance to the here and now of the twentieth century. What has become of myths in the modern world? What has taken the place that myth used to occupy in primitive societies? The world of myth is a continuous source of knowledge which is required for the crucial problems of man's existence – war and peace, life and death, good and evil, truth and falsehood. Myth at an individual level has never disappeared. It exists in dreams, fantasies and in the longings of every one of us. Even what we call myths at the present time are expressions of the experience of earlier times, and what we are willing to regard as myths current in our own time are, for the most part, what we recognise to be the survivals or revivals of those earlier myths. As I have already stated, Marxist Communism is strongly mythic, especially in its eschatological aspects. It has the part played by the just and good and their redemption (the dictatorship of the proletariat). The classless, stateless society is the Golden Age which pre- or post-dates recorded historical existence. Nazism, with its feet embedded in the Teutonic myth, had problems. The racial myth was limited in appeal, and there was the inevitable pessimism of the Teutonic myth, beset as it was with Ragnarok or Gotterdammerung and the total destruction of everything. Teutonic myth was a bad foundation for a political order. It holds out no hope, unlike Christianity. Rather, it faces a climax in total blood and destruction.

Carl Jung, in *Modern Man in Search of a Soul*, suggests that modern man is on a quest for a new myth, which alone could enable mankind to draw upon fresh spiritual resources and renew its creative powers since its profound break (speculated by Jung) with Christianity. If we accept Jung's theory of myth, dealing as it does with archetypes and the subconscious, the popularity of modern media efforts such as *Star Wars*, *Close Encounters of the Third Kind* and *E.T.* are explicable. They appeal to the subconscious desire for the hero, or the desire to touch the hand of a superior being.

Thus, the images and themes remain the same although the mystical or religious basis for myth seems to have faded. Man harks back to archetypes, expresses his primitive fears and seeks universal understanding. For these reasons, and many others, the popularity of the Middle-earth books by Tolkien is explicable. Tolkien set out to create a mythology for England. His was not a mystic mythology, based in symbolic religious rite. His mythology is founded upon the basic symbols which permeate all mythologies that have come to us as part of the heritage and literature of cultures. Tolkien also uses his mythology to explain a language and the development of the linguistic process. His ability to fasten upon the themes, the symbols, the archetypes and the structure of the mythic tales is not accidental but planned. Because he deals with elemental themes he appeals to man's search for universal truths. Such basic ingredients of myth are present in Tolkien's work. But it is appropriate, before we examine Tolkien's myth, that we look briefly at myth as a literary form, for it is upon this that Tolkien constructed the Middle-earth mythology.

CHAPTER 2

The Myth as Literature

Although myth began as a symbolic tale with a ritual or religious meaning, today myths are the stories of a culture, and as much importance is placed upon their position within the literature of a culture, as upon their significance within its religious or social development. The myth collectors or the myth writers were trying to preserve part of the culture or interpret the cultural tales within the field of literature. It is unlikely that the ancient collectors were as motivated as Sir George Grey who studied the mythology of the New Zealand Maori so that he could better understand their culture and thereby deal with them more effectively. At a later date Grey collected the myths together and had them published, but the primary function of the collection was for the purposes of a cultural understanding.

Voltaire was far more cynical, but was dealing with far less practical and essentially primitive people when he said that the study of myths was an occupation for blockheads. However, the transition point for myths into a literary heritage is impossible to place. I believe that history takes over. The myth becomes part of the history of a culture and becomes recorded with it and, in doing so, becomes a part of the literature of the culture. For

15

example, there *was* a siege of Troy. The myth aspect is the part that the gods played. In such a case there is an overlap between myth and history. The great expedition involves aspects of the sacred traditions. There can be no doubt that the Greeks did believe that the gods or supernatural forces were involved. It was only natural to mingle the acts of the gods with the acts of the heroes. Thus we have, in the *Iliad* and the *Odyssey*, a mingling of myth and legend for, in my opinion, pure 'legend' has a hero (be he folk or culture) as the main protagonist, whereas 'pure' myth is more religious in that it deals with the gods – the spiritual creative animi. Yet legend may have within it the raw symbolic power of myth that can lift it above folktale into allegory and indeed higher to the level of myth without the religious influence, although the hero of legend may be viewed with an almost religious awe.

Of course, the historians and writers may themselves create myths to embellish or background their history. Aristotle, for example, believed that myths as devised by Plato were a means of subordinating individuals to the devices of the State. In the sense that early societies were superstitious theocracies dominated by shamans, there is obvious validity in Aristotle's supposition. To cross the line from theocracy to autocracy is not a long step, and would involve a small amendment to the tale but not the theme. Machiavelli, although dealing with historical examples, generalises to such a degree that the ancient power struggles which he describes in *The Prince* in Books IV–VIII become almost mythic archetypes for the political philosophy that he advocates. He has 'mythologised' history as a background for his advice to his patron. *Der Mythus des 20 Jahrhunderts* by Rosenberg is the Nazi ideology incorporated into a mythic form. Communist writers, even today, use quasi-mythic symbols in their writing – 'the valiant soldiers, sailors and workers' or 'capitalist roaders' and 'running dogs'. This is not to say that modern political mythology is restricted to the east of the Iron Curtain. The United States system is full of mythic symbols, heroes and folk-legends. The War of Independence and those who were involved in it have achieved a mythic status. The 'temples' to the heroes of the Republic, the Lincoln and Jefferson Memorials, the Washington Monument and Mt Rushmore all take their places in the sacred political history alongside such relics as the Declaration of Independence, the Constitution and the Bill of Rights. J. Edgar Hoover and Senator Joseph McCarthy also made their contribution to the ritual political language with phrases such as 'Communist front', 'Communist dupe' and 'Are you or have you ever been a member . . . ?' Thus, the myth may be a background to a present history or even a part of it.

In the ancient and not so ancient historical writings, mythic backgrounds are used to place a contemporary leader or ruler into a mythic framework. Virgil links Augustus with Aeneas, the two being the embodiment of Roman virtues. Merovingian tradition traces the ancestry of the Franks to Francus the Trojan. Arthurian tradition claims a link with the Trojan Brutus, grandson of Aeneas who established the British in Albion. Henry VII used the Arthurian legend to give his tenuous hold on the throne more legitimacy. He referred to Monmouth's Chronicles, claiming that 'The Matter of Britain' was unfinished and that another Arthur (his son) would return to rid the land of her enemies. Henry, in tracing his ancestry to Cadwallader and thereby to the Trojan Brutus, claimed to be a 'British' king ruling Britain. Henry's granddaughter, Elizabeth I, was the subject of pseudo-myth in her own lifetime in Spenser's *Faerie Queen*, William Warner's *Albion England* and Drayton's *Heroical Epistles* all of which glamorise Gloriana. Shakespeare had cause to refer to 'mythic history' in *Macbeth*. In Act IV Scene 1, Macbeth's prophetic vision of Banquo as the ancestor of kings points in fact to the legitimacy of the claim of James I to the throne of Scotland and England. It was no accident that the play was written within a few years of James' accession and creates a form of mythic background to give legitimacy to a present state of affairs.

The use of myth over the last five centuries by European writers has taken on an aspect that was never contemplated by those who developed the proto-myths. Most of the names of the heathen gods are nothing but poetical or ritualistic names which have been allowed to assume a divine personality to an extent never intended by the original inventors. Of course, myth today operates on a number of different levels. Children especially appreciate myth which to them is a make-believe reality. The questions, 'Tell me about yourself when you were little?' or 'Is that what it was like in the old days?' demand a mythical response because the information and concepts contained in the answer are beyond the child's concept of reality. Similarly, a child's view of a parent is that of an all-wise, all-knowing person, capable of almost anything. Growing up and adolescence in particular is that time when the myth of the parent undergoes a gradual destruction, often to the resentment of the child.

Yet myth, dealing as it does with archetypes, still functions on different levels in society today. Advertising especially uses archetypes and attempts to create a situation which, if duplicated by the purchase, wearing, eating or whatever of a certain item, will have consequences beyond our normal existence or expectations. Similarly, archetypal animals have been used to portray qualities or characteristics of nations and Sir John Tenniel in *Punch* last century was particularly skilful in such archetypal creation. Many of the characters of modern television soap opera dramas and pot-boiler novels are archetypal. The doctor of the soap opera is the modern magician, all-wise, all-knowing, possessed of the power of healing – a twentieth-century Merlin. The aggressive stick-at-nothing businessmen who sweep all before them embody the image of the all-powerful hero Herakles and his successors in the American Dream, Daniel Boone, Paul Bunyan and others. Furthermore, we develop our own mystical mythic attitudes. Science can solve anything, yet the Saviour Science has within it the seeds of its own downfall in the form of the archetypal Mad Scientist whose ancestor is the tragic Victor Frankenstein. For modern audiences, Doctor Strangelove is an instantly recognisable figure.[1]

Mythic ritual still continues in the religious sense, and is present, alive and well in the form of the Eucharist, the act of recreation. But beyond this, myth provides a richness within the human experience that goes beyond the perpetuation of archetypes or rituals. Myth has had a profound influence in and on literature and the myth in literature is especially important in any discussion of the works of Tolkien.

The first point that must be made is that despite the proliferation of mythologies, tales and names of deities, the types, themes and subject matter of myths are basically the same. The common themes of myth or mythologies are the study of the comparative mythologist who examines the basis of myth, layer by layer, and in doing so finds patterns that express the nature of a society as a whole. An examination of and search for the themes of myth inevitably becomes a search for that which is essential to the human condition and what the symbols embodied in those themes represent. Claude Levi-Strauss has observed that throughout the world there is a great similarity in mythic themes. In such a study one is inevitably drawn to the archetypes of myth. By using the word 'archetype' I am not referring to the Jungian psycho-analytical term, but rather in its common sense – an original or model symbol which constantly recurs. Mythologies carry such models of absolute values or paradigms of human activity. The presence of archetypes assures Man that what he is about to do has already been done, and therefore can be done. The heroes – Jason, Herakles, Perseus, Odysseus, Sigurd, Beowulf, Gawain – all ventured beyond the seas into the wastes or vast mountains, to the Perilous Realm in a fabulous time. All that Man can do is follow their example. Their grandiose feats, which took place in a far-distant and glorious past, can be imitated if only to a degree, and the models of behaviour that are revealed in the heroes give meaning to our present endeavours.

The most common theme in mythology is that of The Creation – the cosmogonic origin myth. This myth sets the pattern for everything else in most traditions, and, at the time of origin, irreconcilable opposites arise. The myth explains beginnings from the existing situation. No one can explain in mythological terms how chaos (be it the vast and dark nature of the Greek myths, or the 'Spirit of God' moving upon the face of the waters in Genesis) began, or from whence it originated. Always is presupposed the existence of something *before*. Creation myths explain the creation of the circumstances leading up to a state of affairs from a particular point. In all cases the cosmos is a divine work and the archetype of every creative situation. In many mythologies it is common for a supreme god to create and leave the governing, ordering or completion of his creation to others. In Tierra del Fuego, although there is an omnipotent god or creative force, his creation is completed by the mythical ancestors. In the Slave Coast cosmogonic myth the sky-god Olorum leaves the completion of his creation to Obatala, a subsidiary deity.

Eliade considers that the myths of primitive societies are always concerned with creation. Myths, he says, always relate how something came into existence, or how a pattern of behaviour, an institution or a manner of working was established. By knowing the myth, one knows the origin of things and can control and manipulate them at will. One lives the myth and is grasped by a sacred exalting power of events recollected and re-enacted. Thus, within the context of Eliade's discussion, the creation myth is a blueprint for everything that follows and is essential for the survival of society. The myth contains vital and essential lore and knowledge.

At the other end of the time-scale is the eschatological myth – the myth of the ending. Of the non-Christian mythologies, the most dramatic eschatological myth, and the most bleak, is the Ragnarok of the Norse myths – or Gotterdamerung as it was called by Wagner. Ragnarok was presaged. All knew that it would come, and certain signs and events evidenced its advent. The year-long winter named Fimbulwinter, which was preceded by a hideous war, was one of the signs. Following Fimbulwinter are mighty earthquakes during which the wolf Fenrir, offspring of Loki the Trickster, breaks loose. A ship bearing the Undead from Hell and captained by Loki journeys to Asgard, the home of the gods. The forces of chaos in the form of fire and frost giants together with the World Serpent and Loki's minions descend upon Asgard. Ragnarok is announced to the Aesir and the heroes of Valhalla by the single crow of a cockerel. A mighty battle follows in which the forces of the Aesir and their enemies consume one another totally. All that remains is Yggdrasil, the World Ash. After Ragnarok, it is said, Midgard will rise again, more beautiful than before. The land, cleansed of distrust and evil, will be a fit place for the habitation of men and gods together. The ancestors of the second race of mankind emerge from the trunk of Yggdrasil. In a sense Ragnarok contains a germ of hope in that there will be a new and better world rising from the ashes of the old. Yet it places present existence within a context of doom and without hope. There will be no reward at Ragnarok – death, doom and destruction will come to all.

The Christian Apocalypse contained in Revelation offers more hope. The final battle is preceded by the advent of Anti-Christ which, as in the Norse myth, is the resurgence of chaos. The Anti-Christ or false Messiah is often portrayed as a dragon or a demon. His coming results in the total overthrow of social, moral and religious values. After the great battle near Jerusalem, Satan is thrown down and God comes among Men in the New Jerusalem. The overthrow of Evil is a characteristic of the Persian apocalyptic myth. After a world age of three thousand years Ormazd, also known as Ahurimazda, conquers Ahriman or The Lie.

A comparison of the Christian and Norse myths reveals presages; the coming of chaos, the rule of Evil followed by its ultimate overthrow. The Christian Apocalypse gives hope for those who believe in Christ for they shall rise again to be judged. The Earth will be renewed, but there will not be the all-engulfing disaster. The Christian end, terrifying as it may be, has overlays of symbolic language and a message of Hope. Common to both myths is the concept of rebirth and renewal. Even the gloom of Ragnarok cannot destroy the phoenix of the human spirit and its hope for better things.

Within the span of aeons between Creation and Apocalypse are many common themes that predate historical time. There is, for example, a common belief in a Golden Age preceding our present brutishness. In some mythologies such a period implies blessedness or wisdom. Golden Age men in the Greek myths were subjects of Cronos, father of Zeus. They lived without care or labour, eating acorns, wild fruit and honey, never ageing, laughing and dancing. Death to them was no more terrible than sleep. The Greeks tell of a silver race, divinely created, who ate bread, were non-violent and were destroyed by Zeus. Following them were the two races of bronze, one warlike and cruel who ate flesh and bread and were destroyed by a Black Death; the other noble and generous, the progeny of gods and mortals. Of this second race are the heroes of Thebes, the Argonauts and the Trojan War who dwell in Elysium. The last race are the men of iron, those of the present. Unworthy descendants of the second race of bronze men, we are cruel, unjust, immoral and treacherous. Graves explains the symbolism of metals in terms of cultist worship. Silver is the metal of the moon Goddess and the myth of the men of silver records the rituals of a matri-archal society. The first bronze men were the Hellenic invaders; the second bronze men were the Myceneans. The men of iron were the Dorians who bore iron weapons. The symbolism of metals in the degeneration of Man is also recorded by Daniel who refers to the kingdoms of gold, silver, bronze, iron and clay which precede the Everlasting Kingdom.

In many myths, the Golden Age and the Apocalyptic Renewal are linked. There is a cyclical pattern with a fresh beginning. The Paradise which was lost will, in the fullness of time, come again in a second or future perfection. Myths of origin too are linked to the end of the old and the beginning of the new. For Christ to die he must be born. While he is with us in the flesh, he symbol-ises the Golden Age. He must die that he may be reborn, return to the Father and come again for the Second Golden Age which follows the Apocalypse. Christ microcosmically embodies so many of the symbolic mythological themes that the attraction of Christianity, dealing as it does with such a powerful archetype, is not hard to understand.

The end of the First Golden Age occurs with a fall from Grace where man loses the perfection which he once enjoyed and descends to the here-and-now realities of existence – life, death, pain, hunger, envy, greed, lust, jealousy and the thousand and one trials of life. Symbolically, the tribulations of life as we know them are released or imposed by the deity following upon a departure from an established mode of conduct. In Greek mythology Pandora, the first woman, was sent by Zeus as a punishment to Prometheus and Epimetheus for stealing fire, and to man for receiving it, although the myth reveals that another punishment was also imposed upon Prometheus. Pandora was said to be endowed by the gods with beauty, persuasion and music. Epimetheus had within his house a box which Pandora, being curious, opened. From the box poured forth all the trials and tribulations of men. Only Hope remained. Another version of the tale is that Pandora had within her marriage chest all the blessings of the gods. These she allowed to escape with the exception of Hope.

Curiously enough, in the Judaeo-Christian mythology it is a woman who initiates the Fall from Grace and places before her man the choice of Good and Evil, although to be fair Evil itself did not emanate from the woman. The expulsion from Eden is indeed the Fall of Man. Yet this is not enough for he falls even further as a result of the first murder by Cain. This demonstrates the depth of the Fall and establishes murder, and especially family murder as the most heinous of crimes.

A further common theme in mythologies is that of the Flood or some similar form of natural catastrophe such as earthquake or conflagration. In the Judaeo-Christian myth the Flood and the reasons for it are still related to the Fall and the way in which Man behaves to his fellows and to God. Similarly, a catastrophe overtakes Sodom and Gomorrah because of sinful ways. Similar catastrophes are set out in the Sumerian epic of Gilgamesh and in the account of Atlantis by Plato, although no rationale of divine wrath is given for the demise of the Atlantean civilisation. Apart from warfare and kin-strife, nothing else seems to have caused Zeus to drown the world, leaving only Deucalion and his wife as survivors. But the catastrophe, although it may seem to be the end of the world to the participants, is not a final end. It is the end of one stage of the development of the human race and the beginning of another.

The flood or catastrophe opens the way to a recreation of the world and a regeneration of humanity.

The theme of the migration of peoples explains the diversity of the human race, yet presupposes not parallel developments but in fact one cradle within which mankind was nourished. This goes back, of course, to the concept of the Golden Age and the time when Man existed in close proximity to Heaven and communed with the gods directly or by way of some link with the home of the gods, such as a tree or a vine. The location of the tree is viewed as the centre of the world (as was the case with Yggdrasil the World Ash) and from this central point the diaspora took place. The wanderings of Abraham and the peoples of Babel are examples, although it is significant that in the Babel tale man wishes to build a tower to re-establish a face to face communication with God.

The themes that have been discussed so far are the more cosmogonic and generalised themes of mythology. From this point on the themes are based more upon the acts of individuals. There is the constantly recurring theme of incest which is linked to a form of sacrifice on the part of the participant(s). In the case of Oedipus there is the ritual sacrifice of a Sacred King, a theme which is the basis of Frazer's *The Golden Bough*. We see the theme of the Tyrant opposed by a returning King or one marked for kingship, as was the case with Saul and David. There is the theme of the Mother Goddess (often representing the Earth Mother) and the Divine Child, exemplified by Isis and Horus and Mary and Jesus. There are the tales of the hero Kings, the *patri patriae*, such as Alexander, Asoka, Arthur, Charlemagne and Frederick Barbarossa linked with the concept of the returning King who will come back from the dead, and the eschatological and apocalyptic themes which are a part of this and which have already been discussed.

This inevitably leads to a consideration of the most common

theme in myth and legend at the individual level; that of the hero and his Quest. The development of the hero and the Quest that he undertakes are often inseparable. For the hero to be a hero depends upon the manner in which he undertakes his Quest. In some cases the Quest is the pivotal issue in the life of the hero and we are not given a full biography, but merely his undertaking of the Quest. Sir Gawain is a well-known figure in the Arthurian legend. His most significant Quest, that related in the tale of the Green Knight, is but one of the many tales surrounding this hero.

The hero is an archetype. In his life he exemplifies man's ideals and aspirations. He represents the higher goals that man can achieve. His actions are the symbolic leaps forward in man's spiritual and moral progress. He has been able to battle past his personal and local historical limitations to serve as a model or example to a wider community. He ventures over the hill of everyday human existence to confront a possibly dreadful unknown, and does so willingly. The hero is symbolic of man's desire to progress, not physically or materially, but spiritually and ethically, to find himself and his place in the nature of things. He is the creature of myth (or legend) in search of the meaning of myth. His goal may not be generalised absolute truth but in his quest he may achieve an absolute truth and self-realisation. Consequently, the life of the hero is a Quest or in the life of the hero a Quest may be a pivotal activity. Thus, in the Arthurian legend, Gawain speaks most significantly and symbolically in the tale of the Green Knight. Perceval's most important function is his role in the Quest for the Sangreal. But the Quest is not restricted to the Arthurian or medieval myths. The Epic of Gilgamesh is entirely a Quest tale, as is the *Odyssey* and the *Aeneid*.

In all the Quest hero tales the hero ventures forth from the world of common or everyday events into a region of mystery or supernatural wonder. He encounters fabulous forces, achieves a decisive victory and returns, enriched and enlightened, to his fellow man and, by his actions and existence, bestows good fortune upon his community. Opposing the hero is the monster who may be a beast or a human tyrant, the latter acting regardless of the rights and sensibilities of those over whom he holds power. The characteristics of the monster are essentially the same. He is the hoarder of the general benefit, avid for the greedy rights of my and mine. He wreaks universal havoc throughout his domain. His ego is a curse to himself and his world. He is self-terrorised, haunted with fear and ready to oppose violently any threat to his rule. Wherever he rules a cry goes up for the redeemer, the saviour, the hero, carrier of the shining blade whose blow, touch or mere existence will liberate the land. By such an act of redemption the hero bestows benefits upon the oppressed victims of the monster and advances further upon the personal quest for self-realisation and moral righteousness. By slaying the monster he symbolically puts aside the black part of human nature, that penchant for evil that lies within us. The hero turns away from lust, greed, cruelty and megalomania and towards the more acceptable modes of behaviour that, theoretically at least, mark Man's moral progress from savage barbarity to moral civilisation. So it is that the hero is archetypal. He represents us all. His actions are an example for us to emulate and follow. By following in his footsteps we become the hero.

Within the life of the hero are a number of steps or stages. These may occur over his whole life or may be reflected within the Quest that he undertakes. His life or adventure follows a pattern, involving separation from the world, the achievement of a source of power and a life enhancing return.

The advent of the hero, his birth or his background, is shrouded with mystery or surrounded by miracle. Quetzal,

Attis and Jesus are examples of the miraculous birth, accompanied by portents and prophecy. The hero may, upon birth, be cast out from his home which is what happened to Siegfried, Moses, Oedipus and Romulus. He may be fostered in a different environment, quite alien from his true origins, or be totally left in the wild, abandoned to nature. Such situations symbolise his universal origins and nature. He is at ease in any environment. He appreciates power and wealth, poverty and degradation. He communes with the wild side of man's soul. He speaks the language of animals. He is at one with nature and with his humanity and is thereby the universal representative of man.

At an early stage of his development the hero will undergo some form of initiation during which time he will reveal a part of his potential as a mover of events. The initiation is a form of rite of passage and as such is as much an indication to the hero himself of his potential as it is to others. It is the dawning or awakening of self-realisation. The initiation may take place in the infancy of the hero, such as Herakles and the serpents or Odysseus and the boar, or at a later time, such as David and Goliath. Jesus had two stages of initiation; one, the Youth Christ at the Temple, is preliminary. The main initiation comes at the Baptism in the Jordan and is a prelude to His ministry. From that point the events in the life of the hero follow swiftly upon one another for Him.

Following the initiation, and preceding his great acts, the hero goes through a period of withdrawal. Having been confronted with the potential of his being he must, psychologically, come to terms with it. He has a choice in the manner of the use of his powers. The choice that he makes, the path that he selects to follow, must be the right one. Consequently the withdrawal phase is a period of inner trial, as well as self-confrontation. Yet from such period of withdrawal the hero emerges to undertake his most important feat, which is the Quest.

28

The Quest, as I have indicated, is a search for the self and the essence of man's being. The hero may receive and refuse the call, as did Perceval. Such a character represents those of us who would rather avoid self-confrontation. Perceval avoided the confrontation with mystic reality. Gawain, on the other hand, asked the question and was held to be a true seeker. He saved the King and the Kingdom and is an imitation of Christ. The Quest inevitably involves magic, beasts or the supernatural, or a combination of all three. The wizards, dragons, demons, giants or mystic dreams and visions are all part and parcel of the effort that the hero must put into the achievement of his goal. They symbolise the darkness, ignorance or temptation that stands in the way of progress towards true understanding, awareness and self-realisation. They must be, and are, overcome. The Quest within the life of the hero reveals an eternal struggle for self-realisation. But frequently associated with the Quest and its achievement is the death of the hero which may be actual or symbolic. I can think of no better example of symbolic death than Aragorn's passage through the Paths of the Dead in *The Lord of the Rings*, which I shall discuss more fully in a later chapter. The actual death of the hero is not final, and may often be linked with nature and the concept of rebirth. Thus, when Odin's Quest for the runes results in his death, and Christ's Quest in a similarly actual and symbolic way, we see the hero in death cradled in the promise of rebirth. The tree, on which both Odin and Christ perished, has its roots in the unknown – that final part of the Quest to be attained.

Associated with death is the descent to the Underworld. Because the death of the hero is so often sacrificial and to conquer death he has first to die, the hero faces that which man fears most – the ultimate unknown from which there is no return – death. The hero becomes the scapegoat for humanity by the frequently sacrificial nature of his death. He carries our sins with him and on our behalf descends to the Underworld to confront Death or the Lord of the Underworld, or the Ultimate Evil itself. If the death of the hero is of a symbolic nature so too is his descent to the Underworld. His descent is not as one who is dead but *as if* he were one dead. Thus, Christ, who physically dies, descends to Hell to deliver His ultimatum to Satan and commence the Harrowing of Hell. Orpheus descends as part of his Quest for Eurydice and conquers death with his musical skill. His is a symbolic descent and a symbolic challenge. His descent represents the power of love and the immortal nature of pure art.

It is by Resurrection that the hero returns – and again this may be actual or symbolic. By rebirth, death is defeated and the cycle of Nature is re-established. The hero evidences his universality as the Man in Nature by actual or symbolic rebirth and the confirmation of the established order of things. He has not only confirmed order but also his self-awareness and self-realisation. His rebirth is a return to the source of his origins, to take up the promised honour, kingdom or throne which was foretold before or at his birth. His resurrection is a fulfilment of being.

The final stage of the hero's development is his Apotheosis, his reception into Heaven or the confirmation of his universal and immortal nature. Christ, Mithras, Dionysius, Elijah and Galahad are received into Heaven. Arthur, Charlemagne and Barbarossa are not dead but sleeping, awaiting a time to return. Their departure from the realms of reality is but temporary and death for them is not absolute. Immortalisation may take a number of forms. The hero may vanish, so that none may confirm his death. He may be received into Heaven or taken to a sacred isle or mountain. He may undergo some change at physical death that makes his passing so unique that it is not a natural death. And in the tales of the returning King the eternal hope and security of the renewal of the natural order of things is assured, such return being the re-establishment of the absolute archetypal and prototype natural order – the Golden Age.

Thus the hero is called to adventure and is set aside as one who is unique. That he may resist the call is evidence of the folly of flight from an omnipotent deity. His adventure involves the supernatural both in the form of aid and hindrance. By undertaking the Quest he crosses the threshold to put on trial himself and, as Everyman, all Mankind. His challenges may involve the eternal opposites – the meeting with the male side and a form of atonement with the father, and the confrontation with the female side; the woman as temptress Death, the Underworld and Resurrection represents a denial of the World, a confrontation with the Ultimate Question and the crossing of the return threshold to the real World. The hero is the master of the two Worlds, spiritual and temporal. He is Universal, Everyman, man in Nature, fulfilled and aware. He is the epitome of existence and achievement.[2]

It has been said by Northrop Frye and subsequently by other literary critics that the Quest myth has been the central myth of literature and the source of all literary genres. T. S. Eliot praised James Joyce for having invented a 'mythical method' or 'continuous parallel between contemporaneity and antiquity'[3] which enables a modern writer to give 'a shape and a significance to the immense panorama of futility and anarchy which is contemporary history'.[4]

Yet the Quest myth in literature is nothing new. Myth telling originally commenced as an oral tradition and, as society developed, the tradition and mythic tales were incorporated into the literature of the society. Ovid's *Metamorphoses* are quaint tales and part of the Latin literary heritage. Yet they are myths of origins – of how things came to be. That myth telling was an oral tradition is confirmed in the Norse word *saga* which means 'things said'. Saga, and its close relation epic which is an extension of saga, deal not so much with 'true' myth but with the ancestors or heroes of a society. Both rely heavily on 'true' myth for a background, and presuppose a knowledge of myth among the listeners. It is wrong to assume that the *Eddas*, the sagas of the North, and the *Kalevala* are representative of a written literary tradition for they are not. The *Kalevala* was not recorded in writing until as late as the 1830s and even though the tales have been written down there is a heavy oral tradition whose function is to stir the spirit of warriors to heroic action by praising the exploits of ancestors in the mead hall or before battle. The *Chansons de Geste* not only tell of deeds, but are also a genealogy. The themes of the epics were heroic and followed the pattern which has already been outlined.

Those who recounted the myths and legends, the priests, shamans or bards and poets, were the keepers of the sacred tradition and the sacred stories. The initiation for shamans and priests was long and complex and, like the Irish 'seauchan' or 'master poet', required passage through various stages of wisdom. Poets, like shamans, were believed to be a medium between man and the gods and were considered seers or soothsayers, yet, as in the case of Homer, Tiresias or the Delphic Sybil, may have had to contend with some physical disability or disorder. By being so disabled they were not totally of the world. The disability set them apart and allowed an acceptable link with the supernatural.

So the poet is not merely an artist, but an inspired artist and a keeper of the sacred tradition. It is therefore no accident that myth, legend and literature were, in early days, so closely linked. Even the use of verse forms is part of the ritual tradition. The *Iliad* and *Odyssey* were written in a dactylic hexameter, a form inappropriate to both Greek and English. But it was the metre of prophecy and religious narrative. In using this form, Homer's work invokes a quality that makes it transcend a mere tale and takes it to the point of religious myth. Of course, an oral tradition results in modifications with the passage of time, although poetic forms would contain mnemonic tricks of metre or rhyme form. An example of the former is the *Kalevala* with its distinctive metre adopted by H. W. Longfellow in *The Song of Hiawatha*. But despite such aids the tales changed, not necessarily in theme but in detail. Much would depend upon the audience for whom the tale was written or created. According to Eliade, Homer created his work for a military and semi-feudal aristocracy. Thus Homer may have avoided some of the themes which would not be of interest to his audience, and rather glorified certain aspects.

Despite such critics as Pindar and Thucydides who rejected the incredible myths and fabulous tales, the Greek myths represent a literary work which documents a religious belief. None of them have come to us in their cult context and, were it not for the work of Graves, it is doubtful that the religious or ritual explanation of them would be available to any but a few scholars. Any myth that has been documented or has been the subject of a literary work is primarily literary in nature. Thus we see the *Eddas* and sagas not as religious documents but as linguistic records and part of the literary history of society.

Myth has appeared throughout the history of literature even down to the present time. Mythical archetypes survive in the modern novel in the symbolic sense. Hemingway's Old Man is Everyman, adrift on the Primordial Waters undertaking his Quest for the Monster of the deep. Dickens returns to the folktale idiom. Nickleby searches for his real background kept hidden by his wicked uncle, Ralph. Dickens' characters may be wicked witches or people or institutions and his heroes are often aided by the guileless fool who leads them to salvation.

The writer, in creating his own myth, will accept the

supernatural as operating within nature. Within the world of nature exist inexplicable forces which are fickle and can turn at will. The use of mythic forms and archetypes by the writer is an aesthetic device for bringing the imaginary but powerful world of preternatural forces into a manageable collaboration with objective and experience facts of life in such a way as to stimulate unconscious passions and the conscious mind. It can bring together the real experience and the submerged impulses of life. The use of myth in the creative sense is the province of the poet or bard; the artist not the historian. The poet may feign a history for his artistic purpose and pattern, using an imagined history or an historical form within which to cast his fictional or symbolic action. Thus the poet's or artist's world is a 'middle-earth' situated between the lower present day historical world and an unexperienced but nevertheless mythically real Heaven.

Fiction, imagination and myth all occupy the same level for the artist. Fiction may be a deviation from reality or an approximation of it. With fiction, the artist can explain the inexplicable. There has been a tendency in modern literature to dispense with the mythic forms and the successful achievement of the Quest or the 'happy ending'. Such literature is literature without hope and says little for Man's ability to transcend or overcome his universal tragedy. But by the same token it is important to consider the element of tragedy in myth. So far we have looked at the hero and his Quest from a positive or 'eucatastrophic' point of view. Tragedy can provide us with a positive point of view, but with anything but happiness for the protagonist. The tragic hero carries within him the well-being of people and the welfare of the State. He engages in a conflict with the representative of darkness and Evil. He suffers a temporary defeat or setback. After a period of shame and suffering he emerges triumphant as the symbol of the victory of light and good over darkness and evil, a victory sanctified by the covenant of the settling of destinies which reaffirms the well-being of the people and the welfare of the State. In the course of the conflict comes a point where the protagonist and antagonist merge into a single challenge against the order of God. The protagonist commits an evil he would not normally do, and fails to do good when he should. At this moment we become aware that the real protagonist of the tragedy is the order of God against which the hero has rebelled. The pride and presumption which is within us all as a result of our mixed state is symbolised and revealed, and it is this hubris which is purged from us by the suffering of the tragic hero.

It is the function of the artist, the writer, the creative myth-maker to highlight and focus the symbols in his creative effort. As Blake says in 'Jerusalem', 'I must create a system or be enslaved by another man's.'

The end product of such creativity may be an eclectic synop-ticon such as W. B. Yeats' *A Vision* or Graves' *The White Goddess*, or a creation-like myth such as that of Wordsworth's personal cosmos in *The Prelude*. Furthermore, it is difficult to achieve a totally clean break with the allegedly extinct mythologies and source studies have been devoted to Blake and Yeats. No matter how hard a creator may try, inevitably he draws upon extant mythology, and the mythopoeic impulse in imaginations as powerful as Joyce and Mann may be impeded by a reluctance to let go of the traditional mythologies. The invented mythology rarely contains the resonances of an inherited one and must always remain private except to the happy few who take the trouble to work it out. Those who advocate that myths are col-lective in nature consider it impossible for any one person to be credited with the creation or invention of a myth. What Melville and Kafka create is not myth, but an individual fantasy express-ing a symbolic action equivalent to and related to the myth's expression of a public rite. Yet initially the myth must have a

THE SONG OF MIDDLE-EARTH

source in the form of ballad, narrative or saga. Someone has to supply the raw material to which others may add or may alter. Thus, anyone can contribute his 'bit' to a myth but is obliged to respect the original integrity of the raw material. In literature myths are moulded and shaped. Imported materials are adapted to fit local custom, landscape or belief and usually suffer slightly. In the continued retelling of a traditional tale, accidental or intentional dislocations are inevitable.

Tolkien created a setting for his mythology. His world was Arda, the realm of mortals, Middle-earth. The themes of his mythology are universal. Many of the themes have been borrowed and reworked to fit the artist's structure. Tolkien's mythology is, however, rare. It is a private mythology but it is available to all. Although it began as a shared experience with a small group, it carries within it elements of universal acceptability. Tolkien's themes, archetypes and symbolism can appeal to us all in that they are universal. It is the use to which they are put, the tailoring within the created mythological world, that makes Tolkien's work one of the most significant of the created mythologies of English literature.

36

CHAPTER 3

The Music of Ilúvatar: Tolkien and the Major Mythic Themes

Also ... I was from early days grieved by the poverty of my own beloved country: it had no stories of its own (bound up with its tongue and soil), not of the quality that I sought, and found (as an ingredient) in legends of other lands. There was Greek, and Celtic, and Romance, Germanic, Scandinavian, and Finnish (which greatly affected me); but nothing English.[1]

Tolkien wanted to create a Mythology for England and his Middle-earth tales are just that. They are a mythic history of the Elves and Men, and how the latter attained dominance of the World. In a way, the whole myth is a myth of origin. Saruman could see what was happening; 'The Elder Days are gone. The Middle Days are passing. The Younger Days are beginning. The time of the Elves is over, but our time is at hand: the world of Men, which we must rule.'[2] Galadriel saw the end of the era dominated by the Elves, Sauron and the physical symbol of evil in the Ring; 'Yet if you succeed, then our power is diminished, and Lothlórien will fade, and the tides of Time will sweep it away. We must depart into the West, or dwindle to a rustic folk of dell and cave, slowly to forget and to be forgotten.'[3] Gandalf reveals to Aragorn on the slopes of Mindolluin the ending of the old and the beginning of the new, and the New Age of Men.

> This is your realm, and the heart of the greater realm that shall be. The Third Age of the world is ended, and the new age is begun; and it is your task to order its beginning and to preserve what may be preserved. For though much has been saved, much must now pass away; and the power of the Three Rings also is ended. And all the lands that you see, and those that lie round about them, shall be dwellings of Men. For the time comes of the Dominion of Men, and the Elder Kindred shall fade or depart.[4]

That is the final point and Tolkien's myth finishes as the new Golden Age of Men begins. He leaves it to other myths to explain the Fall from this new time of bliss that commences with the reign of Aragorn and continues with his son, Eldarion.

The myth ends with hope and a new beginning, but how did it all start? Tolkien does not throw us into a completed world and let us speculate how it all began. He has his own cosmogonic creation myth which tells of the beginning of the cosmos within which Arda is situated.

Naturally enough, there is a Creator, and His existence is presupposed. He is Eru, or Ilúvatar, as he was known to the Elves. He is in being at the very beginning, always was and always will be. He exists in a Void, the Chaos, which is formless and in disorder. Into this disorder are brought the Ainur, the Holy Ones, who are the 'offspring of his [Ilúvatar's] thought'.[5] The fourteen greatest of the Ainur became the Valar. But although the Ainur were powerful and creative, they are subservient to Ilúvatar. The One propounds to them themes of music which are developed. Then Ilúvatar makes a great revelation. He had kindled in the Ainur the Flame Imperishable so that each one could show forth his powers in adoring the theme. At this stage the Ainur are not present in any sort of physical form. They are of the *thought* of Ilúvatar, and are creatures of His imagination. In the spiritual world of Ilúvatar, they exist as beings of the spirit and the Flame Imperishable is that spark which exists within all sentient beings – the flame of creativity. The essence of creativity remains with the Creator because it is not independent or isolated. Melkor, in seeking the Flame Imperishable, sought the power of absolute creativity. His search was doomed to fail, for the power remained with the Creator – 'Yet he found not the Fire, for it is with Ilúvatar'.[6] What Melkor couldn't understand was that the Flame was abstract and did not exist in a physical form. Indeed at that point, everything was abstract. Melkor was yielding to the materialistic side of his nature which developed even more within the Circles of the World at a later stage in the mythology.

In the void the Theme of Ilúvatar and the Music of the Ainur became a vision in which 'they saw a new World made visible before them, and it was globed amid the Void'.[7] This was a vision of a World that would be, but at that stage of its development remained in the spirit of creative fire. Although the Ainur have the power to make and shape, only Ilúvatar can give them the materials and realise the Creation.

> They shared in its 'making' – but only on the same terms as we 'make' a work of art or story. The realization of it, the gift to it of a created reality of the same grade as their own, was the act of the One God.[8]

The realisation in its most absolute sense takes place when Ilúvatar transforms the vision into a reality.

Eä! Let these things Be! And I will send forth into the Void the Flame Imperishable, and it shall be at the heart of the World, and the World shall Be.[9]

Eä is the World that Is. It is a reality and not an abstract vision. It was seen by the Ainur as a fact and 'as they looked and wondered this World began to unfold its history, and it seemed to them that it lived and grew'.[10]

The importance of the Flame Imperishable, the Secret Fire which is sent to the Heart of the World, is that creation carries with it the essential essence of *creativity*. It is the symbol of that categorical imperative, that transformation of a work of art or creation from a vision to an actual reality.[11]

At this point in the creation cycle, Ilúvatar's function fades and the Valar assume more importance. But who or what are the Valar? Why are they so important? The Ainur were the spirits created by Ilúvatar. They were at one with the Creator and with the Music of Ilúvatar. Some of these Ainur later became the Valar and others remained as Ainur in a spiritual or disembodied form. The Valar were those Ainur who descended to Eä and walked upon it in a physical form. They looked like the Children of Ilúvatar – the Elves – whom they had seen in the Vision of Ilúvatar. There were fourteen great Ainur who became Valar – seven male and seven female. There were others also, but they were of a lesser degree, and these were the Maiar, who were the servants of the Valar. The difficulties that some readers may have experienced in understanding these various powerful beings lies in the fact that Tolkien did not say how many Ainur there were in the first place, nor does he tell us how many Maiar came to Eä. We can conclude that Sauron, Olórin (Gandalf), Curumo (Saruman) and the other Istari were Maiar, as were the Valaraukar or Balrogs.[12] The Balrogs were perverted by Morgoth and became the shock troops in his war of fear that he later waged in Middle-earth. It has also been suggested that Tom Bombadil was a Maia because of his power and knowledge, and what he himself says:

> Eldest, that's what I am ... Tom was here before the river and the trees; Tom remembers the first raindrop and the first acorn. He made paths before the Big People, and saw the little People arriving. He was here before the Kings and the graves and the Barrow-wights. When the Elves passed westward, Tom was here already, before the seas were bent. He knew the dark under the stars when it was fearless – before the Dark Lord came from the Outside.[13]

Elrond described him as 'older than the old', 'oldest and fatherless' and 'Last as he was First'.[14]

The Valar were demi-god, Titan-like beings. They were charged with the fulfilment of the Vision and the completion of Arda (the Earth). They each had individual knowledge of portions of the Vision, but of all the Valar, only Manwë *understood* most clearly the Will of Ilúvatar. Manwë's special province was the air, wind and clouds. His companion was Varda (or Elbereth Gilthoniel), the Lady of the Stars. Ulmo was the Lord of the Waters, the Poseidon of Arda. Aulë the Smith is Hephaestos or Vulcan, dealing with matters of the Earth, stone and jewels. His companion is Yavanna, the Earth Mother – Demeter or Ceres. Mandos is the Keeper of the Houses of the Dead, forgets nothing and knows all things that shall be. He pronounces his dooms and judgements only at the bidding of Manwë. He is inflexible and dispassionate and is rather like a recording device. He knows what is going to happen, but unlike Manwë, he does not understand the significance or relevance of it in the greater plan of Ilúvatar. For that reason he can only reveal his knowledge when Manwë lets him. Nienna the Weeper represents pity and suffering, but not despair. Those who hear her learn pity and endurance in hope. She brings strength to the spirit and turns sorrow to wisdom. Oromë is the Huntsman of the Valar, and the only Vala to have come to Middle-earth. He is Lord of animals and beasts. These eight are the Aratar or the Holy Ones of Arda. 'In majesty they are peers, surpassing beyond compare all others.'[15]

The other Valar are Vána, wife of Oromë. She is youth, delighting in fresh new flowers and the song of birds. She is Spring the Renewer. Nessa the Dancer, like her brother Oromë, is of the woods and is a forest spirit. Lórien is the King of Dreams and Visions and is the brother of Mandos. He represents the link between death, the total end of consciousness, and its related state, sleep. Tulkas the Strong is the War Master of the Valar. He is a wrestler and his strength is so great that he has no need of weapons. Estë the Healer lives in the Garden of Lórien, and is gentle, clad in grey, and brings relief from suffering. It would be to Estë that Gandalf the Grey went after his trial by battle with the Balrog of Moria. Vairë the Weaver is the wife of Mandos. She weaves fate into the tapestry of history, long before its time has come. She is an amalgam of the weaving Norns and the Greek Fates. It seems that in mythology, fate is associated with the symbol of weaving or with a thread.

The last of the Valar is Melkor or Morgoth. He is a pivotal Valar and his particular role in the Vision of Ilúvatar will be studied later.[16]

The division of the Valar into two groups represents the two levels of natural order. Aulë and Yavanna are of the Earth. Manwë and Varda are of the Sky. Mandos is Death, an Ending, and the finality of Doom and prophecy. Oromë is lusty, of the living world of animals, the hunt, laughter and anger. Ulmo is the water element, but rather distant, alien and alone. Nienna recognises the sorrow of the World, but represents the positive aspects of sorrow and suffering. Against despair she brings hope and allows wisdom to arise out of sadness.

These are the elemental aspects of the human and natural condition and they are not peculiar to Tolkien's mythology. The symbols may be altered, and in some cases are refined, but not greatly. The elemental qualities of the Aratar point to the importance of nature and the basic things around us as features of a mythology. We are all at the mercy of nature. This was recognised in the earliest of mythologies and was the basis of the ritual re-enactments by which Man sought to move and influence the elements that dominated his life.

The Aratar are those who put into effect the most important parts of the Theme of Ilúvatar. The lesser Valar have their tasks to fulfil as well, but they are more detached from the powerful natural or elemental realities represented by the Aratar. The lesser Valar represent the more spiritual, abstract or transcendental aspects of life, such as youth, springtime or rebirth, art, dreams and healing, history and fate, and raw, unbridled power which is to be used only when needed.

The Valar are the tools of Ilúvatar. It is they who fabricate the Earth and turn the Vision into reality. From the moment that they descend to Arda, Ilúvatar becomes a passive observer. Having made the rules he sits back to watch the game. Tolkien says:

There is no embodiment of the One, of God, who indeed remains remote, outside the World, and only directly accessible to the Valar or Rulers. These take the place of the 'gods', but are created spirits, or those of the primary creation who by their own will have entered into the world. But the One retains all ultimate authority, and (or so it seems as viewed in serial time) reserves the right to intrude the finger of God into the story.[17]

There was strife in the creation of Arda. Melkor caused dissension, even before the work was finished, but he left Arda before the wrath of Tulkas.

After Melkor's expulsion comes the second stage of the creation myth – the formation of light. There was a form of light in Arda, fires which were 'subdued or buried beneath the primeval hills',[18] but Yavanna needed a more substantial form of light to provide the spark for the seeds that she had sown. Aulë built the Great Lamps, Illuin and Ormal. Varda filled them with light, and they were blessed by Manwë. The light was to give effect to an aspect of subcreation and life to those things that grow naturally. But the light was not that of the Sun. That comes later. Tolkien's source of light actually *precedes* the Sun and has a unique quality. In most mythologies the Sun is the first light source, the moon second and the Stars third. Furthermore, the Sun is not predated by another light source, either on the Earth or in the home of the gods. Tolkien's light, like the Sun, heralds and assists the growth of natural life. But the gardens and the forests, not blooming at this stage, are not for Man, nor yet the Elves, but for the Creators, the Valar, who dwelt on the Isle of Almaren.

But Spring is a passing season, and the Spring of Arda did not last long. Melkor, still seeking the Imperishable Flame, yet already becoming the Lord of Darkness, came back to Arda, cast a blight on the growing things, threw down the Lamps and the Light which, as it spilled out, became a destroying flame. The primary design of the Valar was marred and would never return. And after wreaking such havoc and destruction, Melkor hid. The Valar could not pursue him. Their strength and power was required to keep in check the corruption and ruin of nature that Melkor had wrought. They were not aware of the hiding place of the Elves and 'feared to rend the Earth again'[19] in the event that they might destroy the resting place of the special Children of Ilúvatar. The Valar shifted their dwelling to the

Land of Aman and established the realm of Valinor. Those things that they could save from the ruin they took with them, including a great store of light. In Valinor they were able to create a beauty that excelled the Spring of Arda. Valinor was a hallowed and Holy Land, and the Age that followed, the Age of the Trees, is the Golden Age of Arda.

On the sacred mound Ezellohar, Yavanna the Earth Mother, with the tears of Nienna, sang and from the Earth came the Trees of Valinor, Telperion and Laurelin.

The creation of a natural life form is entrusted to the Earth Mother and the Trees were very special. They came direct from the earth without seed or stone and if this is not enough, they had one other extraordinary quality – they gave forth light. The first light of Aman, that of the Lamps, did not spring from the goodness of the Earth as did that of the Trees. The light of the Trees is the light of nature – symbolically the light of artistic creation – and has a purity that is connected with the perfection of nature.

The light of the Trees shone only in Valinor and not in Middle-earth, which was lit only by faint stars created by Varda. When the Elves finally awakened, Varda created special new stars from the dew of Telperion which had been stored in vats. These new stars are thus of an earthly or natural source, yet have a mystic origin, and number among them Menelmacar (or Menelvagor, the Swordsman of the Sky, whose appearance caused such joy to Gildor Inglorion's Exiles in *The Lord of the Rings*), Valacirca the Sickle and Remmirath the Netted Stars. The stars were the blessing of the Light of the Trees to Middle-earth and their creation is part of the myth of the Earth and of the power of Nature.

Until the ending of the Trees and the theft of the Silmarils, the only sources of light that Aman had were the Lamps, the Trees and the Stars. The Sun and Moon that we know, and that order and regulate our lives, had not appeared and their genesis was to be from what little was left of the magnificent light of the Trees, and was to be only a pale reflection of it. The primordial light is pure – far too pure for Man. The pure light of essential creativity is beyond our understanding and too dazzling to comprehend. Yet the light of the stars which we are allowed to behold is the first light that the Elves saw. The stars were the heralds of their arrival and the creation of the new stars from the dew of Telperion was solely for that purpose. It had all been preordained, for the awakening of the Elves was in the hands of Ilúvatar who decreed the hour of their coming which was then pronounced, when that time came, by Manwë. Tolkien says that the creation of the stars was 'the greatest of all the works of the Valar since their coming to Arda'.[20] I would place it second in significance to the Trees without which there would be no dew of Telperion, no Silmarils and no Star-travelling Eärendil.

The manner in which Tolkien deals with the creation of the Sun and the Moon resembles the classic mythic themes. The Sun was made from the fruit of Laurelin, the Moon from a leaf of Telperion, conjured up by Yavanna from the ruin left by Melkor. They were given to Aulë who made vessels in which they were carried, and they were then given to Varda to be placed in the sky. The Moon was the elder of new lights and was first in the sky to be guided by the Maia Tilion. The Sun was second and was guided by Arien. Tilion was a hunter with a silver bow and he loved things silver which explains the colour of the moon and its waxing and waning crescent shape. Arien was a Spirit of Fire who had not been corrupted by Melkor and she was 'as a naked flame, terrible in the fullness of her splendour'.[21] Arien and the Melkor were such opposites that the significant first rising of the Sun after the destruction of the Trees throws Melkor/Morgoth into a panic, and enables the Host of Fingolfin to besiege Angband.

In Tolkien's creation myth, and in the establishment of the basic cosmos, everything is done at every level by living beings, the Valar, brought into being and in accordance with the Plan of Ilúvatar. The Valar exist physically[22] and one commentator suggests[23] that the orders of the Valar and Maiar came from Dionysius the Areopagite who propounded nine orders of angels. (Tolkien propounded two orders of demi-godlike beings.) The Hierarchy was also used by Milton. But the Valar are not orders or classification of levels. They are subcreators – 'they interpreted according to their powers, and completed in detail, the Design propounded to them by the One'.[24] The Valar are the Great of the Ainur. Their power and creativity within the theme is so great that Ilúvatar fades away, leaving to the Valar the ordering of Creation. He only intervenes to awaken the Elves.

In later ages the Valar and Valinor achieve an almost religious, and certainly mythic, significance. In *The Lord of the Rings* Damrod, at the sight of the *mûmakil*, cries 'May the Valar turn him aside',[25] and the Standing Silence involves a ritual of facing towards the ancestral homeland, Númenor, and to the unattainable lands of Elvenhome that is 'and to that which is beyond Elvenhome and will ever be'.[26] It is only at the breaking of their Ban that the Valar call upon Ilúvatar and lay aside their guardianship. Why should they do this? The Valar are capable of shaping, and have shaped, Arda. Surely they have enough power to destroy Númenor and put Valinor beyond the Circles of the World and to effect a transition from a flat earth to a round one.[27] But such a mighty reshaping of the essential cosmos must require the hand of the Great Designer. The other aspect is that this phase of the Theme of Ilúvatar was, like the creation of Elves and Men, within His ambit only, and was a matter that could only be dealt with by Him. It is said that the Ban was imposed through the design of Manwë[28] who perceived the thought of Ilúvatar. The Númenóreans should not be tempted to seek for the Blessed Realm, nor desire to overpass the limits set to their bliss, becoming enamoured of the immortality of the Valar and the Eldar and the lands where all things endure.[29]

Death was the Gift of Ilúvatar, given to Men, his special creation. If Ar-Pharazôn was able to achieve immortality it would radically alter the Design of the One, and only the One could respond to such a challenge.

The Valar are always second to Ilúvatar. The foundation of all that they do is within His design. Any incursion by Evil powers, any attempts to change the theme or the design, are taken and skilfully worked into the Theme so that the conclusion is exactly as it was intended. There is a certain irresistible inevitability to the whole thing. The great cosmogonic myth allows for a few small deviations and trips down side roads but always there is a return to the main highway. Blind chance or pure good luck plays no real part. But powerful as the Valar were, they were not aware of a few private secrets that Ilúvatar kept to himself. When the subject of His own personal and private creation attempts to rend the cosmos, it is He who must step in and take control. In this way, as in other mythologies, sentient life, represented by the Elves and Men, are the province of and created by the Supreme Being.

Elves, Dwarves and Men, the three races of Middle-earth, are not original creations in the Tolkien mythology. He is a literary Ilúvatar only for the hobbits. The other races all had their origins in other myths. The Dark and Light Elves feature strongly in Scandinavian myth, and constitute two forms of the same race. But Tolkien's Elves are more majestic and creative than any of the Elves of previous myth. They

represent really Men with greatly enhanced aesthetic and

creative faculties, greater beauty and longer life, and nobility
– the Elder Children, doomed to fade before the Followers
(Men)[30]... [They are] ... different aspects of the Humane ...
[they] represent ... the artistic, aesthetic, and purely scientific
aspects of the Humane nature raised to a higher level than is
actually seen in Men. That is: they have a devoted love of the
physical world, and a desire to observe and understand it for
its own sake ... They also possess a 'subcreational' or artistic
faculty of great excellence.[31]

Men, the younger Children of Ilúvatar, are mortal and their
life is very brief. They awoke with the coming of the Sun and
their coming was the beginning of the end for the Elves. Men
were forbidden to go to Aman, and they feared the Valar because
they did not understand either them or their purpose. It seems
that Man is doomed always to fear that which he does not know.
But they fell easily under the sway of Sauron and Morgoth who
played upon their ignorance and fear of the Valar, and turned
them to the ways of evil and away from the purpose of Ilúvatar.

Men were equal to Elves in body, but were inferior in craft,
skill, beauty and wisdom. But like the Elves, they were creatures
of light, drawn to the fading glory of Laurelin as the Sun, as the
Elves were drawn to the Stars, the products of Telperion.

The Dwarves are an entirely different aspect of the Plan and
purposes of Ilúvatar. They too appear in many European
mythologies as craftsmen and underground delvers. The
Dwarves were secretly fashioned by Aulë as an offering to
Ilúvatar. The One, by giving life to the Dwarves, and explaining
to Aulë the errors of his creations, shows the nature of the
theme. Ilúvatar subtly changes the fabric of the theme to
accommodate the Dwarves who awaken after the Elves, yet
always remain at arm's length from them. The essence of their
life comes not from Aulë, but from the Supreme Master,

Ilúvatar.

Tolkien's myths of the creation of the cosmos, of the Earth and the life within it fit into the general patterns of mythology. But his eschatology, his myth of the End, is obscure. Those commentators who believe that Tolkien derives his themes and sources strongly from the Norse mythology rather than from the generalised themes of mythology must face the fact that Tolkien's myth is positive and concentrates on continuation and rebirth, unlike the brooding pessimism of the Norse and Teutonic myth. The Fourth Age, which is the ending of the mythological cycle, dreams of a new Golden Age for Men in the Reunited Kingdom and holds a promise of another Golden Age of Númenor, or a Bliss of Valinor. Beyond that, and beyond our present, the references to an Ending are few and are shrouded in mystery.

A curious passage occurs in the Ainulindale describing the uniqueness of the Music of the Ainur, and hints that there will be an end to things followed by a spiritual unification of Ilúvatar, the Ainur and the Children:

> Never since have the Ainur made any music like to this music, though it has been said that a greater still shall be made before Ilúvatar by the choirs of the Ainur and the Children of Ilúvatar after the end of days. Then the themes of Ilúvatar shall be played aright, and take Being in the moment of their utterance, for all shall then understand fully his intent in their part, and each shall know the comprehension of each and Ilúvatar shall give their thoughts the secret fire, being well pleased.[32]

Saruman also comments on the end of things:

> 'For I believe not,' said he, 'that the One will ever be found again in Middle-earth. Into Anduin it fell, and long ago, I

50

deem, it was rolled to the Sea. There it shall lie until the end,
when all this world is broken and the deeps are removed.'[33]

Obviously an ending is contemplated. Precisely when, and its
nature are not clear. The ultimate result of the End will be a
reunification with the Creator. The only other hint that we have
of the nature of the End is that there will be a Last Battle. This
relatively common theme of an 'Armageddon' is not expanded.
But it will happen, and that is presaged by the constellation
Menelmacar with his shining belt 'that forebodes the Last Battle
that shall be at the end of days'.[34]

The mortal men who set foot upon Aman when
Ar-Pharazôn led his ill-fated expedition to the Undying Lands
were buried under falling hills and lie imprisoned 'in the
Caves of the Forgotten, until the Last Battle and the Day of
Doom'.[35] Elendil understood an ending to the World when he
said in the Royal Oath, 'In this place will I abide, and my heirs,
unto the ending of the world'.[36] And when the Last Battle has
been completed Aulë, helped by his dwarves, will tidy up the
mess and remake Arda.[37]

The Last Battle will be with the forces of Evil. Although
Sauron was dispersed at the Fall of Barad-dûr,[38] Morgoth was
'thrust through the Door of Night beyond the Walls of the
World, into the Timeless Void'.[39] The presence of a guard and
the vigilance of Eärendil can only lead to the conclusion that
Morgoth is not utterly destroyed and that he may return.[40] But
the Earth shall not be destroyed and the Valar and the races
shall not be annihilated. The End will not be a Ragnarok or a
Gotterdamerung and, unlike the Aesir, the Valar will not perish.
All the Children shall survive to sing in the new song and be
present at the remaking of Arda. Arda must be remade for it is
marred and needs to be restored to its former beauty, as it was
before the depredations of Morgoth. The breaking of this world

heralds the remaking of the perfect Arda. If Arda were to be totally pulverised there could be no survivors. Saruman speaks symbolically when he refers to the 'breaking'. He uses the word 'this' to indicate Arda as we know it – Arda marred. The marred Arda must end at the remaking and become Arda Restored. The myth of the End is not gloomy or dismal. It is a myth of hope, of what will be, within the Plan of Ilúvatar.

Some commentators feel that the Final Battle is symbolised by the War of Wrath, the Battle of the Pelennor Fields and the Battle before the Black Gates of Mordor. Such views do not stand the test of the evidence that we have of the End. The battles to which I have referred are indicators of a change only, and not the finality that must come with the Last Battle.

In a consideration of the myth of the Creation and of the End, Randel Helms comments:

> Tolkien's mythology in *Ainulindale* thus holds to the Christian pattern of universal history: creation, fall of an angelic being and many of his peers, subsequent universal disharmony for a lengthy period, redemption, end of days, and finally restored universal harmony. We should not be surprised, therefore, to learn that *Ainulindale*, and indeed all *The Silmarillion*, finds a major source for its themes and structures in the Bible, a work, however, which Tolkien feels free to revise and use for his own creation story.[41]

Yet the same author discusses the music of the heavenly spheres as a theme for the creation myth. That theme was developed by Pythagoras and Plato – rational thinkers who wished to offer a logical explanation for the obvious mathematical harmony of the Universe – who despised myth as irrational. The theme of the spheres was developed by later writers and thinkers, but is not a theme that has been developed with any great enthusiasm in Genesis. If Helms's comment is followed to its logical conclusion, he is saying that Tolkien is using the Bible as a source for his themes, and tampers with them. That is not possible of Tolkien, a deeply religious person. The source for Tolkien's myths are the *themes* of all mythologies.

Paul H. Kocher has attempted to pinpoint Tolkien's mythic foundations, suggesting that Tolkien's 'prescription for his new mythology is the number of other mythologies that it *excludes*'.[42] Kocher excludes the mythologies of Greece, Rome, Finland and the Celts. He suggests the myths of the north as being inspirational. Certainly they were, but it is facile to draw parallels between the tales that constitute the mythologies, for these tales contain factual variables within them, even though they are a part of the same mythology. What they do have in common are the same *themes*. For example, Ragnarok and Armageddon are both apocalyptic in theme, but vastly different in realisation. The Norse and Christian myths would be significant if they *lacked* an eschatology.

In *content*, Tolkien's mythology bears a stronger resemblance to the north-west European myths, but to simply *exclude*, for example, the *Kalevala*, is to fly in the face of the evidence. The tale of Túrin Turambar has ingredients of the tale of Kullervo within it. The Silmarils are similar to the Sampo, the jewels of the *Kalevala*. Reams could be written drawing comparisons between the content of Tolkien's tales and those of the great literary myths. The result would be that the tales were – as Gandalf the Grey to Gandalf the White – like, yet unlike. The essence of myth in Tolkien's writing is present in the themes that he uses and develops and the themes present in other literary myths. He uses the language of myth in developing the themes. He is the myth-maker as artist. He is unrestrained by rituals or recreations. He has absolute freedom to create, like the Valar, within the framework of the theme – the theme of myth. To seek the derivative path and to compare Tolkien's stories with others is a fruitless journey.

What happens after death is a matter that is dealt with in almost all mythologies, and Tolkien approaches the question in quite a unique way. The true immortals, Ilúvatar, the Ainur and the Maiar *cannot* die. Even Morgoth Bauglir cannot be destroyed. The Elves are almost immortal in that they do not die of sickness or old age, but there are circumstances in which they *might* perish. Dwarves are mortal and are very long lived, and Men are the shortest lived of all, although long life was granted to the Númenóreans.

Death has been seen in myth as a punishment for some transgression against Divine law. When Man is in the Golden Age he is without sin and beloved of God (or the Gods). He does not die but lives in a state of bliss. As a result of sin, tragedy or foolishness, but usually the first, the perfection of the Golden Age comes to an end. Man learns the meaning of death, and his life becomes a brutal struggle for survival, dedicated to avoiding death for as long as possible.

Was there such a Fall in Arda? Not for Men, for death was not intended as a curse, but was the Gift of Ilúvatar. Why was it a gift? Because upon a man dying, his soul would return to Ilúvatar. This happens regardless of any error into which Man may have fallen. Thus, Ilúvatar can be seen as totally benevolent and totally forgiving. It was within the Plan of Ilúvatar that the desires and fate of Men should extend beyond the pre-ordained pattern of the Ainulindalë. The Elves are not aware of where Men go after death. 'Mandos had no power to withhold the spirits of Men that were dead within the confines of the World, after their time of waiting.'[43] The ultimate End is the return to the loving Creator. Clearly, death was not appointed as a punishment. Speaking to the Men of Númenor, the Messenger of the Valar said:

'Indeed the mind of Ilúvatar concerning you is not known to the Valar, and he has not revealed all things that are to come. But this we hold to be true, that your home is not here, neither in the land of Aman nor anywhere within the Circles of the World. And the Doom of Men, that they should depart, was at first a gift of Ilúvatar.'[44]

It was only after the corruption by Morgoth that Men *themselves* decided that death was a burden. But that was not Ilúvatar's reasoning. Within the Tolkien myth, Man has already fallen. In the early days, Men were befriended by both Elves and Morgoth. In the First Age there is mention only of the Edain and the Easterlings. The Edain were the Elf-friends who knew Ilúvatar and the Valar (in the religious sense) and thus appreciated the true nature of Morgoth. Apart from the Edain, the Race of Men lived in darkness, fearing or worshipping Morgoth.[45]

But if Men do not fall from Grace, do the Elves? Carpenter comments that the Elves are 'Man before the Fall which deprived him of his powers of achievement'.[46]

Unlike Man's original sin and dethronement, which were responsible for the sins of the world, 'elves, though capable of sin and error, have not "fallen" in the theological sense'.[47]

Kocher finds difficulty comprehending this latter concept.

But if the Elves are capable of sinning, and in fact do sin often enough in *The Silmarillion*, it is hard to see how they can have done so without first 'falling' from a state of innocence in the 'theological sense,' whatever the latter phrase means.[48]

'In the theological sense' means in the context of Genesis – wanton disobedience of the Word of God. Although nothing is decreed from the beginning, the Elves have a choice as well as certain moral imperatives which should be followed. If they choose to ignore the moral imperatives, they sin *for the first time* and then, as fallen, they must continue to sin. Sin involves choice. Adam and Eve had a choice – to follow the entrapment of the serpent or obey the Word of God. Their choice was the serpent. They fell. Tolkien suggests that the rebellion of created free will preceded the creation of the World. The World has within it, subcreatively introduced, evil, rebellions and discordant elements of its own nature when 'Eä' was spoken. The Fall or a corruption of all things within the Earth was a *possibility* although not inevitable. 'Elves themselves could do evil deeds.'[49] Elves are considered by Carpenter to be the ideal of every artist.[50] Their resistance to old age, death and disease does not bring their work to an end while it is still unfinished or imperfect.

There is a symbolic Fall among the Elves with consequences which bring them great trials and sorrow. Fëanor was the greatest of artists and craftsmen, a writer and user of words and skilled with his hands. Tolkien conceived in Fëanor the ultimate in Man's creativity. We can imagine Fëanor as a writer, a poet, a philologist, a singer and musician, a painter and sculptor, a builder and designer, a smith and metal craftsman. He is the supreme artist, skilled in every field of creative endeavour. His creativity is symbolised by 'a secret fire . . . kindled within him.'[51] But the Fire of creativity can become a raging inferno of destruction.

The creation of the Silmarils was the ultimate achievement and the beginning of the Doom of the Noldor. Part of the problem was the activity of Melkor. He was insidiously able to attract the Noldor with their love of hidden knowledge. Fëanor resisted Melkor and would not allow him to sully his art. For Melkor there could be only one answer to such impertinence – destruction. Melkor subtly set the Noldor against the Valar, and

Fëanor, while despising the Evil One, did not realise how effective the infiltration had been. And what is more, Fëanor desired the Silmarils for himself. The first obvious step in this downfall was to draw a sword on his half-brother, Fingolfin. For this act he was banished from Tirion by the Valar. Fëanor accepted this punishment, but desired the Silmarils with an increasing love. When the Trees were destroyed, Fëanor was asked to give the Silmarils to the Valar, so that Yavanna could restore life to the Trees. Fëanor would not do so. It would break his heart. But he did not realise that he could not in fact give up the Silmarils, for they had been stolen by Morgoth. When he did find out about the theft, he cursed Morgoth and the Valar who had summoned him, and in his pride, anger and folly, lashed out at all around him, both innocent and evil. He broke the banishment of the Valar and returned to Tirion where he swore the great Oath of Fëanor that bound his House to hatred and revenge at all costs. His desire for the Silmarils was having a disastrous effect. The Valar implored him not to follow Morgoth to Middle-earth but to no avail. The Kinslaying and the Doom of the Noldor followed hard on the heels of Fëanor's foolish Oath.

The Fall for the Noldor and for the Elves in general was from the utmost pinnacle of the Golden Age, the Bliss of Valinor, in which Elves and Valar dwelt together. The highest artistic achievement of one of their number led to their downfall. The Bliss of Valinor came to an end with the destruction of the Trees and for the Elves who determined to go to Middle-earth, 'the Valar will fence Valinor against you, and shut you out'.[52] Fëanor's sin was great. Minor peccadilloes could be tolerated but consistent and flagrant breaches of moral imperatives paid tragic dividends. Fëanor, as the ultimate Elven genius, represents the epitome of Elvendom and Elven potential. His faults are similarly magnified. Because he is what he is to the Noldor, they must follow in his wake. When Fëanor falls he carries with him, like a storm-swollen torrent, the rest of the Noldor. And there can be no doubt – Fëanor falls, and his fall is so great, as Wolsey says in Shakespeare's *Henry VIII*, 'that he falls like Lucifer, never to hope again'. For the rest of the Elves it was a fall too, for Fëanor's Oath could not be ignored or put aside. As an Oath, it had to be worked out, and until it was, the Valar, despite their pity, were unable to assist the Noldor in Beleriand.

Fëanor said that, if he died, he would be the first of the Eldar to do so in Aman. Mandos replied that it was not the first death, for Melkor had slain Finwë, King of the Noldor, and spilled the first blood in the Blessed Realm. Death for Elves was quite a different proposition from death for Men.

> The Elves remain until the end of days, and their love of the Earth and all the world is more single and more poignant therefore, and as the years lengthen ever more sorrowful. For the Elves die not till the world dies, unless they are slain or waste in grief . . . neither does age subdue their strength, unless one grow weary of ten thousand centuries; and dying they are gathered to the Halls of Mandos in Valinor, whence they may in time return.[53]

Tolkien notes the tale of Míriel, mother of Fëanor, who tried to die and which had disastrous results and consequences in the Fall of the High Elves.[54] All her spirit was given to Fëanor[55] which must be the consequence to which Tolkien refers. We can only speculate if Míriel died before Finwë. Fëanor refers to a first *slaying* in Valinor, a word that carries connotations of violent and unwilling death. Finwë was slain. Míriel lost the will to live.

Tolkien also says[56] that the slaying of an Elf did not lead naturally to 'death'; they were rehabilitated and reborn and eventually recovered memory of all their past; they remained identical. From the Halls of Mandos, the Elves could go elsewhere in

Valinor, but could not return to Middle-earth.[57] Of all the Elves, only two truly died in the sense that they received the Gift of Men. Lúthien and Arwen forsook their Elvishness and the Blessed Realm, became mortal and passed away. The other death that is important in the myth is that of Gandalf the Grey. His spirit left him on Zirakzigil and naked he was sent back. Did he die in fact, or did his spirit, like that of an Elf, return to Valinor, to be sent back at the behest of Ilúvatar. Gandalf was angelic in nature, one of the *Istari* or wizards who were 'embodied in physical bodies capable of pain, and weariness ... and of being "killed"'.[58] He passes all the moral tests that are put before him.

> It was for him a *sacrifice* to perish on the Bridge in defence of his companions, less perhaps than for a mortal Man or Hobbit, since he had a far greater inner power than they; but also more, since it was a humbling and abnegation of himself in conformity to 'the Rules'... He was handing over to the Authority that ordained the Rules, and giving up personal hope of success.[59]

Tolkien explains that Gandalf really died, was changed, and explains his reincarnation in terms of Gandalf's angelic nature. He came back, or was sent back, with enhanced powers.[60] In *Unfinished Tales* it is said[61] that Gandalf's return from death was brief, and that he was a radiant flame, although veiled, save in great need. Saruman, on the other hand, died absolutely, and where his spirit went, none can tell. Because Gandalf was a Maia, his reincarnation is understandable. Sauron, another Maia, is different. Sauron's fair form was destroyed in the Wreck of Númenor, but he came back in a different shape. After his mutilation by Isildur, he is never seen again in mortal form, although his embodiment is the subject of suggestion, especially by Gollum.

Man's myths of death and the hereafter are many and varied.

The hope that Tolkien offers for both Man and Elf is encouraging. There is an Elysium in Arda, reached by the 'Straight Road'. Elves could return to Valinor, but it was forbidden to Men, especially after the Valar lifted the land of Aman into the realm of hidden things. But the Edain saw that the Elves could still sail to the Deathless Land by way of the 'Straight Road', running as by a bridge, invisible to Men and impassable to mortal flesh. The precise nature of the way was unknown to Men, although they were aware that it was there. But for all Men, the roads across the sea were bent because the World had become round. A few mariners, and those about to die, did achieve the Straight Road and the concept of the journey to Valinor is one of the most beautifully realised in mythology, a vision of peace and beauty.[62] Those mortals who went to Aman could only dwell there for a brief while, a time of peace and healing, at the end of which they would pass away (die at their own desire and of free will) to destinations of which the Elves knew nothing.[63] Of the mortals who went to Valinor for such a sojourn, we know only of Frodo and Gimli by name, although it is suggested that Sam passed on the Straight Road. The achievement of Valinor is the achievement of a state of perfect bliss, reserved for but a few. It puts the capstone on the mythological concepts of death, life after death and immortality.

Tolkien's myth of the Flood developed from his own fascination with the Atlantis myth.[64] He said:

> This legend or myth or dim memory of some ancient history
> has always troubled me. In sleep I had the dreadful dream of
> the ineluctable Wave, either coming out of the quiet sea, or
> coming in towering over the green inlands.[65]

The manner in which Tolkien places his interest in Atlantis within the history of Middle-earth is creative and novel. The drowning of Beleriand does not constitute the classic theme of the Flood. The Flood theme carries with it an implication of punishment for some transgression or evils after a Fall, a washing away of the old, to be replaced by a newer and hopefully better world.

After the drowning of Beleriand, the Valar raised Andor, the Land of Gift. It was situated nearer to Valinor than to Middle-earth. The breaking and drowning of Beleriand was as a result of conflict between elemental powers of Middle-earth – those that were creative and those that were destructive. Beleriand was the site of the conflict of the Elves and Morgoth and the area of Elvish predominance in Middle-earth. It was not an area of the Golden Age but was more a place for the trials and sorrows of the Noldor. The rest of mainland Middle-earth sees the development of Man beside the Elves, leading up to the Last Alliance and the gradual fading of the Elves from Middle-earth.

But if Elves and Men met in mainland Middle-earth, Andor or Númenor was the exclusive preserve for men. For them, the Golden Age was offered. Unlike the classical theme of a Fall following on a Golden Age, the Edain were rewarded with a Golden Age that they had not had before. In addition, they were given a greater lifespan and a proximity to Paradise, for the sea was not bent at that time. Man had the chance and the choice. He could use his blessings for positive purposes. But despite the great gifts and the chances that were offered, Man became disenchanted. Sauron was able to use the proximity of the Undying Lands to sow the seeds of discontent in the hearts of the Men of Númenor, and played especially upon the Gift of Ilúvatar – death. He turned the blessing into a curse and a fear of the unknown. He was able to use Ar-Pharazôn's overweening pride to such an extent that the Fall of the Men of Númenor took place with the breaking of the Ban of the Valar. It is true that the Númenóreans break other moral rules before the Great

Armament but the Ban of the Valar, by which Men were not allowed to go to Valinor, was an absolute Ban and was tied to the very essence of being of the race of Man.

The Fall of the Númenóreans is a Fall in the theological sense. The actions of Ar-Pharazôn are in direct opposition to a stated Ban imposed by superhuman powers and derived from the authority and decree of the One. By seeking to overturn the ban, Man attempts to tamper with his essential nature and with the Theme of Ilúvatar. When Ar-Pharazôn steps on the Undying Lands, the Valar lay down their government. What else could they do? The purpose of Ar-Pharazôn constituted a challenge to Ilúvatar. So God 'showed forth his power, and he changed the fashion of the world'.[66] A great chasm opened between Númenor and the Deathless Lands, the waters flowed into it and the Earth was shaken. The Great Seas west of Middle-earth were cast back and the Empty Lands east of it, and new seas and new lands were made. The World was diminished. Valinor and Eressëa were taken from it. All the coasts and seaward regions of the western world suffered great change and downpours of rain; the sea invaded the land, islands were drowned and new islands were uplifted; the hills crumbled and rivers were changed into new courses. A few, the Elendili, survived to carry the remnants of the Númenórean civilisation back to Middle-earth, but the true glory of Númenor and of the Golden Age for Men became but a memory.

The Flood is more than just a retribution. It marks an ending of the cosmogonic myth of the Creation of Arda. The Final shape of the Earth is settled; Paradise is a place apart; the boundaries of Middle-earth are defined. These lands are the lands of Men. Within these lands the conflicts must be resolved and whether Man rises or falls will be determined. The Silmarils, the basis of the struggle between the Elves and Morgoth, are gone, Beleriand is broken, Morgoth is expelled and the Elves are exiles in Middle-earth. Sauron is the power of evil, and can only use what Middle-earth can offer to be shaped to his evil ends. Likewise, Man must depend only on the resources available to him. Within this framework the development of the other myths of Middle-earth take place, especially that of the Ring, and the ending of the cycle in the accession of Aragorn Elessar to the throne of the Reunited Kingdom.

Yet, more significantly, in the overall cosmogonic myth, post-diluvian Middle-earth possesses one quality of sadness and truth, not only for the Realms in Exile, but for us today as well:

And there is not now upon Earth any place abiding where the memory of a time without evil is preserved.[67]

CHAPTER 4

Wheels within Wheels: The Submyth and Reality

A study of Tolkien is like a geological exploration. There are different levels or strata of meaning. For this reason Tolkien's writing can mean many things for many people. It can be an exercise in linguistics[1] or Jungian psychology[2]. Yet, when we look at the mythic stratum, we find that there are a number of substrata! Tolkien, within his major mythic creation, has employed the use of submyths, especially within *The Lord of the Rings*. He has developed a mythology for those who live in the Third Age, but when we consider the entire concept, the Third Age is itself part of the total mythic creation.

The development of his languages and words carries mythic elements. According to Treebeard the 'Elves made all the old words: they began it'[3] and this was before the birth of Fëanor. As far as writing was concerned, Rúmil was the first on record to compose a Tengwar, a written alphabet.[4] Fëanor improved upon this, creating the Tengwar of Fëanor. Words for Tolkien are myth. The language that he has devised is, like any language, a living, growing and developing thing. The words embody a story, a mythic origin. This is not uncommon. Ovid's *Metamorphoses* are tales of explanation. They tell us not only how things came to be but also how we arrived at a name for those things. Consequently, the name is placed in a historical context that has its origin in myth. The Eddaic Saga uses this device. All the names of Odin relate to the acts of Odin and are a shorthand means of summing up an Odin myth. Fëanáro – Spirit of Fire – is the most creative and inspired of the Noldor. His name harks back to the Flame Imperishable of Ilúvatar. That Fëanor should embody fire, the symbol of creativity, indicates to us that he is by nature a creative character.

The river Nimrodel is named after the Elf-maiden of the same name. Her tale is part of the mythic history of the Third Age, and is related in verse and prose by Legolas. The myth is expanded in *Unfinished Tales*[5] and provides a background for an etymological discussion of the names of rivers, and especially the River Gilrain of Lebennin in Gondor. Similarly, Amroth and Nimrodel are associated with the development of the *flet* or *talan* – the tree platform used in Lothlórien.

In a chronological context the origin of the flower *elanor* which reminded Aragorn so much of Arwen Undómiel at Cerin Amroth, is first mentioned in the Tale of Aldarion and Erendis in *Unfinished Tales*.[6] It is said that the fragrance of the plant brought heart's ease and was one of the flowers brought by the Eldar to the wedding of Erendis.

Many of the names have a mythic or mytho-historical background. Lothlórien is named after the land of Lórien in Aman. But the very nature of the Lórien in Aman gives us a clue to the nature of Lothlórien in Middle-earth. The first Minas Tirith was a fortress built on Tol Sirion by Finrod shortly after his return to Middle-earth. The Paths of the Dead are so named because of the mythic inhabitants who broke their oath to Isildur. The naming in *The Lord of the Rings* harks back to a prototype or archetype of a concept established in the First Age or earlier and recounted in *The Silmarillion*. The original naming is far back, indeed so far back as to be mythic, except for Eldar such as Galadriel and Celeborn.

A further concept which is developed by Tolkien is the theme of the Quest. Quests feature strongly throughout the Middle-earth works. The essential journey of Man to the achievement of a higher or more complete state of awareness is a common theme in mythic literature. The Quest of Gawain was one with which Tolkien was intimately familiar as was the concept of the hero who maintains his existence but whose essential valour or fortitude is nevertheless challenged or unrealised or reduced. Such is the case with Túrin and Frodo and the true realisation of the human potential is reflected in the Quests of Beren, Aragorn and Eärendil. Certainly, if we view the life of Christ as an example of a mythic Quest, with Christ as the Quest Hero we may see certain similarities in Tolkien's work, but *similarities* only. There has been considerable comment by a number of commentators on the Christian aspects of Tolkien's work and an academic search for Jesus Christ in Middle-earth. The truth is that Tolkien excluded a reference or a parallel to the Son of Man or the Son of God and certainly nowhere do we have a Son of Ilúvatar as the redeemer for the ills of the world. There is the symbol of the King sacrificed for the hurt of his people, or of a willing and selfless death or an end to mortal life to bring about a eucatastrophic event, most obviously in the tale of Eärendil. But all these themes of myth are pre-Christian and some go back as far as the concept of Rex Nemorensis (the King of the Wood) which will be examined in Chapter 9. Many of the actions of Jesus Christ are symbolic as well as real. Christ as the Quest Hero is the ritual sacrifice. He is rebirth in Nature, Easter being the beginning of the northern Spring. He died on a 'tree', a symbol of natural death and rebirth, rooted in the depths of the Earth. In fact, the Bible is a mythic history as well as a sacred Book. The celebration of the Eucharist is a mythic re-enactment of the Last Supper. In the mythic sense there is a *Christ-like* figure in Tolkien's work, but a parallel of Christ as a faithful Christian would understand Him does not exist. What we are dealing with are in fact mythic symbols. Part of the problem is the unfortunate treatment that 'myths' have had. Myth has been said to be a lie. Thus, if we refer to the 'mythic' Christ, are we saying that Christ is a lie? The answer is no. Of all the ancient Mediterranean myths, the Christian one survives. It is a living myth and that is a fact. Whether or not it is true is a matter of faith. The same can be said for all myths. It would have been blasphemous for Tolkien to write a Christ into his cosmos in the way that the faithful Christian understands Christ. Yet as a symbolic and mythic figure, the *similarities* exist.

The successful achievement of the Quest Hero is 'a victory in which all men can rejoice and enjoy because [the enemy] was a monster, hostile to all men and to all humane fellowship and joy'.[7] This is the eucatastrophe referred to by Tolkien in 'On Fairy-Stories' and is the essence of the Quest. We shall see the way in which Tolkien deals with the Quest Hero in Chapter 7.

The Hobbit and *The Lord of the Rings* contain within them by far the greatest number of references to myths of a former age. These myths work on two levels even within the books. For men, the content of the myths took place in a past thousands of years old. For Elves such as Círdan, Elrond, Galadriel, Celeborn and Glorfindel they are a part of the reality which is denied to mortals, emphasising the 'apartness' of the two races.

The Hobbit gives us tantalising glimpses into a developed mythology of Middle-earth. The swords Orcrist and Glamdring have an ancient history revealed by Elrond who identifies them as swords from the city of Gondolin, destroyed eons ago in the First Age – so long ago in mortal terms that its existence lies in the mists of myth rather than in real history. Gondolin then takes the myth further back to the Oath of Fëanor, the Doom of Mandos and, ultimately, to the Will of Ilúvatar.

The War of the Orcs and Dwarves is given a passing reference in the chapter 'Over Hill and Under Hill'. That war, with its climax at the Battle of Azanulbizar in which Thorin Oakenshield and Dain Ironfoot took part, is related to the entire history of Khazad-dûm (Moria) which leads us back to Durin and the Seven Fathers of the Dwarves, their creation by Aulë and their awakening by Ilúvatar.

The nature of the Elvish races is developed in 'Flies and Spiders' and in this chapter there is a reference to the Elves of Middle-earth who enjoyed the light of Trees.

> For most of them . . . were descended from the ancient tribes that never went to Faerie [Aman] in the West. There the Light-elves and the Deep-elves and the Sea-elves went and lived for ages . . . before some came back into the Wide World. In the Wide World the Wood-elves lingered in the twilight of our Sun and Moon, but loved best the stars.[8]

To the men of Lake Town the Dwarves under the Mountain were the stuff of legend for

> some still sang old songs of the dwarf-kings of the Mountain, Thror and Thrain of the race of Durin, and of the coming of the Dragon and the fall of the lords of the Dale.[9]

The return of the Dwarf Lords had become a part of the oral tradition of Lake Town, and the song concerning the return of the King under the Mountain harked back to the legend and yet held that prophetic note that legends of returning Kings contain – upon the return of the King a new Golden Age will begin.

> The streams shall run in gladness,
> The lakes shall shine and burn,
> All sorrow fail and sadness
> At the Mountain-king's return![10]

The dragon was real enough, but his background was veiled in myth. His lineage was old. In *The Silmarillion* we are told of the drakes created by Morgoth, and the nature of Smaug's creation and existence are revealed. The dragon's potential for evil is not revealed until Gandalf told of his chance meeting with Thorin at Bree in *The Lord of the Rings*.

The races of the dragons numbered three and they were Morgoth's minions. The Urulóki or fire-drakes, of which Glaurung was one, breathed fire but did not fly. Those dragons that did fly as well as breathing fire first appeared in the War of Wrath. Cold-drakes did not breathe fire and were only found in Ered Mithrin. Smaug didn't play any part in the War of Wrath, but he came from Erebor and lived there for two hundred years. His mere existence is a connection with the distant mythic history of Middle-earth and with the Master of Evil.

The use by Tolkien of his own mythic history is continued in *The Lord of the Rings* but with greater depth and meaning. The mythic background had been conceived and existed and, as he said,

> a part of the 'fascination' [of *The Lord of the Rings*] consists in the vistas of yet more legend and history, to which this work does not contain a full clue . . . The new situation, established at the beginning of the Third Age, leads on eventually and inevitably to ordinary History . . . Gone was the 'mythological' time when Valinor (or Valimar), the Land of the Valar (gods if you will) existed physically in the Uttermost West, or the Eldaic (Elvish) immortal Isle of Eressëa; or the Great Isle

of Westernesse (Númenor-Atlantis). After the Downfall of
Númenor, and its destruction, all this was removed from the
'physical' world and not reachable by material means.[11]

The mythological background was extremely important to
Tolkien:

> Since the whole matter from beginning to end is mainly
> concerned with the relation of Creation to making and
> sub-creation (and subsidiarily with the related matter of
> 'mortality'), it must be clear that references to these things
> are not casual, but fundamental.[12]

Much of the background mythology had to be reworked so that
it could be incorporated into *The Lord of the Rings* and would
all fit in context. Sauron, as Dark Lord, was not conceived until
The Lord of the Rings although a hint of him as The Necromancer
appears in *The Hobbit*. Nor was the identity and lineage of
Strider developed at the time when he first appeared.
Lothlórien, the Mines of Moria and Fangorn were but names.[13]

Gondolin was the subject of a written tale – 'The Fall of
Gondolin' – and in the Third Age was a far-distant realm hinted
at in *The Hobbit*. It was further developed as the home of
Eärendil, father of Elrond, and a realm wherein dwelt mighty
rulers and great power. The brief mention of Gondolin and
Beleriand in the text and appendices to *The Lord of the Rings*
puts them into the context of an aeons old history, recounted
with such reverence that it has achieved the status of at least
legend or even myth. The action of *The Lord of the Rings*
becomes a part of this tapestry. Sam, when he said that he felt as
if he was 'inside a song',[14] feels that he is within part of the oral
tradition of Middle-earth, for myth is in origin an oral tradition. The oral recounting of tales is part of the heritage of the

Third Age. Aragorn recounts the Tales of Beren and Lúthien in the mode of *ann-thennath*, a mode adopted by the bards and those who maintained the oral tradition. The prose version is given in short by Aragorn and at length in *The Silmarillion* with hints of a longer verse account – the Lay of Leithian. The oral tradition is preserved by the Dwarves for it is Gimli who recounts the glories of Khazad-dûm and the myth of Durin's Crown. Legolas recites the tale of Amroth and Nimrodel. The continuing nature of the oral tradition is preserved by Bilbo, from whom Sam learned passages of 'The Fall of Gil-Galad', and who embellishes upon the tradition by composing his own lays including his verses on the history of Eärendil. This ancient tradition is in sharp contrast to the earthy and day to day verses that are so much a part of hobbit life, such as the walking songs or the bath song.

The concept of the oral tradition is again placed into focus by Sam who comments on the nature of mythic history on the Stairs of Cirith Ungol. Commenting on 'the adventures' he says:

> I used to think that they were things the wonderful folk of the stories went out and looked for, because they wanted them, because they were exciting and life was a bit dull, a kind of sport, as you might say. But that's not the way of it with the tales that really mattered, or the ones that stay in the mind.[15]

He goes on to talk about the tale of Beren and how he wrested the Silmaril from the Iron Crown of Morgoth, a tale that

> goes on past the happiness and the grief and beyond it – and the Silmaril went on and came to Eärendil. . . . Why, to think of it, we're in the same tale still! It's going on. Don't the great tales never end?[16]

The legendary background, the distant and mythic past of Middle-earth is still a functioning part of the present tale, and the actions of the characters in *The Lord of the Rings* are a part of a continuing fabric that is being woven.

The Ents are part of the mythology of Middle-earth. Their existence is revealed slowly, the first hint being a moving tree seen on the North Moors of the Shire. Celeborn warns of the entanglements of Fangorn, yet knows Treebeard and upon meeting him calls him Eldest. Aragorn comments: 'Then there is truth in the old legends about ... the giant shepherds of the trees ... I thought they were only a memory of ancient days, if indeed they were ever more than a legend of Rohan.'[17] To the Elves they were more than a legend. As Legolas says, 'every Elf in Wilderland has sung songs of the old Onodrim and their long sorrow. Yet even among us they are only a memory'.[18] Gandalf must explain the legend to Théoden:

> They are the shepherds of the trees ... Is it so long since you listened to tales by the fireside? There are children in your land who, out of the twisted threads of story, could pick the answer to your question. You have seen Ents, O King, Ents out of Fangorn Forest, which in your tongue you call the Entwood. Did you think that the name was given only in idle fancy?[19]

Treebeard himself clarifies the legend. The Elves taught the Ents to speak and the Ents kept the oral tradition of lists of the living creatures of Middle-earth. Treebeard introduces Merry and Pippin to a part of the mythic reality of Middle-earth, to the Willowmeads of Tasarinan, to the history of the naming of Lothlórien, Laurelindórinan, and the sad and poignant tale of the Entwives. What were myths to the Dúnedain and the Rohirrim, and ancient memories to the Elves become part of the history of Middle-earth.

The treasures of Númenor brought to Middle-earth by Elendil are partly historical and partly mythic. The scion of the Tree, the *palantíri* and, possibly, the Elendilmir, are couched in mystery. The Elendilmir was the symbolic mark of royalty in the North for the Kings of Arnor who wore no crown.[20] The origin of the Elendilmir was obscure but the secret is revealed in *Unfinished Tales*,[21] when, in restoring Orthanc, Gimli found a hidden closet in which he and Elessar located 'a treasure without price, long mourned as lost for ever: the Elendilmir itself, the white star of Elvish crystal upon a fillet of *mithril* that had descended from Silmarien to Elendil'.[22] A second Elendilmir, an echo of the original which burned on the brow of Isildur, had been made for Valandil. The original had been lost with Isildur at Gladden Fields and had been recovered by Saruman but had become part of the mysterious and legendary past of Middle-earth. *Unfinished Tales* makes it clear that the Elendilmir was part of the treasure of Númenor. Silmarien was the daughter and eldest child of Tar-Elendil and her son Valandil was first Lord of Adúnië.

The *palantíri*, on the other hand, had a far greater lineage. In Middle-earth they were 'never matters of ... common knowledge, even in Númenor'.[23] After the loss of the Ithil-stone in TA 2002, they lost their official use and passed out of the general memory of people and 'the rhymes of lore that spoke of them were if remembered no longer understood; their operations were transformed in legend into the Elvish powers of the ancient kings'.[24] They were made in Eldamar by the Noldor and Gandalf speculated that they may have been made by Fëanor himself. Thus a link with the mythic First Age is established and the connection remains, for there were in fact eight *palantíri*, the master stone being on the Isle of Avállonë towards which Elendil gazed with 'Straight Sight' (the visual equivalent of the Straight Way) through the *palantír* of Elostirion at Emyn

Beraid. The comment by Gandalf that 'in Arnor they were remembered only in a rhyme of lore among the Dúnedain'[25] places them within the oral mythic tradition of Middle-earth.

The origin of the White Tree is also part of that oral tradition which establishes a link with the Undying Lands. The White Tree of Gondor originated from a fruit of Nimloth which was taken by Isildur from the King's Court at Númenor. The resulting sapling was planted in Minas Ithil and a seedling was taken by Isildur to Arnor. This was later planted in Minas Anor as a memorial to Anárion. The Tree or its offspring survived until the reign of the Steward Belecthor when it died and the withered remains were left in the Court of the Fountain. The true lineage of the Tree is revealed by Aragorn who called it a 'scion of the Eldest of Trees'[26] when he found the sapling growing on the slopes of Mount Mindolluin. Gandalf traced its history to Nimloth, a seedling of Galathilion which was the White Tree of the Eldar made by Yavanna and was a model of Telperion, although Gandalf says it came from a fruit of Telperion of many names, Eldest of Trees. The significance of the survival of the seedling was symbolic of the survival of the line of Elendil which had remained secret and hidden for so many years.

The significance of the Númenórean treasures is that they establish a link with the world before the Change and with the Undying Lands which are removed. They were real but with the passage of time fell into mystery and memory only, yet took unto themselves in the minds of men a great and mythical significance as symbols of a greater, better Golden Time and they became incorporated into the oral tradition of Men. From another tale of the oral tradition comes the Blade that was Broken. Elendil's broken sword Narsil was used to cut the Ring from Sauron's finger. The sword was taken by Ohtar, esquire of Isildur, who bore it away from the disaster at Gladden Fields.[27] Upon its return to Imladris it became a memory in the minds of all but the Dúnedain and the Elves of Imladris, and it became one of the many myths surrounding the end of Isildur. For example, because Isildur was slain with arrows, an arrow was believed to be Isildur's Bane.[28] This version of the death of Isildur was the only one that Faramir knew. The mystical riddle that was spoken to Faramir and Boromir in a dream – 'Seek for the Sword that was broken' – indicates the validity of Elrond's prophecy[29] that the sword would not be forged anew until the Ring should be discovered again, and the imminence of a legend becoming reality is a theme which is prevalent in *The Lord of the Rings*.

Galadriel is a figure of myth and mystery both in Rohan in an oral tradition – 'In Dwimordene, in Lórien'[30] – 'Then there is a Lady in the Golden Wood, as old tales tell! . . . Few escape her nets, they say'[31] – and in Gondor,

> You passed through the Hidden Land . . . but it seems that you little understood its power. If Men have dealings With the Mistress of Magic who dwells in the Golden Wood, then they may look for strange things to follow . . . *O Boromir . . . What did she say to you, the Lady that dies not?*[32]

Few understood the nature or the true history of Galadriel and Celeborn, the latter being the true ruler of Lothlórien. Naturally the image of a beautiful and mysterious witch in Lórien is far more perilous than the magnificence of an Elf-Lord from the Undying Lands. As it is said in *Unfinished Tales* the myths surrounding Galadriel and Celeborn, like so many myths of mystical persons, are problematical and 'there are severe inconsistencies "embedded in the traditions"'.[33] In terms of symbolism, Galadriel must represent the unknown and unseen perils that can be associated with such an extraordinary natural phenomenon as Lothlórien. She is one of the elemental creatures of the

Earth and, as a figure of mystery and peril, she is the progenitor of a later and similar, but somewhat reduced perilous sprite, Titania.

The hobbits themselves represent creatures of legend who walk the Earth. Halflings are part of the legendary tradition of Rohan and Gondor. As Théoden said:

> Now here before my eyes stand yet another of the folk of legend. Are not these the Halflings, that some among us call the Holbytlan? ... All that is said among us is that far away, over many hills and rivers, live the halfling folk that dwell in holes in sand-dunes. But there are no legends of their deeds.[34]

In Gondor, Halflings were named in the prophetic poem that drew Boromir on his fateful mission. Peregrin became a person of some importance in Minas Tirith, being honoured with the title *Ernil i Pheriannath* – the Prince of the Halflings.

But the central legend of the Third Age which becomes reality has its origin in the Second Age. The legend, of course, is that of the Ring.

The One Ring was one of a number that were made in the early years of the Second Age. They worked in different ways and different fates befell them. In the Third Age they vanished from the reality of Middle-earth and, with the exception of the Dwarf Rings, fell into the realms of memory and legend. As far as the High Elves were concerned the existence of the One Ring was never in doubt. Elrond and Círdan were aware that Isildur took it, notwithstanding their protestations. Furthermore, the fate of the Elven Rings was bound up with the One, for when the One was destroyed the Three would lose their power.

> The chief power (of all the rings alike) was the prevention or slowing of *decay* (i.e. 'change' viewed as a regrettable thing),

the preservation of what is desired or loved, or its semblance
– this is more or less an Elvish motive. But also they enhanced
the natural powers of a possessor – thus approaching 'magic',
a motive easily corruptible into evil, a lust for domination.[35]

The Three were made by the Elves of Eregion and were directed
towards the preservation of beauty.

It is quite apparent that the High Elves of Middle-earth have
a lot less power than the Elves of Beleriand or of the Blessed
Realm. Elrond is Half-elven. The Ring Vilya enhances and
amplifies the powers that he possesses to a considerable degree.
Círdan, an Elf from the Blessed Lands, possessed Narya until
he relinquished it to Gandalf. Galadriel holds Nenya. She too
came from the Blessed Lands. The importance of the One to
these High Elves can only be viewed in the context of a dimin-
ishing power of the Elves that, as at the end of the Third Age,
has been taking place for some time. They have been absent
from the Blessed Land and the end of Beleriand saw the
destruction of much of the glory of the Elf-realm. The end of
the One means the end of the Three which enhance Elvish
power to such a degree. Men never associated Elvish power in
the Third Age with the Elven Rings. To Men, Elves were
magical. It was a part of their elvishness. Even without the
power of an Elven Ring Elves such as Legolas had a sense of
heightened awareness and highly acute senses of sight and
hearing. And Legolas did not sleep but let his mind wander in
the paths of Elvish dreams.

It was in SA 1200 that the Gwaith-i-Mírdain of Eregion and
their greatest craftsman Celebrimbor, grandson of Fëanor, fell
under the promises and wiles of Sauron, who came to them as
Annatar, Lord of Gifts. He promised to aid the Elves in enrich-
ing Middle-earth and he taught the Gwaith-i-Mírdain much
and Rings were made under his guidance. The Three were not

sullied by Sauron, but he was aware of their existence although without the One he could not know where they were.

In SA 1590 the Three were completed. In SA 1600 Sauron forged the One. Into this Ring passed a great part of his own power, 'a frequent and very significant motive in myth and fairy-story'.[36] The One enhanced and amplified Sauron's power, and even though he may not wear it he would be in rapport with it, and he was not diminished unless someone else came into possession of it. The power of the Ring to render its wearer invisible is, like the passage of the Maker's power, a common feature of magic rings in myth.[37]

The Ring was a very potent reality in Middle-earth in the Second Age. War never ceased. Eregion was destroyed. The Elven ring-maker Celebrimbor was killed. Khazad-dûm was no longer open. Sauron's power, enhanced by the Ring, seemed irresistible. The Rulers of Men were enslaved by the Nine Rings although Ringwraiths or Nazgûl did not appear until SA 2251. From SA 1693–1700 Sauron ravaged west of the Misty Mountains over-running Eriador to Ered Luin. Only the intervention of the Númenóreans under Tar-Minastir drove him from Eriador, ending the Black Years. It was this action more than any other that aroused the wrath of Sauron against the Númenóreans although the Edain had had contact with Middle-earth long before Tar-Minastir and were well aware of the rising power of Sauron.[38] A fortress was established at Umbar and Ar-Pharazôn 'captured' Sauron and returned with him to Númenor. It is obvious that Sauron allowed this to happen, notwithstanding the Ring.

> He perceived that the power and majesty of the Kings of the Sea surpassed all rumour of them, so that he could not trust even the greatest of his servants to withstand them; and he saw not his time yet to work his will with the Dúnedain. And

he was crafty, well skilled to gain what he would by subtlety when force might not avail.[39]

No doubt Sauron's war with Ar-Pharazôn would have been a victory for him given the power of the Ring. Yet it would have been a terrific contest of wills and a Pyrrhic victory for Sauron in terms of retaining his sway over his Middle-earth territories. Instead of using the raw and violent power of the Ring, Sauron preferred to use more subtle forms of power – persuasion and infiltration – to bring about the conquest but not the ruin of Númenor. But not even Sauron's power could overcome the power of Ilúvatar, and the Ring was not with him for after he returned to Middle-earth 'he took up again his great Ring in Barad-dûr'.[40]

Ten years later he was in a position to challenge the realms in exile until his overthrow in SA 3441 when the Ring was taken from him. What was it that allowed the Last Alliance to overcome Sauron who wielded the One? The Elven Rings worn by Gil-galad and Círdan were Rings of making, healing and preserving. They were not Rings that would enhance power for war. The host of the Last Alliance

was fairer and more splendid in arms than any that has since been seen in Middle-earth, and none greater has been mustered since the host of the Valar went against Thangorodrim.[41]

None could stand against Aeglos, the spear of Gil-galad, and Elendil's sword Narsil filled orcs and men with fear. Sauron's force was so beset that he wrestled *corps-à-corps* with Gil-galad and Elendil. In such a fight the Ring could have no power for the contest was one of strength and will. Sauron fell taking Gil-galad and Elendil with him. The Ring passed to Isildur and thence to the River at Gladden Fields and into memory.

And there in the dark pools amid the Gladden Fields . . . the Ring passed out of knowledge and legend; and even so much of its history is known now only to a few, and the Council of the Wise could discover no more.[42]

Its existence became a matter of the past, forgotten even in legend. Certainly there was knowledge of a powerful token or amulet possessed at one time by the Dark Lord. Yet even he was thought to have passed from Middle-earth and it was not until TA 2850 that Sauron's return to Middle-earth was confirmed by Gandalf. But Sauron did not have the Ring. The nature of the amulet was known to only a very few. In Gondor it was referred to in Faramir's dream as 'Isildur's Bane' but the nature of the Bane was a matter of speculation and was thought, as we have seen, to be an arrow. To those who interested themselves in the lore the Ring became a matter of fascination, either for the power that it could bring to its finder or for the terror that it could bring to Middle-earth if, as it must, it found its way back to the hand of Sauron. Gandalf and the Elves realised that Morgoth's servant could only be vanquished if the Ring were destroyed. Saruman, who propagated the myth that the Ring fell into Anduin and was rolled to the Sea, wanted to use it to enhance his own power. Thus, when a Ring was found by Bilbo, no one could be sure that it was the One. Many, no doubt, would have preferred to imagine that it was not rather than face the horror that it could bring. It was not until Gandalf cast it into the fire at Bag End in April TA 3018 that its true nature was revealed. Gandalf preferred to complete all his investigations before he went to the Ring itself and confirm the truth. And having found the truth, it could not be kept a secret forever and decisions had to be made. The Ring had to be destroyed. Thus, 3,016 years after the Disaster of Gladden Fields, the Ring appeared from the mists of myth and legend. Sauron's amulet of power, that had enabled him to overrun almost all of Middle-earth, that had caused the myths and tales of the Dark Years, that was the basis of nameless fear and all-pervading evil, had returned; the worst and most dreadful myth of the Third Age was found to be a reality.

For those who live in primitive societies, myth is a day-to-day reality, an explanation for why things have been, are and will be. Myth provides the basis for the rituals that ensure survival. We have seen how the mythic tales become a part of the cultural and literary heritage of a society. Tolkien has engrafted his own mythic development into his essentially mythic world. Within the overall tapestry of his myth, Tolkien has woven sub-myths. They begin as a reality and become a part of the culture. Then they disappear and become a distant memory. But at a later time, in the form of a loose thread, they come back into the reality of the developing mythology. Tolkien's submyths are substrata within the greater stratum of his myth; they are wheels within the greater wheel of the overall mythic history that he has created.

CHAPTER 5

The Eternal Conflict: Good and Evil in Middle-earth

Some reviewers have called the whole thing simple-minded, just a plain fight between Good and Evil, with all the good just good, and the bad just bad. Pardonable, perhaps (though at least Boromir has been overlooked) in people in a hurry, and with only a fragment to read, and, of course, without the earlier written but unpublished Elvish histories. But the Elves are *not* wholly good or in the right. Not so much because they had flirted with Sauron; as because with or without his assistance they were 'embalmers'. They wanted to have their cake and eat it: to live in the mortal historical Middle-earth because they had become fond of it (and perhaps because they there had the advantages of a superior caste), and so tried to stop its change and history, stop its growth, keep it as a pleasaunce, even largely a desert, where they could be 'artists' – and they were overburdened with sadness and nostalgic regret.[1]

This explanation that *The Lord of the Rings* was more than a Good versus Evil story was written by Tolkien to Naomi

Mitchison. His comments could not have been made known to another reviewer (and one more erudite than those to whom Tolkien referred), W. H. Auden, who said:

> If, as I believe, Mr. Tolkien has succeeded more completely than any previous writer in this genre in using the traditional properties of the Quest, the heroic journey, the Numinous Object, the conflict between Good and Evil while at the same time satisfying our sense of historical and social reality, it should be possible to show how he has succeeded . . .
>
> To present the conflict between Good and Evil as a war in which the good side is ultimately victorious is a ticklish business. Our historical experience tells us that physical power and, to a large extent, mental power are morally neutral and effectively real: wars are won by the stronger side, just or unjust.[2]

Tolkien's comments on this review were lengthy, and on the question of good and evil he wrote:

> If the conflict really is about things properly called *right* and *wrong*, or *good* and *evil*, then the rightness or goodness of one side is not proved or established by the claims of either side; it must depend on values and beliefs above and independent of the particular conflict.[3]

Tolkien commented that he did not deal with Absolute Evil and likened such a concept to Zero, in that the evil beings fell – Satan, Morgoth – although Sauron, he says, represents as near an approach to the wholly evil will as is possible. Paul Kocher comments, 'Running through all three histories is the central theme of a contest between Good and Evil',[4] and then goes on to demonstrate the conflict in *The Silmarillion*, the *Akallabeth* and

The Lord of the Rings. Randel Helms[5] takes a more interesting line, inferring that the conflict between Good and Evil is biblical in nature, with the difference being that evil in Tolkien's cosmos is never totally overcome but surfaces again in a different form.

Tolkien's themes are much more subtle than a mere out and out conflict between Good and Evil. Rather, the study is one of the justice that exists within the writer's framework that he has created. Those who obey the moral imperatives that have been set down are not necessarily good in the sense that they display a form of moral rectitude. Those who disobey are not moral degenerates. Within Tolkien's world are personifications of Evil – Melkor/Morgoth and Sauron – who are essential opposites to the forces of creation and creativity. They are the forces of darkness, ugliness and destruction and are the antithesis of the forces of light, beauty and creativity – Ilúvatar and the Valar. Melkor/Morgoth wished to be a Creator but his activities became a parody and ultimately, being unable to succeed, he became antithetical to the Themes of Ilúvatar.

Tolkien's starting point is that nothing was bad in the beginning. How could it be? In the beginning was Ilúvatar. All things came from him. All things were good and those things that flowed from the themes of Ilúvatar continued to be good until such time as evil took a hold of them for 'nothing is evil in the beginning. Even Sauron was not so'.[6] Orcs, trolls, wargs and the other minions of Sauron and Morgoth cannot really be termed evil. They are the slaves of evil and have no minds of their own. They cannot choose for good. They have been under the aegis of evil from their beginning and were perverted from the previously created beauty of Ilúvatar. To use modern science, orcs and trolls were genetic mutations of Elves and Ents and Saruman's Uruk-hai were genetic mutations of Orcs. The tragedy for Orcs and trolls is that they cannot know good.

They are mindless and committed to an evil course through no choice of their own.

The Master of Evil is Morgoth, the fallen Vala. He is a real and physical presence upon Middle-earth. But he began as a spirit where his fall took place and evil or antithesis had its beginning. Morgoth, like Satan, was the most privileged of the Ainur and had a share of the gifts of the others. His greatest gifts were power and knowledge. Initially he wanted to be a creative force and bring into being things of his own. He wanted to create something from nothing, including sentient life. He really wanted to be another Ilúvatar. But such creative powers were Ilúvatar's alone. To even desire to emulate or equal Him was an unharmonious thought. If Morgoth were to emulate Ilúvatar he could not remain on his level of power and he would go beyond the place and powers assigned to him. His desires took him outside the Plan of Ilúvatar and he interwove his disquiet with the themes of the Ainur. The resulting conflict caused some of the Ainur to follow Morgoth's music rather than Ilúvatar's. Thus, from a desire to emulate or become equal with the One, did Evil and discord first arise in the Tolkien cosmos.

Ilúvatar tolerated Morgoth's discord throughout two of his themes. Finally He called the themes to an end and made it clear that Evil could not subdue the Grand Plan, and the final result would be 'the devising of things more wonderful, which [Morgoth] himself hath not imagined'.[7] Morgoth was ashamed for he was acknowledged as one of the mightiest of the Ainur, but he was still just an instrument of the One. All his devices would result, not in his own desire or wish, but in a conclusion devised by Ilúvatar. From this shame, and the revelation that he was caught in a no-win situation, flowed hatred. His humiliation was made even more bitter when Ilúvatar revealed the Music in the history of the World which began 'to unfold its history', in which even Morgoth 'wilt discover all the secret thoughts of thy mind, and wilt perceive that they are but a part of the whole and tributary to its glory'.[8] As the history unfolded, Morgoth started upon a path of deception, indeed self-deception for he thought that he would 'order all things for the good of the Children of Ilúvatar, controlling the turmoils of the heat and the cold that had come to pass through him'.[9]

Self-deception was fleeting. Deception of others remained. Morgoth's wish was to subject Elves and Men to him. He wanted to have subjects and servants, to be called Lord, to be a master of the will of others. Part of his motivation was envy but there were other motives. He could not be Ilúvatar, but he could challenge Him. Such a challenge, however, would be unsuccessful in the final result. Morgoth could impede and confuse. The awe with which the Ainur treated Ilúvatar would be mirrored in the awe with which the Children treated Morgoth. But Morgoth was not Ilúvatar, although he was the greatest of the Ainur. He was not benevolent, kindly, or a spirit of Love. The act of creation of a thing of purity must be accompanied by a spirit of Love – a spirit which Morgoth did not have. Rather, Morgoth's desire was for subjection, power and to rule through fear and terror. There could be no other option to Morgoth's rule but obedience. To disobey meant horror. Such an attitude was in sharp contrast to that of Ilúvatar.

Ilúvatar could have eliminated Morgoth. The designs of the latter were laid bare to the One, but they were also within the Great Plan. Morgoth was also at odds with the other Ainur, or Valar as they became when they entered Arda. Morgoth desired Arda as his own. He could not control the cosmos, so he would have the Earth. The Valar would have none of it. His antithesis to creation in the cosmos continued on Arda, but his opposition was not now Ilúvatar. It was from his peers, the Valar.

When Morgoth finally took on a form, it reflected his attitudes of malice, evil and ill will. His initial conception was one of magnificence, but he is the antithesis of creation. His contradictions are set out in the *Valaquenta*. Where art and purity seek splendour, evil is wasteful, pitiless, selfish and contemptuous. Where goodness is equated with understanding and sympathy, evil perverts these characteristics to intolerance and lies. Where grace and purity are symbolised by light as illuminator and creative force, light as fire becomes a destructive force.

A part of Tolkien's justice and a common moral theme in Middle-earth is that sin which is regretted and confessed is followed by a form of retribution and redemption. There is no suggestion that this morality has been decreed by Ilúvatar or that it is a divine imperative. Certainly it has its roots in the Catholic concept of a confessed sin necessarily being punished, but the punishment will not be infinite. At the end is forgiveness and redemption. In Tolkien's cosmos the difference is that purgatory and redemption take place on earth – in the temporal rather than spiritual context.

Théoden falls under the spell of Gríma Gálmód's son and Saruman. He despairs. His kingdom suffers. As a result of his departure from the path, he loses Théodred his son whom he loves. But Théoden arises and casts out Gríma. He acknowledges his wrong and rides to redemption and a glorious death. This death is his purgatory or punishment. But the means of his death is glorious and so within his punishment also lies his redemption.

Denethor, who does not repent and passes from pride to total despair, dies an ignominious, horrible and degrading death. Boromir's fall is gradual and tragic as the desire for the Ring gnaws at an otherwise strong-willed Captain of Gondor. His attempt to take the Ring is followed immediately by repentance. He is not entirely frank about his activities to the Fellowship but he does act well in defending the hobbits. He confesses in full to Aragorn and is permitted the privilege of dying a heroic death, as opposed to an ignoble one. His funeral is that of a warrior hero. Thus he is redeemed.

Saruman falls into evil and his fall is even greater because he is the greatest of the Istari. It is his lust for power and knowledge that brings his downfall, fuelled by his desire for the Ring. Unlike Boromir, Denethor and Théoden, he does not die after his fall at Isengard. He is allowed to go free. Why is this so? Saruman has not confessed. He is unrepentant. But because he is a Maia he is spared death at the hands of Gandalf. He is allowed to go free, but he is powerless. He, like Morgoth, is given another chance. He can move away from the evil that he has embraced. But Saruman does not take his chance and continues and his end is absolute. Like Sauron, he will never return to the Undying Lands.

Tolkien's justice may seem harsh. There are no epitaphs for Denethor or Saruman. Yet Théoden and Boromir will survive as long as there are skalds in Middle-earth to keep alive their memory in song. The redemption of the repentant is that they have been forgiven and they can resume their former greatness. The concept of forgiveness had its origins with the evil of Morgoth in Middle-earth.

When Morgoth was chased from Arda after the First War, he remained in Outer Darkness. As the Lamps were built he was kept informed of progress by Maia whom he had perverted to his Way. The Spring of Arda was diametrically opposed to the attitudes that he had adopted. Rather than covet the beauty for his own, he sought to destroy it. First he built Utumno which was a mockery of the products of the Spring. Where Spring grew and flourished, Utumno Was corruption; where the Lamps shone Utumno was dark. Morgoth's malevolence flowed from Utumno, blighted the Spring and the Lamps were destroyed. Morgoth hid in Utumno and, for fear of rending the

Earth further, the Valar were unable to overcome him. They left Middle-earth and went to Aman.

Upon the awakening of the Elves, Morgoth ensnared this special creation of Ilúvatar and corrupted it in such a way that it became a ghastly mockery in the form of the Orcs. His shadow began to grow, his power to increase. He built fortresses and harassed the westward-moving Elves. His continuing corruption of all creation impelled the One to counsel Manwë. The Valar were to aid the Elves against Morgoth, and he was overcome. Morgoth never forgot that his defeat was in a war fought for the sake of the Elves. He was dragged from his craven refuge in the Uttermost Pits of Utumno and was brought to Valinor in chains where he was imprisoned until he should be retried or crave pardon.

It would have been reasonable for the Valar to rid the world of Morgoth. He had caused so much strife, misery and destruction from the beginning of visible creation. But such an act would be an act of vengeance and if vengeance rested with anyone, it was with Ilúvatar. Morgoth's imprisonment was not a punishment but a withdrawal from circulation. The Valar, as forces of creativity, could not destroy Morgoth. To destroy would put them on the same level as Evil, because Evil is the antithesis of creativity. The destruction of Evil would taint Good. The act of destroying *anything*, for the sake of its destruction, is contrary to the very nature of creativity. In this way, Frodo was caught in an inextricable web. As the agent of Good, he had to destroy the Evil of the Ring. Frodo's act becomes tainted, as he himself was, as we shall see in the next chapter.

Therefore, because they could not exercise vengeance or the power of destruction, the only option for the Valar was neutralisation. This is the paradox of Good and Evil. Evil will destroy and overrun Good, but Good can only defend. It cannot take the offensive and it cannot *eliminate* Evil, for to do so would be contrary to the very nature and essence of Good. At best it can tolerate, cajole, persuade or neutralise, but it cannot destroy. To rend the fabric of creation in such a way can only rest in the hands of an omnipotent (and usually eternally patient) Superior Being – The One.

After three ages, Morgoth sued for pardon, which was granted. He was freed from his chains but was required to dwell within the Gates of Valimar. After a period 'on probation' he was free to go about the land. The forgiveness and pardon were because Morgoth was a reformed soul and because Good can have no idea of the true nature and machinations of Evil.

> For Manwë was free from evil and could not comprehend it,
> and he knew that in the beginning, in the thought of Ilúvatar,
> Melkor had been even as he; and he saw not to the depths of
> Melkor's heart, and did not perceive that all love had departed
> from him for ever.[10]

This does not mean that Good is naïve. It is in the nature of Evil to deceive. Forgiveness is that attribute of Good that co-exists with mercy. It is an attribute of Good to give a repentant soul another chance. But Evil does not know forgiveness. For the unrepentant, only destruction awaits. Morgoth was not truly repentant. He worked his wiles by infiltration and deception. So subtle was Morgoth that even whilst he was ensnaring Fëanor, the latter held a passionate hatred for the Master of Lies.

It was Fëanor who provided Morgoth with the Silmarils, although not directly, of course. The Silmarils Morgoth did not want to destroy. He wanted to possess them. They had within them the Light of the Inner Fire of the Trees and that was the Light of Creation and the Light of Creation was related to his first all-consuming desire – the Secret Fire. If Morgoth could possess this form of Secret Fire, he could deny it to the Valar and mock the Elves with their greatest treasure. So he sowed the seed of distrust and discord among the Elves. He was preparing the way for chaos in Paradise, a chaos of vengeance, lust and destruction. Yet Good could not see this was happening. It could not anticipate the wiles of Evil. The idea of an assault upon the Trees was as unthinkable to the Valar as it was logical to Morgoth.

The theft of the Silmarils plunged Valinor into darkness and the destruction of the Trees and the chaos that followed was total and horrifying. It set in motion the circumstances that would pit Morgoth against the Elves in battle and this was a form of organised chaos and perpetual destruction. The Elves, angelic, higher than Man, capable of absolute Goodness, would be plunged into Evil by using the methods and tools of Evil to combat it. Small wonder that the messenger of Manwë said to the departing Fëanor, 'For the hour is evil, and your road leads to sorrow that ye do not foresee. No aid will the Valar lend you in this Quest; but neither will they hinder you.'[11]

The attributes of Good are thus revealed. It seeks to deter by persuasion rather than by coercion. The Valar saw that the path being taken by the Elves could only lead downwards. The Fall from Grace would be inevitable. But the forces of Good allow such a choice to take place. Good cannot compel. Compulsion is the province of Evil and infers coercion in the event of disobedience. In this way, free will is destroyed. Good cannot destroy free will. A being must choose Good or Evil by his own unfettered free will. If persuasion cannot produce the desired result, Good cannot hinder, but can only mourn, the descent to Hell.

But Morgoth was blind. Ilúvatar had said to him that he would become the instrument of making more wonderful things and this is just what happened. Two new sources of light were created – the Sun and the Moon – pale reflections of the glory of the Trees, but a shock to Morgoth, and something that he could not endure. As was said in *The Lord of the Rings*, 'oft evil will shall evil mar'[12] and although Morgoth created and saw chaos in Valinor, his evil actions resulted in another phase of the Great Plan coming into effect. How blind evil is. The rising of the Sun had another consequence that Morgoth could not have forseen. It heralded the coming of Man in Middle-earth.

Morgoth turned Middle-earth into his battleground and used all the evil arts and powers that he had at his command. His powers were very great and his motives were evil, tainted and destructive. Lies and deception were major weapons in his armoury in his desire for the downfall of Elves and Men. With his deceit the truth was distorted so the actions following would be tainted. His lies sowed the seeds of distrust between Elves and Men. His capacity for untruth was so powerful that it caused Fëanor and his brother to challenge the Valar and set out on the path of ruin. The Oath of Maedhros and the Doom of Fëanor even divided the Elves against one another, and divide and conquer was a helpful reality for Morgoth.

Fear and terror, the weapons of coercions and destruction, were more effective against Men than against Elves. The majority of Men lived in darkness. They were a prey of Evil and feared and worshipped Morgoth. The great fear that Morgoth created and that was used so effectively by Sauron was the fear of death. The Gift of Ilúvatar became a curse after being twisted by Morgoth, and the fear of the unknown after death was a great fear for evil to play upon. Of course, this fear had no meaning for the Elves. Their future after a physical death was known. It took considerable will power on the part of the Edain to overcome the fear of a permanent end and side against Evil. But ambition was also a quality that Men had and that Evil played upon. It turned ambition to a force that would stick at nothing to attain its end and use any means, including evil ones to get there.

Evil also used naked and destructive force. War with the Elves was a constant activity, either by way of guerilla activity or by out and out confrontation in battle. Time was an ally for Evil. With it, Morgoth could create destructive fires, poisonous vapours and hideous monsters. Lies, treachery and discord prevented the Elves from raising an effective opposition when the hammer of war was raised. In addition to his Orcs, Morgoth had other powerful allies – wolves, bats, dragons, trolls and Balrogs. Werewolves were particularly favoured by Sauron. Draugluin and Carcharoth were of this breed. They were horrifying spirits imprisoned in the body of a wolf. Bats were bred in darkness as imitations of the birds and beasts of Middle-earth. Thuringwethil, the vampire woman, was supposed to be the spirit of a corrupted Maia in the form of a bat. Ordinary wolves were inhabited by corrupt spirits brought under the sway of Evil.

Dragons were the epitome of Morgoth's corruption of life. We do not know where they had their origin but they were very powerful, with added powers of intelligence, williness and knowledge. They were vain, gluttonous, greedy, deceitful and wrathful. So great was their power that even Gandalf was concerned that Smaug could be used by Sauron. Dragons were greater in power than Balrogs, the corrupt and fallen Maia who chose to follow Morgoth. Certainly with this collection of hideous forces Morgoth could wage a blitzkrieg of a devastating nature.

In the Second and Third Ages there were other servants of Evil, especially the Nazgûl and their steeds, the latter being bred by Sauron and fed upon fell meats.

The essential feature in all the servants is that they have been corrupted physically or in spirit. The corrupt creations like the Orcs have no alternative but to follow Evil because they have no choice. The Balrogs and Thuringwethil have fallen.

The rogue factors in the pantheon of Evil in Middle-earth are Ungoliant and Shelob. Ungoliant descended from the darkness that surrounded Arda. Morgoth lured her to his service. Lured though she was, she was not subservient! As mistress of her own lust, she hungered for and hated light. If Morgoth wanted domination and was prepared to use a form of chaos for that end, Ungoliant desired the utter chaos of utter darkness. She sought the sort of chaos that came before the ordering of things by Ilúvatar. She is the mythical equivalent of a black hole – a rent in the fabric of the universe that absorbs everything including light. Even Morgoth feared her and was unable to control her to the point where she nearly overcame him.

Shelob is an echo of Ungoliant. She is described as the last child of Ungoliant and dwelt in the Mountains of Terror. In the Third Age she lived in Cirith Ungol, and Sauron thought that she was his servant. From Shelob's point of view the relationship was commensalist, born out of opportunism. She was not owned and her power was great. She was mistress of her own obscene self. Where Ungoliant tried to devour light, Shelob found the light of the Silmaril in Frodo's star-glass unendurable. Her evil powers, although great, were not as great as those of her predecessor.

When the Valar finally did interfere in the affairs of Middle-earth, Morgoth's end quickly followed. But although he was defeated, Evil did not come to an end. The bitter seeds that he had sown continued to the tragic fulfilment of the Oath of Fëanor, for as the sons of Fëanor came into possession of the Silmarils and found that they could not hold them, they cast them into earth and water. Morgoth himself was

thrust through the Door of Night beyond the Walls of the World, into the Timeless Void; and a guard is set for ever on those walls, and Eärendil keeps watch upon the ramparts of the sky . . . He cannot himself return again into the World, present and visible, while the Lords of the West are still enthroned.[13]

There was no way that Morgoth would be forgiven. But he was not destroyed and nor was the evil that he had loosed upon the Earth destroyed. And if that were not enough, Morgoth's most powerful lieutenant was still at large – Sauron.

Sauron was a Maia of Aulë, learned in lore, who fell under the sway of Morgoth. He was

> only less evil than his master in that for long he served another and not himself. But in after years he rose like a shadow of Morgoth and a ghost of his malice, and walked behind him on the same ruinous path down into the Void.[14]

After the fall of Thangorodrim, Sauron confessed his evil ways to Eönwë, and said that he would turn away from darkness. He was certainly dismayed at the fall of his Master but he was not pardoned by Eönwë. For that, he had to humble himself before Manwë. An act of contrition was required before forgiveness was complete. Sauron couldn't do it. He hid himself in Middle-earth and became an evil force that in many respects was more subtle and finely realised by Tolkien than was Morgoth. Although Morgoth was the Master, his power was more elemental than that of Sauron. Where Morgoth succeeded with raw power and force, Sauron and his evil had to be more subtle and insidious. But as is so often the case with evil, it sowed the seeds of its own downfall in trying to arrogate to itself even more power. Sauron's big mistake lay in the One Ring.

Sauron is described by Tolkien as representing

> as near an approach to the wholly evil will as is possible. He had gone the way of all tyrants: beginning well, at least on the

level that while desiring to order all things according to his own wisdom he still at first considered the (economic) well-being of other inhabitants of the Earth. But he went further than human tyrants in pride and lust for domination, being in origin an immortal (angelic) spirit ... Sauron desired to be a God-King, and was held to be this by his servants; if he had been victorious he would have demanded divine honour from all rational creatures and absolute temporal power over the whole world.[15]

Sauron could use raw power when it suited him, as he did in the invasion of Eregion and Eriador and the attack on Minas Tirith. But he preferred subtlety, persuasion and fair speech. As Annatar, Lord of Gifts, he appeared to the Gwaith-i-Mírdain and perverted their talents to his uses. He surrendered to Ar-Pharazôn as a pragmatic act. He could not use his raw power. His forces had deserted him. By surrendering, he obtained free passage to Númenor where he began the infiltration of the Edain. He played, as Morgoth had done, on the fear of death, turning the Gift of Ilúvatar into a curse. He corrupted the Golden Civilisation, and reduced Men to a barbarism of the mind and spirit to the point where they no longer heeded the decrees of the Valar.

The Great Armament was a tool of Evil that ended the Golden Age of the Men of Númenor. For all men afterwards, Eressëa would be a memory of some dim and distant glory which, by the folly of their ancestors, had been snatched from them. For Elendil, Isildur and the descendants of the Elendili, Sauron and his actions which led to the Fall of Númenor could only be viewed with implacable hatred. But he who destroys even a destroyer carries within him the seeds of his own destruction.

Words, raw power, infiltration, these were Sauron's tools. But he had even more potent weapons in his armoury – the Rings.

Nine Rings to corrupt the Men and Seven to subvert the Dwarves. The Men became his servants in the form of the Ringwraiths or Nazgûl. The Dwarves were made of stronger stuff but their rings brought out a part of their baser nature – lust, greed and a desire for gold and the precious metals of the Earth. And then there was the One Ring.

Saruman was corrupted by his lust for the power of Sauron that the One Ring held. Through the Palantír of Orthanc he made an alliance with Evil. Sauron knew that Saruman was hooked. Saruman thought that whilst he was tugging on the line, yet the hook was not lodged. That was his mistake. He underestimated how his desires would betray him, and it was upon these desires that Sauron played.

Sauron was a merciless user. Those who would not act as his minions, either knowingly or in ignorance, he destroyed. He caused Denethor to fall, not by allying with Evil but by abdicating his responsibilities. Denethor was a proud man. He thought that he could use the Palantír of Minas Anor to ascertain the will of Sauron. Sauron tried and failed to subvert the old man, and then played on his grief to such a point that it became absolute despair, culminating in self-destruction.

But despite these atrocious aspects of Sauron's nature, he was 'but a servant or emissary'.[16] Gandalf in saying this refers to the fact that Sauron fell to the wiles of the ultimate Evil represented by Morgoth. But in the use of his powers, Sauron the servant exceeded the Master. But it is the Ring that is critical to an understanding of Sauron and the nature of Evil.

The One Ring contained the powers of all the others

and controlled them, so that its wearer could see the thoughts of all those that used the lesser rings, could govern all that they did, and in the end could utterly enslave them ... He rules a growing empire ... wielding the One Ring.

98

But to achieve this he had been obliged to let a great part of his own inherent power (a frequent and very significant motive in myth and fairy-story) pass into the One Ring. While he wore it, his power on earth was actually enhanced. But even if he did not wear it, that power existed and was in 'rapport' with himself: he was not 'diminished'. Unless some other seized it and became possessed of it. If that happened, the new possessor could (if sufficiently strong and heroic by nature) challenge Sauron, become master of all that he had learned or done since the making of the One Ring, and so overthrow him and usurp his place. This was the essential weakness he had introduced into his situation in his effort (largely successful) to enslave the Elves, and in his desire to establish a control over the minds and wills of his servants. There was another weakness: if the One Ring was actually *unmade*, annihilated, then its power would be dissolved, Sauron's own being would be diminished to vanishing point, and he would be reduced to a shadow, a mere memory of malicious will. But that he never contemplated nor feared. The Ring was unbreakable by any smithcraft less than his own. It was indissoluble in any fire, save the undying subterranean fire where it was made – and that was unapproachable, in Mordor. Also so great was the Ring's power of lust, that anyone who used it became mastered by it; it was beyond the strength of any will (even his own) to injure it, cast it away, or neglect it. So he thought. It was in any case on his finger.[17]

In *The Lord of the Rings* the nature and power of the Ring is revealed both by explanation and by incident. Thus, Gandalf says:

These Rings have a way of being found. In evil hands it might have done great evil. Worst of all, it might have fallen into the

hands of the Enemy . . . Yet the way of the Ring to my heart is
by pity, pity for weakness and the desire of the strength to do
good. Do not tempt me! I dare not take it, not even to keep it
safe, unused. The wish to wield it would be too great for my
strength.[18]

The Ring also gives power according to stature. In the hands of
Gollum it was used for malicious and crooked acts, small-
minded and petty vengeance and mischief.

There was no option but to destroy the Ring. It could not be
given to Bombadil, for although it had no power over him,[19] 'he
would soon forget it, or most likely throw it away. Such things
have no hold on his mind. He would be a most unsafe guard-
ian'.[20] Quite clearly the Valar would not allow a token of such
Evil into the purity and bliss of the Undying Lands. But how to
destroy it and by whom? The Ring, out of the hands of Sauron,
was a mighty temptation. To most it was a total mystery. Its
nature and true origins were not understood. Boromir and
Faramir cannot comprehend the true nature of Isildur's Bane,
although they were aware of the rough outline of Sauron's token
of power. But they could not see it as a Bane.

For Boromir and Faramir, the Ring works in different ways.
To Boromir, a proud, fearless, powerful captain, the Ring represents the power of command. The temptation to take it is with
him from the first moment that he sees it. After Lothlórien, his
desire becomes more potent until he meets his fate upon Amon
Hen. On the other hand, Faramir does not fall into temptation
at all, although he has a better opportunity than Boromir, for
'not if I found it on the highway would I take it'.[21]

For Frodo and Bilbo the desire for the Ring is the desire for
possession. They cannot properly use it. They do not have the
depth of understanding. When deprived of the Ring, they lower
themselves and become wizened, pathetic, mean and grasping.

They echo the attitudes of Gollum. Bilbo uses the Ring for party tricks and vanishing. Frodo uses it as a means of escape and not an arrogation of power. The Ring allows him to see Nenya on the finger of Galadriel and, as he develops, the inherent power of the Ring gives him power over Gollum, even although he is not wearing it. He becomes 'a tall stern shadow, a mighty lord who hid his brightness in grey cloud'.[22] On Mount Doom, holding the Ring, he becomes 'a figure robed in white, but at its breast it held a wheel of fire. Out of the fire there spoke a commanding voice'.[23] His statement to Gollum is prophetic – 'If you touch me ever again, you shall be cast yourself into the Fire of Doom.'[24] Even though Frodo tried to claim the Ring as his own, the power that it held over Gollum drove the creature to destroy the Ring and himself.

Tolkien describes 'the primary symbolism of the Ring, as the will to mere power, seeking to make itself objective by physical force and mechanism, and so also inevitably by lies'.[25] But the Ring represents more than this. It is not only an inanimate symbol of evil that inspires lust for its possession and the power (for whatever purpose) that will flow from it. It is a symbol of a far more basic problem that highlights the nature of Good and Evil and a fundamental tenet of the Christian faith. Although Tolkien was not telling or retelling the Christian tale (and the Middle-earth books are not so blatantly allegorical as say *The Pilgrim's Progress* or C. S. Lewis' *Perelandra* and *Out of the Silent Planet*), a Christian aspect is present. God gave Man the right to choose the path that he would follow – the path of Good or Evil. The fundamental proposition of Christianity is to choose the path of Christ – the path to salvation – or otherwise. This right to choose, free will if you like, is essential in both Tolkien's cosmos and the Bible. One could hold the Ring and not be tainted. But to choose to use the Ring is to choose an object of evil and to use an evil means, no matter how noble the end may be.

Preceding the exercise of choice must be temptation. Gandalf is *tempted* to take the Ring. He resists. Bilbo is tempted to kill Gollum. By not yielding to the temptation his possession of the Ring is not tainted. Had he killed Gollum, Bilbo would have been lost. But he began his possession of the Ring with a sentiment alien to the talisman – pity. Boromir's temptation is long and bitter, for it is in the nature of temptation to work on a Man's mind, gnawing at it and sapping his will. Temptation for Faramir does not exist. His strong will rejects Evil.

For Elves, Men, Dwarves, even the Istari, Evil is not something that appears out of the blue. To follow Evil and depart from the path of Good involves a decision that is consciously made. The wiles of Evil may have reduced a man's will and played on his baser instincts of pride, despair, envy, lust for power and covetousness, yet there must be a choice– an act of will. It is not only the Ring, the physical manifestation or symbol of evil that is the problem – it is the thought of it, the temptation, the potential that becomes available. Saruman never sees the Ring but the desire for it destroys him. With it he hopes to establish a rule of Knowledge, Rule and Order. He deceives himself and falls before he gets even so much as a glimpse of his goal.

The Ring, therefore, is not only the safety deposit of Sauron's power or the symbol of his evil ways. It is the symbol of the forked road that we all so often face and at which we must choose a path.[26] As is the case in all myths, the symbols are larger than life, the decisions more earth shattering and the consequences more immediate. As Tolkien says:

> Having mentioned Free Will, I might say in my myth I have used 'subcreation' in a special way ... to make visible and physical the effects of Sin or misused Free Will by men. Free Will is derivative, and is ... only operative within provided

circumstances; but in order that it may exist, it is necessary that the Author should guarantee it, whatever betides ... when it is 'against His Will', as we say, at any rate as it appears on a finite view. He does not stop or make 'unreal' sinful acts and their consequences. So in this myth, it is 'feigned'. . . that He gave special 'sub-creative' powers to certain of His highest created beings: that is a guarantee that what they devised and made should be given the reality of Creation ... But if they 'fell', as the Diabolus Morgoth did, and started making things 'for himself, to be their Lord', these would then 'be'. . . [his] greatest Sins, abuses of his highest privilege, and would be creatures begotten of Sin, and naturally bad.[27]

Thus we are faced with another allegory that is represented by the conflict between Good and Evil – the purposes and effects of creativity. Tolkien believes, as any Christian would, that creativity is a gift of God, and the purposes of 'subcreation' are to honour the Creator. Tolkien has given us a study of his concept of the function and method of the artist in the creative process in 'On Fairy-Stories'. He places considerable emphasis upon subcreation and the subcreator, the latter working within an already created cosmos. Art, he says, is the operative link between Imagination and the final result, Subcreation.

The Themes of Ilúvatar represent Imagination. Art, the act of creation, is contained in the word 'Eä' – let these things be. Ilúvatar does not subcreate – he creates and through Him we see creation. The Valar physically manifest the themes and are subcreators using the means of Art. Pure creativity, pure Art, the rendering of an unsullied imagination into a stainless reality is the epitome of Goodness. In so doing, Man the Subcreator becomes an imitator of the Creator for the glory of the Creator. To create solely for oneself is to deny that all creativity flows from God. Morgoth wanted to usurp absolute creativity and deny the creative power of Ilúvatar. Thus, he was counter-creative. The Valar realised Art by creating beauty and purity. Morgoth sought to destroy the works of the Valar and the special Children of Ilúvatar. He is set against Art and Creation and is thus the Destroyer and the Ultimate Evil.

Tolkien continues the symbol in the actions of his counter-creators. On the one hand, we have the beauty of nature and its sanctity as a created life form. On the other hand, Sauron, Saruman and Morgoth employ manufacture as a means of creation. They cannot manufacture life, but those things that are manufactured are created by the smoking fume of destruction, using fire the consumer, set against the Secret Fire of Creativity. Good may create material things – the Silmarils, Andúril, the Elven Rings – but these are corruptible. But their creation requires a skill akin to Art. Andúril is lovingly handforged at the Elven smithy at Rivendell. Orc scimitars are punched out on production line presses, lacking creativity, care and craftsmanship. The horrors of the industrial cities that arose from the fields of England in the nineteenth century and covered the Midlands with smoke and fume of pollution, and which inexorably invaded the countryside are reflected in Thangorodrim, Isengard and Mordor. Such 'creation' is the antithesis of creation – the use of art to realise the imagintion. In this sense, the struggle between Good and Evil deals with whether or not Art and its purity will survive as a creative force.

Thus, the Middle-earth tales are not simply tales of Good versus Evil. They constitute an examination of the nature of evil and the way that it works on a number of levels. They are tales of the origin of evil as we know it. They show us the consequences of Evil, of Sin and the counterproductive essence of Evil.

From the beginning to the end of the Third Age, Evil is presented as having a physical and real form. The nature of Evil is given form and substance. Today it does not physically exist. It is viewed as a philosophical concept, although there may be a Master of Lies, a Prince of the World, lurking in the shadows. But he is spiritual and, like Morgoth, waits off-stage for the Last Battle. With Sauron gone, evil did not vanish from the World. The prior existence of an Evil Being meant, tragically, that there would be evil forever in the Earth. Other forms of Evil have come and the spirit of Sauron and his master, Morgoth, are spirits of malice that gnaw in the shadows of the hearts of Men. The end of Tolkien's myth of the rise and fall of the Evil Ones is the beginning of the reality of Evil in our existence.

CHAPTER 6

The Tragic Hero

The tragedy as a literary form is one which has an irresistible attraction to writers. Its most commonly recognised realisation is in drama. When one speaks of tragedy, one thinks of the Greek tragedians, Euripides, Sophocles and Aeschylus, or one's mind springs to the well-known tragedies of Shakespeare – *Hamlet, King Lear, Othello,* and so on. The themes and characters of tragedy have become almost standard, available for reworking by different authors in different times. Christopher Marlowe has given us the Elizabethan interpretations of Faustus and the same theme has been examined by the German genius Goethe.

Tragedy is an examination of the doom of man and his short-comings. The form was first developed by the Greeks and even today, from a distance of two and a half thousand years, the Greek realisation of the formula is still seen as the epitome of tragedy, a formula from which there has been little departure over the ages. But the tragic form has not been the exclusive property of the ancient Greeks. The tragic awareness occurs in the literature of many peoples and is demonstrated in many of the heroic sagas, such as the *Edda,* the Icelandic sagas, the *Kalevala,* even to the soul-searching tragic realisation of Sir

Gawain in his second encounter with the Green Knight. The tragic awareness in the heroic sagas is demonstrated by a conquering glorious hero, possessed of skill in arms and special weaponry, engaging in great and important acts. Yet 'he appears against the sombre background of inevitable death, a death which will tear him away from his joys and plunge him into nothingness; or, a fate no better, into a mouldering world of shadows'.[1] The tragic man (or tragic hero) carries within himself the seeds of his own downfall. His humanity, at times a blessing and a virtue, can be a curse. His good acts are magnified, demonstrating him as the epitome of the potential goodness in man. His failings are enlarged, heightening the contrast and making his fall that much more poignant. And fall he must, for fall is the essence of tragedy. And the tragedy is that one so demonstrably noble and so potentially great must fall, not as a result of external influences, but as a result of the failings or shortcomings of the man within. It is, however, impossible to devise a short formula or definition for tragedy. This has been recognised by all who attempt so formidable a task. The best that one can do is point out the essential ingredients of tragedy. Goethe said, 'All tragedy depends on an insoluble conflict. As soon as harmony is obtained or becomes a possibility, tragedy vanishes.'[2] As a result of certain actions by one of the protagonists of the tragedy, who may even be the tragic hero, the balance of the various conflicting forces of nature has been upset. The forces of nature represent order and harmony. The upsetting of the natural order results in chaos. The resolution of the conflict must be the restoration of order. Consequently in tragic drama, the murder of a King, or an incestuous relationship, or usurpation, or an abandonment of filial duty are all seen as actions contrary to an established order of things. The tragic hero may be responsible for upsetting the order or he may be the character through whom order must be re-established, but who, at the same time, may have to be sacrificed that the balance may be restored. Thus, when Hamlet cries,

> The time is out of joint; o cursed spite,
> That ever I was born to set it right![3]

he is not only defining the present circumstances in which he finds himself, teetering on the edge of a disordered universe. He is lamenting the nature of the tragic hero, that fate has decreed that he must restore the balance and in doing so must not only face disorder, but face himself as a human being. In such a case the insignificance of one man is measured against the primaeval and cataclysmic forces of nature. Fate has decreed that he shall attempt to restore the balance. The question is, can he face this? Hamlet is one of the few tragic characters whom we view from within as well as from without. His continued procrastination is that of a man who is trying to avoid his fate rather than that of other tragic heroes who confront it head on.

On the more macrocosmic scale, the balance of nature theme is representative of the great cosmogonic myth – the continuing struggle between light and dark, order and chaos. In some aspects of the Greek idiom the tragic hero is but a piece in a larger game played by the gods. Even in Hamlet's case, he is one man pitted against vastly greater elemental forces.

Tragedy is often presented to us in the tales of the heroes. The protagonists are frequently kings, statesmen, princes or warriors of great renown which makes more poignant the depth of their fall. Macbeth, formerly a doughty warrior and faithful subject, recognises the depth of his own fall with the words:

> I am in blood
> Stepped in so far, that should I wade no more,
> Returning were as tedious as go o'er.[4]

Likewise, the famous soliloquy 'Tomorrow, and tomorrow, and tomorrow'[5] is the statement of a fallen man for whom life has become a futile exercise. But the tragedy must mean something to us, the audience or readers. The fall of the tragic hero must affect us, come close to us, have meaning for us, become something that we recognise and which must have relevance. The tragedy must be something to which we can react and which affects us emotionally. This is what is known as catharsis.

To make the tragedy even more meaningful, the tragic hero must be fully aware of his situation. He must suffer, know that he is suffering and know why he is suffering. He cannot complain by asking, 'Why must all these things happen to me?' He is master of himself and of his fortunes and misfortunes. He may berate himself for committing a certain act which led to a certain consequence, but he cannot question why the consequence has befallen him.

Of course, in tragedy there can be only one end for the character who has captured our imagination by his nobility and has heightened our dismay by his fall, and that is death. By his death, the tragic hero returns the balance to nature, whether he was responsible for the upset or not. His death is the final action in a number of actions that he must undertake to dispel disorder. The tragic hero is always within a state of conflict to which Goethe refers. If he is the perpetrator of disorder he is opposed to the forces of order. If, like Hamlet, he is man alone, he is in the midst of the conflict, struggling to restore order to a disordered world.

A further element of tragedy is that it deals with an essential ingredient of the human condition in that it inevitably raises questions of a moral nature. It need not be a *purely* moral failure which causes the tragic fall. The tragic hero must fall into moral error which *contributes* to his fall. As a consequence of this the tragic hero, like Oedipus, must carry with him a moral guilt. The tragic hero suffers both the external consequences of his fall and an awareness of his downfall and of the events which led to it.

The Greek nature of tragedy contains another factor relevant to this discussion. The three great tragedians to whom reference has been made drew for their material upon mythology. The full range of Greek myth mirrors human existence itself, a perception of the world so rich, so immediate as to be unequalled.

Beyond all those heroes who through their combats set countries free from terrible oppression or heroically succumb to overwhelming forces, who achieve their own deliverance through bold action or clever ruse, we perceive what ultimately determines the life of us all: human existence imperilled and asserted. And when we see that what is at stake here is always man's entire existence, that there is no question of compromise, no evasion of hostile powers, no turning aside of man's unconquerable will, then we have already defined one of the essentials of tragic man which these figures from Greek myth also epitomise.[6]

The Greek tragedians drew upon their myths and the essential nature of tragedy embodied within them and produced monumental works of literature. The perpetuation of the myth in literature and the continuing examination of the nature of man disposed of the ritual aspects of myth and focused upon the basic questions – why are we here and what will happen to us on the way?

Tolkien, in his myth, has made tragedy an essential part of his tale. Indeed *Quenta Silmarillion* is a tragedy in itself, containing within it many subtragedies. Fëanor demonstrates that essential quality of the Greek tragic hero Achilles – hubris or overweening pride. It is this element within his character that causes Fëanor's fall, but the tragedy of Fëanor is linked with the race tragedy of the Elves which would go beyond an examination of the tragic hero. Therefore I shall examine the tragic heroes Túrin Turambar and Frodo Baggins and consider the duality of spirit represented by Sméagol Gollum.

Tolkien observes of Túrin that he is 'a figure that might be said (by people who like that sort of thing, though it is not very useful) to be derived from elements in Sigurd the Volsung, Oedipus and the Finnish Kullervo'.[7] There can be no doubt that Túrin bears some similarity to the three characters mentioned by Tolkien but Túrin, Sigurd, Oedipus and Kullervo are all tragic heroes. Rather than examine Túrin from a derivative point of view, it is more profitable to examine his development as a tragic hero.

'Narn i Hîn Húrin' in *Unfinished Tales* is the 'long version' of the tale of Túrin. The shorter version 'Of Túrin Turambar' appears as chapter 21 of *The Silmarillion*. The short version is a summary of 'Narn', recounting events and omitting the subtle detail that assists us in fleshing out the nature of Túrin. In the course of the 'Narn' reference is made to *The Silmarillion* account. It is not possible to consider one account in isolation from the other and consequently I would caution the reader, who is familiar with one account but not the other, that I shall be taking an overview of both accounts.

Túrin, the son of Húrin and Morwen, came from noble stock. However,

> he was not merry, and spoke little, though he learned to speak early and ever seemed older than his years. Túrin was slow to forget injustice or mockery; but the fire of his father was also in him, and he could be sudden and fierce. Yet he was quick to pity, and the hurts or sadness of living things might move him to tears.[8]

At an early age we observe the nobility of spirit in Túrin exemplified by his relationship with the crippled Sador, known as Labadal or 'Hopafoot', a name given by Túrin 'in pity and not in scorn'.[9] A further example of Túrin's worth comes at his eighth birthday. The knife given him by Húrin is given freely by Túrin to Sador. In commenting on the gift, Húrin warns and prophesies of the danger of steel – 'It will cut your hand as willingly as aught else'[10] – for it is with steel that Túrin carves the events that mark his downfall, and the steel that will earn him such renown will also be a vital force in his tragedy. Túrin's explanation of the gift to Sador was that he gave the gift out of love for the cripple and out of pity. Húrin praised his son with the words, 'All three gifts were your own to give, Túrin: love, pity and the knife the least.'[11]

After the capture of Húrin by Morgoth and the enslavement of his people by Brodda the Easterling, Túrin was sent to the Kingdom of Doriath where he was received by Thingol as his own fosterling. Upon entering the forests that surrounded Thingol's realm he met Beleg Strongbow – a fateful meeting and the beginning of a friendship which would end during one of the states of Túrin's fall. Indeed, Túrin's fall began early in his career and was a long process. Túrin was proud but his pride was not the hubris of Fëanor. He was swift to anger and in his rage committed acts which, by degrees, destroyed the nobility that he had displayed even from an early age. There was no doubt that he was a doughty fighter held in high regard even by Thingol Greycloak whose love for the race of Men was not great. Túrin's argument with Saeros and the death of the latter, although accidental but precipitated by Túrin's wrath, was the beginning. After the death of Saeros, Túrin questioned the judgement of Thingol, abjured the King's law and joined outlaws, taking the name Neithan, the Wronged. But the wrong was within Túrin who yielded to the flash of his anger and fled from a confrontation with Thingol.

113

Beleg finally found him and told Túrin of the pardon of the King. Where previously anger and fear had caused Túrin to flee, now pride forbade him to return. Beleg returned to Doriath and took as gifts to Túrin the dread sword Anglachel and the Dragon-helm of Dor-lomin and sought him again. When Beleg found Túrin for the second time since the self-imposed exile, Túrin had formed an alliance with Mîm the Dwarf. The reunion of Túrin and Beleg was deadly to the servants of Morgoth, and was not to the liking of Mîm who betrayed Túrin and Beleg. Túrin was captured and Beleg sore wounded. It was when Beleg again sought Túrin, and found him, that the next great step in Túrin's downfall took place. Túrin mistook his liberator as a foe and he slew Beleg with Anglachel. He recognised Beleg after the deed and 'stood stonestill and silent, staring on that dreadful death, knowing what he had done'.[12] Húrin's warning about steel began to take on new significance:

Thus ended Beleg Strongbow, truest of friends, greatest in skill of all that harboured in the woods of Beleriand in the Elder Days, at the hand of him whom he most loved; and that grief was graven on the face of Túrin and never faded.[13]

For a time Túrin wandered mad accompanied by the faithful Gwindor who carried Anglachel until Túrin's recovery at Eithel Ivrin, where he was able to mourn his former companion. Then Túrin came to Nargothrond, naming himself Agarwaen son of Úmarth – Bloodstained son of Illfate.

Túrin's self-naming catalogues his downfall for on each stage he takes a name significant for the tragic step that he has taken. Each name is a recognition of his falling star – that he was wronged is a cry against his nature; that he was the son of Illfate continues this cry, but his self-name of Bloodstained is a recognition of his deadly capacity to kill those he loves and who love him. Gwindor recognises his fate, saying, 'A doom indeed lies on him, as seeing eyes may well read in him, but a dark doom',[14] and he remarks upon this to Túrin – 'The doom lies in yourself, not in your name.'[15] Túrin re-establishes himself after his sojourn in Nargothrond as a folk hero, becoming known as Mormègil, Black Sword, after the reforged Anglachel renamed Gurthang, Iron of Death.

It is at this stage that Glaurung enters the tale. Túrin is bewitched by Glaurung who misleads him with lies, convincing him that his mother and Nienor his sister are slain or in torment. Túrin returns to his birthplace, slays Brodda, but realises that his actions only bring further woe to his people. He becomes a Wildman of the Woods, an outcast but is restored from his grief by Brandir. After putting the black shadow behind him he takes for himself his last name, a name that is a recognition of his nature and indeed the nature of all tragic heroes and is prophetic of the fate that awaits him – Turambar, Master of Doom. Following upon this are the final stages of his tragic decline: his incestuous relationship with his sister and the murder of Brandir. His marriage with Nienor was, of course, unwitting in the same way that the marriage of Oedipus to Jocasta was unwitting incest. Nienor had been bewitched by Glaurung and Túrin, never having seen his sister, took her as a stranger. It is only when Túrin slays Glaurung that the dragon reveals the truth to Nienor saying:

> I give thee joy that thou hast found thy brother at last. And now thou shalt know him: a stabber in the dark, treacherous to foes, faithless to friends, and a curse unto his kin, Túrin son of Húrin! But the worst of all his deeds thou shalt feel in thyself.[16]

Nienor in horror and distress killed herself, but the truth was overheard by Brandir. It was after an argument with

Brandir, and an unjustified insult delivered as a result of Túrin's uncontrollable temper, that Brandir revealed what he had heard. Túrin, hearing 'the feet of his doom overtaking him',[17] accused Brandir of lying and of leading Nienor to her death. Being unable to acknowledge the truth and thinking that he could destroy it with murder Túrin slays Brandir. Only when Mablung confirms the dreadful tale does Túrin take his own life, beseeching the sword Gurthang to slay him swiftly. The sword recalls the two great wrongs of Túrin, the deaths of Beleg and Brandir. Thus, Túrin comes to the only end possible for the tragic hero – death.

It has been suggested to me that the tragedy of Túrin is not true tragedy at all, because his marriage to Nienor was unwitting. Not only was it unwitting but it was also as the result of the deception of Glaurung. I cannot recall any tragic hero who has committed incest, knowing at the time of the act that his partner was related. It is not so much the incest as the horror and revulsion that it causes upon its discovery that contains the tragic element. It is the burden of guilt which the tragic protagonists have to bear that is the tragedy. As audience or readers we know of the incest and that it is wrong. We also know that it must be discovered. We are aware that the revelation will destroy the otherwise noble character of the tragic hero. The question that must be asked is how the tragic hero resolves the knowledge of the discovery and the burden of guilt within his own frame of reference.

However, the incestuous relationship with Nienor is not the sole tragic element in Túrin's history. It is one of the contributing factors to the spectacular downfall that he must suffer. It is perhaps because of the nature of incest and its use as a tragic theme in Oedipus and the *Kalevala* that it has a tendency to obscure the other equally important tragic aspects of Túrin's career. The fall of Túrin is continually associated with death.

The death of Saeros is accidental. It is Túrin's anger, pride and fear of injustice that prevents him from returning to Thingol. But he cannot flee from the justice that pursues the tragic hero and which must inevitably overtake him. His major fault is his violent anger. This is set against his generosity, his love of justice and his obvious filial piety. He recognises in his self-naming the error of his ways and the faults that beset him. Yet he cannot run from his own nature or from the violent anger that flares and results in the deaths of Beleg and Brandir. The curse upon Túrin lies within himself and is not laid upon him by Morgoth. Although some tragedies have been tied in with a curse of the gods and the inevitability of some predetermined fate, the House of Húrin is not blighted by the gods as was the House of Atreus. When one considers the very nature of Túrin, the curse of Morgoth does nothing to influence his destiny. The deceptions of Glaurung are relevant only to one aspect of his total tragic career. If anything the curse of Morgoth is more prophetic than determinative. The totality of the tragedy of Túrin and his ever downward path to his final doom meets a contrast in *The Lord of the Rings* in the tragic hero of that work.

Frodo Baggins is a more modern form of tragic hero; more in line with Ibsen than with Euripides. Frodo is an ordinary individual who becomes involved in the great affairs of the world. His involvement allows us to see in him the nobility and at the same time the weaknesses or flaws of his character. In a sense we can more easily identify with Frodo than with Túrin. Frodo has been cast unwittingly into, and to a degree unknowing of, the nature of the events in which he will be involved. We see him as a Ring-bearer leaving the Shire, not really sure of the events that will take place, not really aware of the full impact of his decisions. His initial destination is Rivendell and from there no plan has been determined. On the way he meets characters who aid, hinder, teach or terrify. By the time he reaches

Rivendell he has endured Barrow-wights and the terrors of the Witch-realm of Angmar, had the advantage of a sojourn with Bombadil, learned of the terrors of Mordor in the form of the Black Riders, most horrifyingly revealed on Amon Sûl, and has been led through paths seldom trodden by the mysterious figure of Aragorn. During this time, and particularly on Amon Sûl and at the Ford of the Bruinen, he demonstrates a depth of courage unknown even to himself. It is not his courage alone that causes the dispersal of his enemies but the assistance of friends and of forces the true depth of which he hardly recognises or comprehends. His use of the Ring is for escape from danger or, in the case of Bombadil, the unknown, and not for the use of the incredible power that lies within the talisman.

At the Council of Elrond he presents as a naïve hobbit among the Great, accepting the burden of the Ring with the words, 'I will take the Ring, though I do not know the way.'[18] By assuming the burden Frodo is demonstrating that courage and strength of will that allows one to undertake the course of action that is fraught with danger and the unknown, yet, by the same words, he makes it clear that he is dependent upon the assistance of others. He is not yet ready to be the Man Alone against the World.

It is at the Mirror of Galadriel, at a time when he is tested, that he turns the tables. When he offers the Ring to Galadriel he is demonstrating a subtlety and strength that indicates to us that he has ended his simple naïveté, yet has not ended the simplicity of his character. His next most decisive move comes at the Seat of Amon Hen. With the power of the Ring he is able to see for the first time the true nature of the forces that he must overcome. The Ring, which was used as an escape from Boromir, is transformed into a tool in Frodo's hands. No longer is it a retreat into invisibility for, as Gandalf observed, the power of the Ring is only as great as the power of its user. That Frodo is able to use the Ring with the power of Sight indicates that he is growing. Because he is aware of his danger he is reluctant to draw his companions into it. He cannot bear that burden as well as that of the Ring. It is selflessness that determines his decision to undertake the destruction of the Ring alone, although unintended by him he is joined by Samwise.

A further nobility of spirit is displayed by Frodo's treatment of Gollum. Here, like Bilbo, he displays attributes of pity and mercy that give the Ring-bearer a certain resilience against the awesome power of the Ring. Although Frodo uses the Ring to dominate Gollum to the last prophetic threat – 'If you touch me ever again, you shall be cast yourself into the Fire of Doom'[19] – his use of the Ring is tempered with mercy. The cynic may say that Frodo was merely using Gollum to find the secret entrance to Mordor, but if that was Frodo's only motive the actions of the hobbit towards Gollum do not indicate it to be so. Even at Henneth Annûn Frodo pleads for the life of Gollum, and it is only as a result of his entreaties and his oath to take Gollum under his protection that Faramir is prepared to spare the life of the miserable creature.

There is no doubt that Frodo was aware that Gollum could and probably would play him false. The pity and mercy that is demonstrated by Frodo flows from a natural magnanimity of spirit (contrasted with Sam's intolerance) and an understanding of the torment of Gollum as a former Ring-bearer. When Gollum finally does turn against Frodo he is not slain, although on the journey to Mount Doom such an opportunity presented itself. Gollum is exiled from the band as having proved unworthy to accompany them further. Gandalf's admonition that it is not within our purview to determine when a person should die holds good.

The imprisonment at the Tower of Cirith Ungol and the arduous trek across Mordor represent a triumph of will for

Frodo. The power of the Ring and the nature of the burden are all-consuming. Yet in the midst of his torment he discards his weapons vowing to kill no more. It is with awe and wonder that we see him reach journey's end, standing in Sammath Naur. Up until this moment, Frodo's struggle and his development have elevated him from a rustic and ordinary hobbit to an individual possessed of great attributes – courage, determination, justice, pity, mercy, wisdom, compassion and sympathy. He deserves to achieve his Quest. But at the moment of his triumph comes his tragedy. Having achieved the heights of respect, admiration and achievement, he falls. 'I do not choose now to do what I came to do. I will not do this deed. The Ring is mine!'[20]

Frodo's tragedy lies within his *choice*. He does not choose to destroy the Ring. Here he exercises free will, knowing the consequences of his act; and his act is indeed a tragic one. Having resisted the allure of the Ring for so long he falls to the temptation of its power at the final and most critical moment. And by making such a choice, the fate of the Ring is taken literally out of his hands as the frantic Gollum gnaws off Frodo's finger and the Ring and plummets to his death.

Why, you may ask, doesn't Frodo die? His tragedy is that he must live on. The celebrations on the Field of Cormallen, the Coronation and the Wedding – none of them mention that at the final, critical moment Frodo wavered. The secret is known only to Sam and Frodo but although it may be a secret the truth is nevertheless inescapable. This is known to Saruman who notices Frodo's growth but foretells that he will have neither health nor long life. Frodo remains cursed by his wounds, his experiences, his memories. He has little honour in the Shire and his involvement in affairs diminishes. As he acknowledges, he tried to save the Shire, and it was saved, but not for him. His reception and return to the Shire is not that of a hero. He is realising the consequence of his tragedy and must bear the burden of his guilt. But it is as Ring-bearer, enemy of Sauron and as a person possessed of noble attributes such as pity and mercy that he is granted the rest that he seeks. But his rest is not in Middle-earth but in the Undying Lands. Frodo's tragic death is not the oblivion sought and achieved by Túrin, but is the restful release granted to one whose efforts to succeed were marred only by his fall on the brink of achieving success. Frodo's end shows that even in tragedy there may be mercy and we mourn the fact that he fell, rather than passed away.

But as important in the development of our tragic heroes are the parts played by the villains, Gollum and Glaurung. In a sense Gollum is a reflection of what Frodo could become – a spirit torn between his former nature and his present desires, a spirit broken by his lust for the Ring. The lust is not for the power of the Ring, for Gollum is too small in character to use it effectively. For Gollum, the desire for the Ring is for the possession of the object. He has been almost totally broken by the Ring but the treatment of him by Frodo allows a spark of humanity to flicker within him from time to time. The rare occasions of tenderness, sympathy and caring for Frodo show us that Gollum can attain mastery over his ruined self. Yet he is a potential alter ego for the tragic hero, a snivelling, whining, treacherous, self-seeking individual; a certain beastliness that lurks within all of us, that we keep submerged, but which may awaken. For Frodo to become a Gollum would be more tragic than the fate that he suffers. Yet while Frodo is alone, he must face a being and a spirit which he could conceivably become. It is to his credit that with pity, caring and mercy he is able to keep that spirit down. Yet, for a flash it emerges as he demands the Ring from Sam after the rescue from the Tower of Cirith Ungol.

Glaurung is Túrin's alter ego for the dragon is the symbolic beast in man; a slimy, reptilian, destructive, hideous monster that lurks in the psyche only too able to destroy the good deeds that the hero is capable of achieving. In slaying the dragon, George, Sigurd, Beowulf and Túrin slay the beast in man, the beast of sin, degradation, barbarism and ignorance. For Túrin, although he slays the beast, release from truth does not follow. He cannot escape the fact that it is the beast within him that has led him to his ghastly fate and the havoc that surrounds him. The slaying of Glaurung results in the final recognition of his truly tragic nature.

But perhaps the last word, particularly for the tragic hero Frodo, should be left to Tolkien who describes the tragic element that he sought to portray:

> It was not only nightmare memories of past horrors that afflicted him, but also unreasoning self-reproach: he saw himself and all that he had done as a broken failure.[21]

Perhaps that is as valid an analysis of any tragic hero, and particularly the Tolkienesque one, as we can get.

CHAPTER 7

The Quest Hero

Beren, Aragorn and Eärendil are the Quest Heroes of Middle-earth, and the way in which they have been developed by Tolkien shows an adherence to the classical theme of the Quest Hero. He has given each of his Quest Heroes specific tasks or quests to undertake, but he has also used the theme of an entire life as a quest – a quest for fulfilment of one's potential and for self-realisation. Furthermore, Tolkien's Quest Heroes are related to one another. The line begins with Beren and Lúthien. Their child Dior was the father of Elwing who became the wife of Eärendil. The children of Eärendil were Elros and Elrond. Aragorn is a distant descendant from Elros, who later became the first King of Númenor, and his wife Arwen Undómiel is the daughter of Elrond. Each Quest Hero marries into the Elven race and thereby creates a union between the two races beloved of Ilúvatar.

The quests undertaken by these three heroes are representative of different aspects of human development. Beren, in seeking the Silmaril, is seeking the hand of Lúthien. His quest is motivated by love and his goal is the fulfilment of that love. Eärendil, in seeking the shores of Valinor, seeks succour for the beleaguered peoples of Middle-earth. Aragorn seeks his heritage as King of the lands of Middle-earth, and to re-establish the Númenórean realms in exile and bring to Middle-earth the blessings of enlightened rule and order. Beren's quest may, at first glance, appear to be a more personal goal than the altruistic ends sought by Aragorn and Eärendil but the nature of his achievement involves an attack upon the fallen Vala, Morgoth, and an indication of the ability of the individual to overcome incredible odds, especially when that individual is motivated by a pure intention.

All three heroes are born in circumstances that are out of the ordinary and their early years are disrupted. They lack the peace, warmth and security of a normal family background.

Beren was the son of Barahir and Emeldir. Barahir was a great warrior and distinguished himself by rescuing Finrod Felagund during the battle of the Sudden Flame (Dagor Bragollach). Finrod swore friendship with Barahir and promised to aid him or his kin at any time of need. He gave Barahir his ring, the Ring of Felagund, which later became one of the heirlooms of the House of Elendil.

After Dagor Bragollach, Barahir continued his resistance against Morgoth and was aided by his wife Emeldir (named Man-Hearted) who chose to stay with her family, rather than take refuge. Barahir's band was beset and was reduced to twelve, who became outlaws, living off the wild. Finally his hiding place was revealed to Sauron by Gorlim, who had been taken prisoner and fell foul of the deceits of Morgoth's lieutenant. Barahir and his band were slain by Orcs in Dorthonion, but Beren escaped death, having been sent on a mission. He foresaw his father's death in a dream and, after returning and burying the bodies near Tarn Aeluin, swore an oath of vengeance. He traced the Orcs to Rivil's Well where he slew them, and recovered the Ring of Felagund which the Orc chieftain had taken by cutting off

Barahir's hand. Barahir's enmity for Morgoth and for the ways of evil passed to Beren. After Barahir's death Beren became his own man and an individual mover of events. As sole survivor of the outlaw band he is fatherless in a world that seems to have turned its face against him. His father's death, and the wreaking of his revenge, is for Beren a form of initiation or rite of passage and represents the transition from an adult but subservient son to a Man Alone who must shape his own destiny.

Eärendil was the son of Tuor and Idril Celebrindal, daughter of Turgon of Gondolin. His birth is unique in that he was the offspring of the second union of Elves and Men. His coming had been foretold and was part of the structure of the history of Middle-earth and was therefore a part of the Music of Ilúvatar. He was no ordinary child. 'Of surpassing beauty was Eärendil, for a light was in his face as the light of heaven, and he had the beauty and the wisdom of the Eldar and the strength and hardihood of the Men of old; and the Sea spoke ever in his ear and heart.'[1] Eärendil lived in Gondolin until he was seven, and at that time Gondolin fell to Morgoth. Idril, Tuor, Eärendil and other refugees from the Fall of Gondolin escaped down a secret way that Idril prepared, and came to the Vale of Sirion by the sea. There they found other refugees from the Fall of Doriath, among them Elwing.

This, for Eärendil, was a form of initiation. His home was destroyed and he and his family were cast into the wild as exiles. The normal security of a safe and secure home was denied Eärendil and his flight from Gondolin dooms him to become a wanderer and unable to rest. His introduction to the sea came from his father who sang to him the song of the Coming of the Vala Ulmo to the shores of Nevrast. This song awoke a longing for the sea in the heart of Tuor as it did in Eärendil, who is initiated into that part of his Elvish ancestry that desires the sea, and, once awakened, it determines his fate.

Aragorn was the son of Arathorn and Gilraen. Gilraen's parents, Dírhael and Ivorwen, were opposed to the marriage of their daughter to one of the Dúnedain. The life of the Rangers was hard, dangerous and severe. Dírhael, particularly, felt that his daughter was too young to marry and, if she did so, he thought that the marriage would be short-lived. His wife, Ivorwen, felt that a child of the union could bring hope for the Dúnedain. Both were right. Arathorn was killed when Aragorn was aged two. Mother and child were taken to Imladris where he was fostered by Elrond, who treated him as his own child.

Aragorn was given the name 'Estel' which means 'hope'. Although the circumstances of his birth were not miraculous or mystical, his upbringing was, to say the least, different. He was raised in foreign surroundings and given a prophetic name. By his fostering he became a part of the Elvish realm in terms of culture and upbringing. He re-establishes a link with his ancestry that had been broken for over six thousand years. By these events, and by the duality of his background and cultural upbringing, he is able to establish his universal origins and nature.

His initiation or rite of passage takes two stages. When Aragorn was twenty, Elrond revealed to him his true name and glorious ancestry. He was given the heirlooms of his House, although the Sceptre of Annúminas was withheld until he became King. By this revelation, Aragorn passed from being an orphan Dúnedan raised by the Elves to being the heir to Isildur, and by his pedigree has the potential of reuniting the Kingdoms of Gondor and Arnor, and re-establishing the former glory of the Númenórean realms in exile. But he has to prove his worth.

The second stage of his initiation involves Arwen. At his first meeting with her at Imladris they revealed their backgrounds to one another. But, like Beren, his love was to be unrequited. Mortals could not marry Elves (although it had been done before in the mythic past). Gilraen explained to her son the futility of such a desire. Elrond also perceived the situation and explained the problem in far more precise terms. Arwen, as an Elf, was immortal and was of a lineage far greater than that of Aragorn. As an Elf, she could accompany her father to the Undying Lands, something that Aragorn could never do, or remain in Middle-earth and become mortal, thus denying herself her true destiny as an Elf. Aragorn could see that to cause Arwen to make such a choice would be to cast far too great a burden upon her, and so he decided to leave Imladris and walk in the wild alone.

It is a common theme in Quest tales for the hero to spend some time away from civilisation and their fellow men. This is known as the period of withdrawal, a time when the hero builds up his inner strength, prior to undertaking the great quest.

Beren withdrew from the world for four years, during which time he was an outlaw in Dorthonion. During this time he learned to communicate with animals and birds. This attribute is common to many of the heroes of mythic or legendary literature. In stories of, say, Romulus and Remus, we find that communication with animals was one of the attributes that they developed as a result of their upbringing by wolves. Indeed, the concept of assistance from the wild by the help of animals, or communication with animals, is common in the development of the Quest Hero. Aragorn was able to understand the languages of birds and beasts, and it was Elwing as a seabird who brought the Silmaril to Eärendil, while Beren and Lúthien adopted the shape of animals during the Quest for the Silmaril. Beren, during the period of his outlawry, became friendly with birds and animals and he sealed his contract of love and affection with them by not eating any living thing for sustenance that was not in the service of Morgoth. In this way he forges a strong link with nature as a force for good, respecting the positive aspects of the natural world, and, by so doing, becomes more closely identified with it. It is clear that not only is he a man who depends upon the good will of Nature, but he also becomes absorbed into Nature herself and can be identified as a Good Man in harmony with his natural surroundings.

Tolkien takes the importance of this symbol even further once Beren embarks upon his Quest. Beren comes to the Gates of Angband in the shape of Draugluin, the great werewolf of Sauron which had been slain by Huan, the wolfhound of Celegorm. Although he is in the shape of a servant of evil, he is not corrupted by it. The potential corruption that he might otherwise have suffered is counterbalanced by his identification with the inherent Good of Nature that he grew to understand and identify with during his period of withdrawal.

The nature of Lúthien is important in any consideration of Beren as a Quest Hero. From their meeting, their fates are intertwined. Unlike the heroines of so many of the Gestae, who remain imprisoned in a tower or who simper in the Courts of Kings awaiting the return of the Hero, Lúthien becomes actively involved and is vitally important in the successful resolution of the Quest. The simple explanation for her involvement is the power of the love that Beren and Lúthien have for one another. On a deeper level, they represent Man and Woman in Nature. They are, if you will, the essential Yang and Yin. Because of their very being as they are, individually they are destined for great works. Together, they constitute an almost unbeatable force, especially because they combine essential spirits of nature. Beren realises his universal nature during his withdrawal and Lúthien, through her descent, is Universal Woman. She is one with nature but, as a Woman alone, is an incomplete entity. She is made complete by her union with the Universal Man. United they represent the elemental forces of natural Good derived from the essential forces of earth and life. They are the completeness of Good, united against the chaos and darkness of Evil.

The nature of Beren's Quest, to take one of the Silmarils from the Crown of Morgoth, is the retrieval of that essential natural light that originated from the Trees of Valinor. So the Quest is made by a man and woman, united in nature, for the essence of nature. Because the trees are symbolic of the purity of light and nature, and the light of the Silmarils came from that source, the Quest becomes symbolic of the search for the salvation of purity from the hands of corruption, darkness and Evil.

Eärendil's withdrawal involves the development of his fascination with, and understanding of, the sea. After Idril and Tuor departed west, Eärendil became the leader of the refugees and married Elwing. As a result of an attack by the sons of Fëanor, the refugees of Doriath fled to the sea. But Eärendil was not with them. He too had gone to sea, ostensibly in search of his parents, and hopefully to find the shores of Valinor to plead with the Valar to relieve the sorrows of Middle-earth. We certainly know that he voyaged far and long and if the withdrawal period is seen as a time for preparation by the Hero for his great undertaking, Eärendil's voyages, although not documented, were the basic learning experience that he required before departing upon his most important voyage. Furthermore, this period establishes the link for Eärendil between the land and the sea. Instead of obtaining the overview of Man's condition in nature (as is the case with Beren and Aragorn), Eärendil's preparation is elemental. It makes him one with the two basic earthly elements – earth and water. By his withdrawal he becomes man upon the waters; a creature of earth who becomes a creature of the sea. When he sets out upon his Quest he has established this elemental universality. All that remains for him is the air and the sky.

Of Aragorn's acts during his withdrawal we know little. Five years after leaving Imladris he met Gandalf. He then travelled east and south, learning of Men and their ways, acquiring that knowledge of the world that would enable him to become a good ruler if and when that time should arrive. At all times he was directing his energies against the servants of Sauron and of Evil. He served Théoden of Rohan and Ecthelion of Gondor and in Gondor he was known as Thorongil – Eagle of the Star – and led what could be termed a guerilla raid against the Corsairs of Umbar. In Gondor, it seemed that he came into conflict with Denethor, son of Ecthelion, and in the minds of the Gondorians Aragorn took first place. After the raid on the Corsairs, Aragorn left Gondor and went to Lórien. There Galadriel clothed him as an Elf-Lord from the Isles of the West for a meeting with Arwen. For a season he and Arwen (who was staying at Lórien with her grandmother Galadriel) remained in Lórien, and on a midsummer evening they plighted their troth on the hill known as Cerin Amroth. Galadriel's matchmaking had brought them to this point on the road to the fulfilment of their desires, but Elrond, when he found out, made the marriage conditional upon Aragorn becoming King of Gondor and Arnor. Thus Elrond becomes like Thingol, although perhaps not quite so scheming, in setting the Quest Hero an impossible task. It is on 29 September TA 3018 that the withdrawal phase ends. When he sets out to accompany the hobbits to Imladris he takes the first steps upon the road that will lead him to his ultimate destiny.

Life is a Quest for Quest Heroes. They are all seeking their potential and journeying along the road to self-realisation. But each of our Quest Heroes has a specific Quest.

Beren's Quest is for the Silmaril and really begins when he first sees Lúthien. Thingol will allow Beren to legitimise his relationship with Lúthien if he can prove himself and bring one of the Silmarils in his hand from the Crown of Morgoth. Beren's Quest was long and is detailed. He undergoes many trials. He is captured by Sauron, is wounded by Curufin, one of the sons of Fëanor, and only by the arts, herblore and love of Lúthien is he saved. At times he regrets his task, not because of any personal peril or frustration, but because of the danger to which Lúthien frequently exposes herself on his behalf. Ultimately they penetrate the fastness of Angband and wrest the Silmaril from the Crown of the Fallen Vala. Indeed, Beren is able to hold it in his hand. This is a mighty indicator of his nature. When the Silmarils were made, the Valar hallowed them and mortal flesh, sullied hands or anything that was evil could not touch them without being scorched and withered. Beren can bear the Silmaril without hurt and because of his very nature is able to transcend his mortal being. The Silmaril, as a symbol of enduring light and Goodness, suffers Beren to hold it, recognising a kindred, or even identical, nature.

But as nature itself is cyclical and suffers rises and falls, so Beren suffers a fall. Nature as a spirit may continue unsullied, but the physical side of nature must wither and ultimately die to be reborn. Wild, untamed forces enter the arena in the form of Carcharoth who, with his jaws, severs Beren's hand that holds the Silmaril at the Gates of Angband. Lúthien once again heals Beren who suffers from the shock of the wound and the dreadful venom from the jaws of the hellhound. Although he survives, he is maimed for the rest of his life.

When Beren returns to Thingol he does not have the Silmaril which remains clenched in his hand in the belly of the wolf. Thingol recognises that Beren is no ordinary man and that he has transcended his nature. Thus the unity and love of Beren and Lúthien is recognised. Finally, Carcharoth is run to earth by Beren and Thingol, but in the final conflict Beren is killed, as is the faithful hound of Valinor, Huan. Beren does survive long enough to see the Quest achieved, and the Silmaril passes to Thingol.

In a sense, Eärendil's Quest first started when he set sail. One of his objectives was, as has been observed, the Shores of Valinor. But the actual event that precipitated the final move towards the successful achievement of this goal comes as a result of the Oath of Fëanor. The sons of Fëanor, aware that the Silmaril was not in the hands of their family, attacked the exiles in Sirion. Elwing, bearing the Silmaril, escaped and finally cast herself into the sea. Ulmo came to her aid, and she was transformed into a seabird and she flew to Vingilot and to Eärendil. She resumed her normal shape and Eärendil headed west, wearing the Silmaril upon his brow.

That he could bear it is a testimony to his goodness, purity and universality. Only one bearing the Silmaril could reach Valinor intentionally to obtain sympathy from the Valar. The Silmaril increased in power and brightness as it went west. But it is not merely the Silmaril that aids Eärendil to Valinor. It is his own essential goodness that is a prerequisite. Were it not for this most important quality, he would be unable to bear the jewel in the first place. Thus, the achievement of his Quest is a realisation of his elemental nature and his goodness rather like Galahad's achievement of the Grail.

Eärendil's successful attaining of his end carried the seeds of a greater end for him. Having come to Valinor as a mortal, he could not return to Middle-earth in a living form. For Eärendil, the end of his Quest was also the end of his mortal life.

That a man might undertake a Quest, the successful achievement of which means his own end, is, of course, the highest form of sacrifice. The Valar and Manwë are aware of this fact. Because of the nature of his sacrifice and the totality of it, although he dies, nevertheless he conquers death. His is a sacrifice of his own being and nature, so that the very nature that he is bound to protect may survive.

Aragorn commences his quest from his foster home,

Imladris. It is here that he is first identified before strangers as the heir of Isildur. The disclosure of his lineage and the presentation of the shards of Narsil, the Sword that was Broken, constitute a formal declaration that he is the rightful heir, and he will now embark upon the Quest to retain his throne and his rightful heritage. In the course of the Quest we see Aragorn develop in more subtle ways than we see Beren or Eärendil develop. In the assault upon the mountain passes and in the journey through Moria, Aragorn is not the dominant force, and it is Gandalf who takes the lead. Although Aragorn bears Andúril, the Sword Reforged, he has yet to demonstrate his true self. It is all very well to *declare* oneself in the security of one's home. The Quest must be achieved by the demonstration and discovery of the inner self. Even his revelation clad as an Elf-lord in the Hall of Fire is only indicative and not demonstrative. The curious thing about Aragorn's leadership of the Fellowship is that it is not assumed but thrust upon him after the Fall of Gandalf at the Bridge of Khazad-dûm. Even the decision to go to Lórien is not wholly his for he says, 'I shall take you by the road that Gandalf chose.'[2]

It is at Lórien that Aragorn is revealed as the returning King and takes upon himself further symbols of his declared kingship. At Cerin Amroth he is seen by Frodo as a young lord, tall and fair, clothed in white. Most importantly he is acknowledged as the returning King at the parting feast by Galadriel. At the welcome to Lórien she called him Aragorn, son of Arathorn. Now, as he takes full leadership of the Fellowship, she gives him the green gem, the Elessar, and gives him the name that was foretold – Elessar, the Elfstone of the House of Elendil.[3]

Aragorn's progress from the declared King to the King as leader is slow and beset by trouble. The Breaking of the Fellowship indicates to him that he has let his control slip. There is a lack of decision-making capability on his part. He yearns for the guidance of Gandalf. He berates himself that his choices have gone awry, and that all he does goes amiss. His decision to follow the Orc band that has captured Merry and Pippin is based on the fact that the fate of the Ring-bearer is no longer in his hands. But it is not a complete abdication of responsibility for, in taking this course, he has set himself and his comrades upon a positive course of action which leads to further opportunities to pursue his Quest for the kingship and for himself as King.

One of the most significant things that Aragorn does is to make more declarations of his kingly heritage before strangers. At the Argonath he makes a private declaration to those who already know who he is, but he enlarges upon his lineage – 'Elessar, the Elfstone son of Arathorn of the House of Valandil Isildur's son, heir of Elendil.'[4] This declaration is the first one made outside a place of sanctuary. The second is made to Éomer on the Plains of Rohan. It is made to a potential ally whose position is not wholly clear. By making the declaration, Aragorn forces the issue and places Éomer in a position of having to acknowledge his dominance. As he said the words, 'Elendil! . . . I am Aragorn son of Arathorn, and am called Elessar, the Elfstone, Dúnadan, the heir of Isildur Elendil's son of Gondor. Here is the Sword that was Broken and is forged again! Will you aid me or thwart me? Choose swiftly!',[5] it seemed to Legolas and Gimli that he grew in stature and his face became majestic, akin to the Argonath figures. By declaring he is King he affirms his status and increases his own majesty and self-awareness. Subsequent declarations flow more easily once the ice has been broken.

At Meduseld, Gandalf describes him as Aragorn son of Arathorn and leaves it to Aragorn himself to make the full declaration to Háma when the question of the surrender of the sword arises at the door of the Golden Hall. On this occasion

Aragorn displays the attributes of a wise ruler, affirming his status, yet bowing to the etiquette that demands compliance with the rules of the house in which one is a guest. He plays a secondary role in Gandalf's debate with Théoden, and does not ride as leader to Helm's Deep, deferring to the lordship of Théoden in his own lands.

At Helm's Deep Aragorn becomes the King in Battle. He is at the forefront of the fighting and uses his powers of leadership to rally the defenders. But he does not declare himself to the enemy when they make reference to the skulking King. The time is not ripe, and Théoden is King in name and fact. But most importantly, throughout the Battle of Helm's Deep, Aragorn's inherent majesty is revealed.

At Isengard, Aragorn realises that the dispute is between the two Istari. He steps down from his post as leader, and for a brief moment becomes Strider again, smoking a pipe with the hobbits. But Strider the Dúnedan is gradually fading as Aragorn the King emerges. Most significantly, on the return to Edoras, Aragorn claims the *palantír* of Orthanc from Gandalf by right and it is yielded to him by Gandalf who says, 'Receive it, Lord! ... in earnest of other things that shall be given back.'[6] Aragorn uses the *palantír* to confront Sauron, revealing himself and his sword. He carries his declaration now straight to the heart of the enemy, and confronts him. He confirms his majesty to Gimli, who questions the use of the *palantír*. 'You forget to whom you speak ... Did I not openly proclaim my title before the doors of Edoras?'[7]

The Hero has progressed from Ranger to self-proclaimed King, sufficiently confident in his role to challenge the enemy. Although the Quest for the crown must continue, the line of self-awareness and self-realisation has been crossed. Now the Hero must conquer death itself, symbolically in Aragorn's case, for:

> From the North shall he come, need shall drive him:
> he shall pass the Door to the Paths of the Dead.[8]

Aragorn's symbolic death and passage through the Underworld are mirrored to a certain degree by Beren when he enters the fortress of Angband and faces the Lord of Evil. But for Beren, the conquest of death is actual as well as symbolic. After his mauling by Carcharoth he was returned to Menegroth and was bidden by Lúthien to await her beyond the Western Sea. Beren's spirit tarried in the Halls of Mandos, the Houses of the Dead, and despite the unbending nature of Mandos, Lúthien was able to persuade him to be flexible, and an appeal was made to Manwë who released Beren on the condition that Lúthien would give up her immortality. And so it was that Beren was returned to the land of the living. His conquest of death was engineered by Lúthien who, as I have observed, is the female side of nature. She can be likened to the Earth Mother, Demeter, who pleaded with the God of the Underworld, Dis, for the release of Persephone. However, Lúthien, the female side of nature, is pleading for the release of the male factor, and for the unity of nature. Thus the release of Beren represents the restoration of the balance created by these two elementals and makes more explicable the reason for the death of Lúthien, for to leave her alive would result again in an imbalance.

Unlike Beren's actual resurrection, and Aragorn's symbolic rebirth from the Paths of the Dead, Eärendil does not return to mortal lands save on one occasion, and that reappearance is somewhat mystical. Although Eärendil does not return to mortal lands, yet he is within mortal gaze, perpetually transfigured. He who bore the Silmaril away from Middle-earth carries it for ever, so that its light shines on Middle-earth. Eärendil and Elwing elected to assume the Elvish side of their nature, with the near immortality that that gave. Eärendil's night-time voyages, in the ship built of *mithril* and of elven-glass, returned him each day to Valinor. His conquest of death is affirmed in the Undying Lands, and his apotheosis is confirmed in Middle-earth, set, as he is, as a star.

But what of his mystical reappearance in Middle-earth? During the War of Wrath, when the Valar came to aid the beset land, Eärendil returned with birds and eagles, creatures of the air, thus affirming the totality of his universal nature, and slew the dragon, Ancalagon the Black. To do this, he must have returned in a physical form. He does not return as a man of the sea or of the land, but as a being of the air. Tolkien does not explain whether he descended in his star ship, but we can safely assume that he did, and that his return was as a transfigured being of great power. Thus Eärendil has achieved a totality of being. He has achieved his Quest, is symbolic life-giver and a light-bringer in the darkness, illuminating and reminding his watchers of the universality in nature.

Aragorn's symbolic death takes place when he passes the Door of the Dead at Dunharrow. Behind the Door and under the mountain are the Oathbreakers who swore to assist Isildur against Sauron, but reneged on their promise. They remain as restless spirits until their oath should be fulfilled. Only the King could pass the Door of the Dead for only he would have the power of will to do so. Only the True King could command the Dead to his service, as Aragorn does. The symbolism is intense and archetypal. The paths of the Dead, situated as they are in caves under a mountain, admirably meet the image of death, and the emergence at Erech is a symbolic rebirth. So it is that the King commands his followers, descends to the underworld, and emerges, commanding the Host of the Dead. Aragorn's strength of will increases step by step. He conquers death where others have failed. In the tale of Orpheus and Eurydice, the hero, on the verge of achieving his quest, does not have the strength of will to heed the command of the King of the Underworld and, as he approaches the light, casts a glance behind him, and thereby loses forever his beloved. Aragorn has the strength of will not to look behind, and his will holds his followers, especially Gimli, who is terrified of the cave.

The returning King now goes forth, having conquered death, to go to war against the forces that besiege his kingdom, and against the Evil One. With the aid of the Dead, Aragorn deprives Sauron of his allies at Pelargir, and moves on to the relief of Minas Tirith. Throughout the account we see the ever increasing growth of Aragorn's might, majesty and strength of will. But, at the hour of his triumph, he withdraws and remains apart from his inheritance. He furls his banner and takes off the Elendilmir and camps outside the City.

It is at this stage that Tolkien introduces a medieval touch to his character, although one that is common to the great rulers of myth, and that is the concept of the King's Evil or the power of the monarch to heal by the laying on of hands. Aragorn displayed a touch of this talent when he used athelas to heal Frodo's wound from the Morgul-knife. But at the Houses of Healing he proves to be more than a mere master of herblore and folk medicine. He fulfils the prophecy that the hands of the King are the Hands of a Healer. It is from this point that the word goes out within the City that the King had returned, and the people gave him the name Elfstone, thus fulfilling another prophecy that he should be given his name by his people.

Aragorn elects to prove his kingship by deeds rather than by declaration and at the Last Debate it is he who makes the final decision. Gone is the self-doubt or the questioning of choices that he had before. The King, although uncrowned, has assumed his proper role.

His coronation and his honouring of Frodo and Samwise are indicative of his position and the level of his self-realisation.

His marriage to Arwen is the culmination of his personal quest for happiness, but to achieve that end he had to succeed in the greater Quest. Although Aragorn's fulfilment is complete, the symbolic renewal of the Kingdom is not. Although the power of the One Ring has gone from the Earth, and the power of the Elves must fade, to be replaced by the dominion of Men, nature itself has not given evidence of the renewal until the discovery of the sapling of the White Tree. With this event, the circle is complete. The link with the First of Trees is re-established and the planting of the sapling in the Court of the Fountain heralds the completion of the natural cycle of death and rebirth. The spirit of the old days, dominated by the brooding presence of Sauron, is over. The new sapling heralds the New Age and the completion of Aragorn's Quest. His marriage with Arwen completes the link with his ancestry.

As is so common in tales of Quest Heroes, there is a form of apotheosis, whereby the hero is admitted into the ranks of the Gods or the Immortals or is allowed to dwell in the form of Elysium. We have seen that Eärendil is transfigured as a star, and dwells in Valinor and thus his apotheosis is complete.

Beren returned to Middle-earth for a while and his return heralded a period of restoration. Menegroth was healed and Beren and Lúthien passed through Ossiriand and dwelt at Tol Galen. Nothing is told of their passing, but whilst they dwelt in Middle-earth they were creatures of wonder. This may be a form of apotheosis, but perhaps what is more significant is what they represented within the structure of Middle-earth. They were the first of the unions of the two kindreds, and from that union formed one half of the line of descent of the Peredhil, the Kings of Númenor, and, of course, the King of the Reunited Kingdom.

The apotheosis is not so much a reception into heaven as the extraordinary respect and honour with which they were accorded by Men, Elves and, indeed, the Valar themselves. For they were one man and one Elven woman who achieved what the might of the Atani and the Eldar could not, the taking of a Silmaril, the invasion of the Realm of Evil and the Conquest of Death itself.

A similar situation takes place with Aragorn. He must suffer physical death, the Doom of Men, and cannot pass to the Undying Lands. But such is his nature that he was given a longer life than most men and one other great gift was given to him. He could nominate the time when he would pass beyond the Circles of the World. He foresaw his death as more than just a mere passing for, as he said, beyond the Circles of the World is more than mere memory. As he passed away, there was revealed in him a great beauty, the grace of his youth, the valour of his manhood and the wisdom of his majesty and age, and so he remains until the breaking of the world. His apotheosis is not an ascension to heaven, but the nature of his death was so unique, and his mortal remains were unsullied by decay, and his memory was so honoured that he lives in memory as if he were immortal.

In depicting his Quest Heroes, Tolkien has not been casual in relating their development to the development of other Quest Heroes in myth, legend and literature. He has concentrated on the common themes and symbols of the Quest. True, there are hints of Gawain in Aragorn, especially in his recognition of self-doubt, or Galahad (and even Christ, although Eärendil is not the Christ of Middle-earth) in Eärendil, or the heroes of *The Mabinogion* and the Scandinavian legends in Beren. And that he has created a relationship between his heroes is not uncommon either. In most of the European and Near Eastern mythologies, heroes beget heroes, and the son may be greater than the father. But again there are the layers of meaning that so often appear in Tolkien's work. Although he despised allegory, the creation of his characters and the layers of meaning that we can derive make it impossible to view the Quest Heroes in other than archetypal terms if we consider their activities within the mythological framework that has been created. Beren is related to the Earth. Eärendil brings earth, air and water together, but his influence in the later history of Middle-earth is more oriented to the air. Aragorn is the ultimate synthesis of the two, and brings the greatest qualities of his ancestry together and forms, with Arwen, the third and final union of Elves and Men.

CHAPTER 8

The Importance of Being Eärendil

In a consideration of the history and mythology of Middle-earth, Eärendil is the key figure. Although Elves such as Elwë, Fëanor, Turgon and others are important figures and men such as Beren epitomise the heights to which humanity may scale, and Túrin the depths to which he may fall, there is none that can match Eärendil. He is the link between the reality of life on earth – suffering, privation, hardship – and the Bliss of Valinor and the Undying Lands. In the context of Middle-earth he was born flesh and underwent an apotheosis to virtual godhead and immortality. He is the link between Elves and Men even more effectively than Beren or his own father, Tuor, and becomes the focal point for both races. He is the character who joins the myth of Creation and the Undying Lands with the here-and-now life of Middle-earth. He is one of the few living myths of Middle-earth. He once was Man and is now Morning and Evening Star. He is more than a simple explanation for a natural event. Without necessarily engaging in simplistic comparisons, he occupies the same *position* as Christ within our framework. He is man, sacrificial object, one who intercedes, saviour in battle and a constant reminder of the past to the present.

In the history of Middle-earth his presence is foretold but the time of his coming is not known. His coming is foreseen in the early stages of *The Silmarillion* when Valinor was hidden 'and of the many messengers that in after days sailed into the West none ever came to Valinor – save one only: the mightiest mariner of song'.[1] And in the account of the Making of Men 'and in the glory and beauty of the Elves, and in their fate, full share had the offspring of elf and mortal, Eärendil, and Elwing, and Elrond their child'.[2] The recounting of the Houses of Men singles out not only those who are great among the Edain but also Eärendil's father, a leader of the Edain in his own right, who was overshadowed by his son. 'And the son of Huor was Tuor, father of Eärendil the Blessed . . . But the son of Barahir was Beren One-hand, who won the love of Lúthien Thingol's daughter, and returned from the Dead; from them came Elwing the wife of Eärendil, and all the Kings of Númenor thereafter.'[3]

The foretelling does not lie only with the narrator. Huor says to Turgon:

> Yet if it stands but a little while, then out of your house shall come the hope of Elves and Men. This I say to you, lord, with the eyes of death: though we part here for ever, and I shall not look on your white walls again, from you and from me a new star shall arise.[4]

Huor's words epitomise the traditions of prophecy, laden with metaphor and perhaps even more far-sighted than appears on the surface. Huor refers to the hope of Elves and Men, obviously Eärendil, who will intercede successfully with the Valar and obtain their assistance. This indeed proves to be the case. Perhaps we can look further into the future to another descendant who was to be the hope of Elves and Men through the line of Elros Tar-Minyatur and whose name at birth was given as Estel (Hope) – Aragorn. Aragorn's coming resulted in the destruction of Sauron, implacable enemy of Elves and Men. Aragorn freed the Elves from a defensive position to one where they could in fact fulfil their destiny and return, as most of them did, to the Uttermost West.

The use of the word 'star' by Huor is metaphorical but also direct. A 'star' may be one who blazes more brilliantly than his fellows in his deeds, and in the direct sense Eärendil did become a star, thus literally fulfilling Huor's prophecy.

The coming of Eärendil was known to the Valar and was expected, although the precise time was unknown and was a secret that lay with Ilúvatar. As Eönwë said when Eärendil arrived at Tirion:

Hail Eärendil, of mariners most renowned, the looked for that cometh at unawares, the longed for that cometh beyond hope! Hail Eärendil, bearer of light before the Sun and Moon! Splendour of the Children of Earth, star in the darkness, jewel in the sunset, radiant in the morning![5]

Thus Eärendil's destiny was clear and in his category of laudations Eönwë refers to him as a star. Such words could only apply to the bearer of the Silmaril and is the realisation of the wealth of prophecy that surrounded Eärendil throughout *The Silmarillion*.

Eärendil's importance goes beyond his intercession with the Valar, his actions in the War of Wrath and the guiding of the Edain to Númenor. By his pedigree he is linked to the noble houses of Middle-earth. His son Elros elects to become mortal, rules Númenor and is the patriarch of the Númenórean Royal Family. Eärendil is the super-patriarch of all the rulers of Men in Middle-earth. The ruling house of Númenor fails with the expedition of Ar-Pharazôn to the west. But the line of rulers does not die. Elendil establishes the Númenórean realm in exile and his sons, Isildur and Anárion, establish the Royal Houses of Gondor and Arnor. Anárion's line fails, but Isildur's does not. The Dúnedain continue after the last ruler of the Northern Realm, Arvedui, passes away. The line of Isildur is re-established in Gondor and Arnor by Aragorn Elessar. Aragorn fulfils the destiny that his name envisaged as did his ancestor Eärendil before him for, although the bloodline has been weakened, Aragorn can trace his ancestry directly back to the Great Mariner. So too can Arwen. Elrond, Eärendil's other son, elected to be Elf. As a direct descendant of Eärendil he still resides, in *The Lord of the Rings* in Middle-earth. As he says, 'Eärendil was my sire'[6] and by so doing links the myth to reality.

At the end of the Third Age Eärendil is a part of the realm of myth. But he is not merely a bright star placed in the heavens eons ago. His heritage continues in fact. Thus he functions in both a mythic and realistic sense. He is both myth and reality in *The Lord of the Rings* – mythic in the part that he plays, and reality in so far as he is Elrond's father. As a mythological character Eärendil is introduced in Bilbo's 'Lay of Eärendil' at Rivendell. In the true bardic or Homeric tradition, Eärendil is portrayed as a creature of legend. His acts are dramatised and embellished and become the subject of a literary work. In a sense the 'Lay' is the myth within the literary form, within Tolkien's literary retelling of a greater myth. It is not until we see the short prose account of Eärendil's acts in *The Silmarillion* that we are able to comprehend some of the obscure poetic references in Bilbo's poem. Bilbo, in the true bardic tradition, has made his own literary contribution and has drawn on sources apart from *The Silmarillion* in the same way that Aragorn no doubt drew on sources such as the

'Lay of Leithian' for his rendering of the tale of Beren and Lúthien.

Eärendil is introduced in Bilbo's poem to establish his importance in the affairs of Middle-earth and to set the stage for the part he has to play as a symbol in the later stage of the book. When the Fellowship leaves Rivendell, Eärendil is a character of song and an ancestral hero. When Galadriel captures the light of Eärendil's star in the star-glass, the symbolic power of Eärendil and the Silmaril returns to Middle-earth. Galadriel is Fëanor on a smaller and feminine scale. As Fëanor captured the light of the Trees in the Silmarils, so Galadriel captured the light of the Silmaril in the star-glass. The power of the Silmaril is still vital and potent in Middle-earth. But despite this power, the use of the star-glass is more accidental than planned. Before the gates of Minas Morgul Frodo, in reaching for the Ring, touches the star-glass instead. Its power gives him strength to turn his mind from the compellingly evil power of the Nazgûl Lord and resist the temptation to reveal himself by using the Ring.

At this point Eärendil's importance in the affairs of the Third Age becomes more apparent. Sam's comment 'don't the great tales never end'[7] and the observation that he and Frodo are part of a continuing train of events, inextricably woven into the far-distant and mythological past, re-establish the concept of the myth as reality. The discussion on the Path to Cirith Ungol sets the stage for the circumstances which represent Eärendil's final participation in shaping the events of Middle-earth. It is Sam, common and unversed in Elvish traditions, who seizes on the star-glass in Shelob's Lair. It is the duplicated light of the Silmaril that stops Shelob and causes agony to her wounded eye. It was Shelob's ancestor, Ungoliant, who hungered for the light of the Silmarils, hidden in the hand of Morgoth, but the duplicated subject of Ungoliant's lust becomes an instrument that, more than any other, results in salvation from the Lair of the Spider. In a way this is a symbolic re-enactment of Eärendil's part in the War of Wrath. As Eärendil descended with eagles to the Siege of Thangorodrim and slew the monster dragon, Ancalagon the Black, so the Light of Eärendil descends to the depths to confound the monster black spider Shelob. The use of the star-glass is a symbolic Third Age re-enactment of a First Age mythological–real event. The star-glass is also used by Sam and Frodo to pass and repass the Watchers of the Tower of Cirith Ungol. In Shelob's Lair, the Vala Elbereth was called upon for aid. At the time of this later use, the phrase 'Aiya Eärendil Elenion Ancalima' is used. The spirit of light that had its origin in the First Age is called upon for succour in the Third. The phrase itself is a reworking of the words 'Eala Earendel engla beorhtast ofer middangeard monnum sended' from the *Crist* of Cynewulf.[8] The translation of the first four words bears a remarkable similarity to the Elvish invocation to Eärendil. In both phrases Eärendil is the man as a star. He is no ordinary star, but one of exquisite brightness. In the Old English he is the star of bright religious significance. In Middle-earth he is the heaven-borne Silmaril and, as we know, the Silmaril carries within it a brilliant and unequalled light. Eärendil's significance is not only restricted to the acts of the Man/Star, but as a bearer of light also. To understand this most important symbol we must look at the nature of light both as a reality and a symbol in Middle-earth.

The Silmarils are not so important for the fact that they are jewels – it is what they contain that matters. They hold the light of the Trees and it is that light that gives them their primary value. Again, it is not the Silmaril that Eärendil bears but the light within it that strengthens and inspires, and sets the Flammifer of Westernesse apart from other stars.

On the most elementary level, light in Tolkien's myth equals hope and especially in the context of Eärendil. As we have already observed, he is the hope of Elves and Men. As light-bearer on Earth, he successfully reaches the Undying Lands to plead for the relief of sorrow in Middle-earth. It is what he bears that allows him to pass the delusions and despairs of the western ocean. Without the Silmaril, his quest would be without hope. It is the light of the Silmaril that touches the Valar where no other token could.

As heaven-traveller, Eärendil brings hope and wonder to those who see him. Although the Silmaril had been a token for the view of a privileged few, as a star its glory is free to all, to inspire and comfort and assist. As a star, Eärendil's light is a symbol of hope for better things and as a relief from the toils and misery of evil. Eärendil's light can dispel darkness and the fear of the unknown. Only light can render the lurking mystery of fearsome things unseen in the darkness as mere figments of the imagination. Light negates darkness and goes beyond Gandalf's observation that black is greater than white, for there Gandalf is referring to colours only.[9]

As a star, Eärendil leads the Edain to the new Kingdom of Númenor which was a land set aside for the pure flowering of the culture of Men. The concept of a new land and a Golden Age for the purer flowering of a culture is a well-established theme in myth, as we have seen. Examples can be seen in the Camelot of Arthur, the Christian New Jerusalem, the Elysian Fields of the Greeks, and so on. The idea behind the 'new land' is that it will be a place above the toil of the present, a place where man will be a better individual and the human community a better society. This was the hope of the Valar in establishing Andor. Its inhabitants were given wisdom, power and longevity. They were given a fruitful land. In that framework rests the hope that mankind would transcend the ways of evil and become a new high culture, as great as the Elves before the Oath of Fëanor and the various incidents of kin-slaying, suspicion and contrariness to the Will of the Valar and Ilúvatar.

Eärendil was a precursor of the Men of the new high culture. As the guiding star he carried the hope of the Valar in leading the Edain to Númenor, as well as the hope for the Men of the New Golden Age. Eärendil also represents to those who follow him in later ages an image for which to strive, a goal in one's performance as a human. His example can only rarely be matched, if at all, yet he is there in the upper line of man's achievement. The light of Eärendil is a potent force against evil as well as the light of hope, the last of the inhabitants of Pandora's box.

Randel Helms comments, 'Tolkien knew from the beginning that his Eärendil was a poetic representative or type of Christ, and so he appears in *The Silmarillion*.'[10] Eärendil's ancestry (although not as Ilúvatar Incarnate) and various actions in his life such as his wandering and his ultimate sacrifice can be considered as Christ-like. Certainly Tolkien wrote from a Christian point of view, but it is too easy to take the acts of Eärendil and quotations from the Bible to establish that Eärendil is Tolkien's Christ. That is not what Tolkien intended. What is important in so far as Eärendil is concerned is the importance of light. Tolkien himself states:

As far as this has a symbolical or allegorical significance, Light is such a primeval symbol in the nature of the Universe, that it can hardly be analysed. The Light of Valinor (derived from light before any fall) is the light of art undivorced from reason, that sees things both scientifically (or philosophically) and imaginatively (or subcreatively) and 'says that they are

150

good' – as beautiful. The Light of Sun (or Moon) is derived
from the Trees only after they were sullied by Evil.[11]

The Light of Valinor, the light before it and the light of the
Silmaril are the purest form of beauty and embody the essential
light of nature created by infinitely sublime creative forces. To
understand this concept of light it is necessary to go back
to Telperion and Laurelin and the creation myth.

As we have seen, the categorical imperative of Tolkien's
cosmos is Eru or Ilúvatar. Although the Valar are imbued with
God-like qualities, they are as archangels to Jehovah. The
concept of song or music is the foundation upon which all is
based, but there is one other force – the Flame Imperishable.
This flame is not a flame as we understand it, which contempo-
raneously creates light and consumes and destroys. The Flame
Imperishable is the essential flame or light source of being. It is
the divine spark of life – that uncreatable essence that sets apart
a laboratory made body from a living person. It is not the soul or
conscience – these are attributes peculiar to human beings. It is
that essential yet indeterminate factor which separates animate
from inanimate.

In the Gospel of St John[12] there is a reference to the Word as
the source of light (or life in the modern translation). This
source of light comes into the world and shines on all mankind.
Although this is not the place to deal with the Christian aspects
of Tolkien's work, to understand the concept of the Flame
Imperishable as a symbol of the creative spark of life, the
opening didactic verses of St John's Gospel assist.

Another aspect of the Flame is that it *is* imperishable – it
cannot be extinguished. It transcends all other types of flame. It
is God-created and eternal. To emphasise the nature of the
Flame, we see that Melkor sought it in the Void in the deluded

thought that it was other than from the absolute Creator. Melkor desired the Flame so that he too could be a Creator. Yet all these aspects of the Flame remained abstract until Ilúvatar materialised the Music with the word 'Eä'. The Flame was sent into the Void and became the Heart of the World. Although all was dark within the material creation, the light burned. Thus God created light and light was at the heart of creation in its first and purest form.

As the antithesis of created light, Melkor kindled great fires. Because Melkor wished to stray from the path of Ilúvatar's thought and therefore plunged into Evil, the fire of Melkor is a destructive force. It consumes rather than creates. It heats the forges for the hateful machinery that, throughout all of Tolkien's works, is inextricably meshed with things evil. Although it is a light source, the fire of evil is anti-good and therefore anti-pure light; pure light being the light that derives from creativity and nature.

Once the Song had become visible, the Ainur were enamoured of its beauty. They longed for the pure light and this influenced all their subsequent efforts to create a form of light. Melkor desired light for himself. He negated the nature of light as being glorious in itself and to be marvelled. By his covetousness of the Light of Creation, his desire to have it as his personal property, he confounds himself. The Light of Creation is of the Creator. Setting himself up against the Creator for possession of the light is a demonstration by Melkor of his evil nature. And he goes further in creating his burning fume and by living in darkness. He was away from the light of good and determined upon a path of evil on Earth. From that time, the creation and the pursuit or destruction of light becomes a significant theme through all Tolkien's works. In the presence of pure light, good works may be done. In darkness or in the fume and smoke of fires, evil dominates.

After their descent to Arda, the Valar created the first of their lights. Yavanna asked Aulë to provide light for the fruits of the Earth. The need for light comes from the Earth Mother to the Earth Father who has dominion over the substances of the Earth. So Aulë made the Lamps of the Valar and the light was put in them by Varda, Lady of the Stars, but it could not rival the Flame Imperishable. It was not a carbon copy, nor an antithesis like Melkor's fume. It was a light designed by and created for nature. The bias of the light was towards life on earth and the beauty that such light would provide. There was within that light a purpose for purity and goodness that rendered the light pure in itself. The lights were destroyed by Melkor because they gave forth light and not primarily because they were good. Melkor was jealous and wanted to dominate the Valar. He had a hatred for the beauty that they had created. By destroying the lamps he ruined the work of the Valar and ended the Spring of Arda. But he did not subdue the Valar, nor did he absolutely destroy light for, when the Valar retired to the West, they gathered a 'great store of light and all the fairest things that were saved from the ruin'.[13]

The second great source of light in Arda was that of the Trees. Again there is a 'light-in-nature' image and again the Trees were devised by the Earth Mother, Yavanna. The Trees contained light within themselves. If light in nature is the light of pure creation and of life, then the Trees are a powerful symbol of that concept. Tolkien loved nature and natural life. He did not like or appreciate artifice or things manufactured. When he talked of the beauty of a tree, he talked reverentially of life embedded in the good earth, growing and nourished by the goodness of the earth. Its beauty is inherent and will continue to be so. All trees have within them their own natural life. They are not concerned with the day-to-day struggle for survival. They survive in their beauty as an essential part of nature. If light is a symbol of life, it is a natural step to the proposition that pure life emits its own radiance. The quintessential goodness of the Trees allows them to emit their silver and gold light. There is no need for Tolkien to engage in facile explanations for the source of the light. Life which springs from natural goodness carries its own light which is so pure that it can be no other than superlative goodness itself. The light of absolute goodness goes beyond mere illumination and enters a realm of sanctity and holiness and sanctifies that upon which it falls.

The light of the Trees was captured in the rain and the dew and was stored by Varda in great vats. The light of the vats must be of a secondary nature to that of the Trees but its quality is still far more sublime than that of the Sun (which is yet to come) and, when used by Varda to make new stars, places in the heavens pinpoints of the magnificence of the source. With such a source, the stars are pure – symbols in the heavens of light as a source of goodness.

It is this starlight that is the first light seen by the Elves and with which they become enamoured. The beauty of the light is one thing; the love for what it represents is another. Within the Elvish spirit is a constant yearning for purity and the excellence of absolute goodness. Although many of the wanderers find this purity in Valinor, those who remain in or return to Middle-earth are still drawn to it and seek to achieve it. But the yearning for light in the hearts of the Elves produces aberrant behaviour in some of them. Fëanor and his kin are motivated by the all-consuming desire to recover what they consider to be theirs. But on a more basic level they are motivated by the desire to seek the light and the purity that it represents. The problem that they face is that those who would possess the Silmarils for other than a noble purpose and who are prepared to use whatever methods they can to achieve them must fall. One cannot selfishly desire or attain elemental purity. One cannot use other than pure means to attain a goal of purity. Thus, kin-slaying, warfare, hatred and feuding as actions on the road to achieving a Silmaril must finally fail. The machinations of Evil produce subtle and deadly results as Fëanor and his family not only attempt to confront evil face to face to regain the Silmarils, but also taint their goal with internecine strife among the Elves themselves.

Thingol's desire for a Silmaril is not really positive. In setting Beren his task, Thingol considers that he is well protected. Only when the Quest is achieved does Thingol take the Silmaril for himself. Beren's motive in undertaking the Quest was not to attain a Silmaril for its own sake – rather he seeks one form of purity to achieve another in the form of Lúthien.

The problems of Fëanor do not only flow from the use of questionable means to attain an end. The end itself is questionable because of his very attitude to the jewels. The purity of the light of the Silmarils is not Fëanor's own. No one has a freehold on absolute goodness. It is to be shared or achieved by all. Without the light created by nature and nurtured by the Valar and captured in the Silmarils, the Great Jewels would be no more than beautiful but lifeless gems. In claiming the Silmarils, Fëanor attempts to claim ownership of their essence and to claim pure goodness as his own creation. But the goodness came from the earth and from the Valar. Such pride and arrogance on the part of Fëanor was intolerable. The actions that followed from such an attitude resulted in the two edicts from the Valar, forbidding the departure from Valinor and the Doom of the Noldor.

Morgoth perverted the sensitivities of the Elves and their desire for pure light into a lust for possession and domination of light. Adam's fall was as a result of disobedience. The Fall of Fëanor and the Doom of the Noldor also flow from disobedience, rather than a mere desire to regain the Silmarils. Even within his own name, Fëanor carries the seeds of his own downfall. He too is a form of embodiment of light – his name meant 'Spirit of Fire'. In his skill and creativity he represents fire as a catalyst for the creation of beauty. Yet fire in its malignant aspect can consume, and consume Fëanor it does. The destructive element of fire scours the noble aspects of Fëanor away, leaving him a debased and ignoble character. The fire of creation that drove him ultimately consumed him. In the creation of the Silmarils he was motivated by the highest goals, to preserve the light of the Trees and the glory of the Blessed Realm. For such an action, he earned the praise of Yavanna. But the fire of his own creation perverted him, for he 'began to love the Silmarils with a greedy love, and grudged the sight of them to all save to his father and his seven sons; he seldom remembered now that the light within them was not his own'.[14] It was the lies and deceit of Morgoth that eroded the will and the standards of the Noldor to the point where they could act only in a self-destructive way.

The destruction of the Trees and the theft of the Silmarils is the act of dark evil attempting to destroy or conceal the goodness of nature. Yavanna's creation is one of purity. Morgoth is the ultimate polluter. He could not destroy the goodness of light itself, but he would not allow it to be free to all. This was coupled with his own perverted lust for light – to possess it and treat it as his own creation. His actions in destroying the Light of Valinor are absolute and grotesque. He is aided by Ungoliant, a spirit of malevolent evil and emptiness, a creature like Morgoth, of absolute darkness who hated and hungered for light. Like her offspring, Shelob, she was only a nominal servant of evil, going her own way and aiding evil only when it suited her. Ungoliant was evil as a light extinguisher and symbolises the absolute qualities of chaotic evil; anarchy and total despair. When she and Morgoth ventured forth they were concealed in the terrible

Unlight – the most absolute of evil concepts. Ungoliant consumed light, satisfying her lust to negative good by absorbing it. The darkness that flowed from the malice and spirit of evil 'had power to pierce the eye, and to enter heart and mind, and strangle the very will'.[15]

Morgoth himself was only able to avoid destruction at the claws of Ungoliant by the timely intervention of his Balrogs. The moral is clear that an evil power can suffer at the hands of an equally evil instrument. Ungoliant, as a mindless spirit of evil, departed and ultimately consumed herself. Yet her importance in the context of light as goodness is essential. Morgoth wanted to possess light. Ungoliant went further – her end was the absolute and total annihilation of light. Her role as a figure of evil goes beyond the satanic.

But all was not lost. From the Flower of Telperion and the Fruit of Laurelin, Yavanna created the Sun and the Moon. Although they were pale reflections of the Light of the Trees, yet their light derives from nature and they are representatives of good. The light of the Moon cannot disperse the Ringwraiths as can the Sun. As allies for Good, the Sun and Moon are more limited than the light in nature of the Trees. Only the Silmarils have that power, and because of that the star-glass was such a potent weapon for Good in the hands of Frodo and Sam, being distilled, not from the Sun or the Moon, but from the Silmaril of Eärendil.

In *The Lord of the Rings* evil functions in darkness whereas light aids good. Gandalf, as Servant of the Secret Fire and Wielder of Narya the Ring of Fire, is a light-bearer. But he is not the source of light. Although his powers are great he is not omnipotent. Sauron, as the embodiment of darkness and evil, is ranged against him. He functions most effectively in darkness as do his servants. The attack of the Ringwraiths on Amon Sûl, the Wargs on the Misty Mountains, the assault by the Balrog in

Khazad-dûm all took place in darkness. Sauron could manufacture his own darkness such as the light-defeating fume at the Siege of Minas Tirith and the light-extinguishing darkness of Sammath Naur. Only in darkness can evil flourish. Only with light can a plant survive. If nature is the embodiment of goodness, then the light that helps it thrive must be the source of that goodness.

In an examination of the quality of purity, Tolkien takes the symbol a step further. No matter what steps evil may take to destroy or sully the light, it will still remain, even if it is fragmented or dissipated. The goodness of light will still survive. Goodness and purity have their source with Ilúvatar. The Valar by their efforts achieved light from nature in the Lamps and the Trees. The light of the Trees was captured in the Silmarils and was rejuvenated in a much less potent form in the Sun and the Moon. Although two of the Silmarils were destroyed as a result of the arrogance and greed of the House of Fëanor, one survived to shine in its magnificence upon the earth, a constant reminder of the absolute nature of light and the ultimate source of creative good.

Eärendil as bearer of the essential light of goodness, purity and creativity is a symbol of man's potential to attain a state of grace, and a constant reminder of the shining potency of good in the midst of darkness. He symbolises hope for Elves and Men; hope for relief from evil, hope in the sense that Man may look up and aspire to greatness. He is patriarch of the lines of Elros and Elrond; of the Kings of Númenor and Lúthien reborn in Arwen.

He is also myth. His reality in history can be proven to those who dwell in the Third Age and he is a star and always has been. His high heroism has gone, passed into the mists of time, and is the subject of song, yet there may be an opportunity for man to emulate or call upon Eärendil to recreate the mystic tale and ensure that the ancient story has not come to an end. And above all, the Flammifer of Westernesse is the only surviving memory of the glory of the Silmarils and the beauty of the Light of the Trees of Valinor.

CHAPTER 9

Tree and Leaf: The Idiom of Nature

One of the images that predominate throughout all Tolkien's work is that of the world of nature and of growing things. We know that Tolkien loved the natural, and especially the botanic, world. Growing things, the fruits of the earth, the seasonal cycles of nature are so often used to represent purity or a world unsullied. Juxtaposed against this image is that of the Pits of Utumno, the bleakness of Thangorodrim, the desert of Mordor, the industrial wasteland of Saruman's Isengard and the blighted Shire of Sharkey and Wormtongue. Yet this is only one use of the image in the myth. The use of the world of nature is fundamental in most myths. As I have observed, Man used mythic ritual in an effort to control, influence or encourage nature. The pantheistic religions have their major gods, responsible for the essential forces of nature, as well as minor deities who reside in and are responsible for certain areas – even to the *lares* and *penates*, the household gods of hearth and home.

Graves tells us of the cult of the Great Goddess of Syria – the matriarch. The hearth was the earliest social centre and the miracle of life via motherhood was a great mystery. The first victim of Greek public sacrifice, so Graves tells us, was offered to Hestia of the Hearth. At once she was the representative of the essential nuclear family group who used the fire for warmth, cooking and for the making of implements, and of the greater family of the tribe, ensuring its ongoing survival. She was represented in the Sun and the Moon, and in the seasonal changes by Selene, Aphrodite and Hecate – a triad – maiden, nymph and crone. Thus it becomes clear that essential attributes of existence become embodied in and represented by deities, and the ritual that surrounds them is of invocation as well as celebration of what it is that they symbolise. It is only natural to expect that all the essential elements and miracles of the natural world would become embodied in religious ritual.

Now within this complex mythic ritual and re-enactment come the priests, or more correctly, the priest-kings. Frazer in *The Golden Bough* refers to the King of the Wood (Rex Nemorensis) and the fate that he assumed when he slew his predecessor. Frazer points to the combination of priestly functions with Royal authority.

> Kings were revered, in many cases not merely as priests, that is, as intercessors between man and god, but as themselves gods, able to bestow upon their subjects and worshippers those blessings which are commonly supposed to be beyond the reach of mortals, and are sought, if at all, only by prayer and sacrifice offered to superhuman and invisible beings. Thus kings are often expected to give rain and sunshine in due season, to make the crops grow, and so on.[1]

Frazer, in examining the nature of the King as a god and a natural force, examines and exemplifies the departmental Kings of Nature, Tree Worship, the symbolism of the sacred marriage, and so on. The essential aspect in all this mythic ritual, for what is sympathetic magic but a form of mythic ritual, is the emphasis that it has upon nature and its elemental forces. Graves also makes reference to the Sacred King whose reign was for a year and which was related to the cycles of nature.

As the myths became part of the religious or folk history of cultures, the significance of the rituals gave way to the essence of the tales which were as much a form of teaching as anything else. The rituals became complex symbols, which nevertheless retained the basic elements of the myth and the relationship to nature. Graves' analysis of the meaning of the Greek myths, for example, makes this clear and he places the tales in their ritual, anthropological and archaeological context.

Yet the later myths of the West European cultures maintained these themes. For example, the Grail myth has at its heart 'the idea of an object of awesome sanctity and power which holds the secret of life'.[2] If we look at the early Grail legends and in particular Chrétien de Troyes' *Conte du Graal*, we are confronted with the Fisher King who is crippled. He must be healed or the fabric of society will crumble, his lands will be devastated and the inhabitants will die. The health of the land is reflected in the health of the Sacred King. The healing of the Fisher King will restore prosperity in the land, demonstrating the link between the fertility of the land and the virility of the King. Certainly, the wound of the Fisher King between 'the two thighs' is a reference to impotence or emasculation. The healing of such wound is total and restores fertility. The symbol is a strong one. 'The prosperity of the land was threatened if the King grew old and feeble and lost his virility.'[3] In the context of the Priest-King, the old and feeble pontiff is unable to carry out his sacred duties of propitiation of the natural elements and so the land is subjected to the whim of nature and uncontrolled natural elements.

There is no clearer example of the Wounded King symbol than in the form of Théoden whom we meet in the narrative as the weakened or Wounded King, but who becomes the King Restored.

Théoden son of Thengel was born in TA 2948. He became King of Rohan in TA 2980 at the age of thirty-two. It is recounted that

> In the days of Théoden there was no man appointed to the office of First Marshal. He came to the throne as a young man . . . vigorous and of martial spirit, and a great horseman. If war came, he would himself command the Muster of Edoras; but his kingdom was at peace for many years, and he rode with his knights and his Muster only on exercises and in displays; though the shadow of Mordor reawakened grew ever greater from his childhood to his old age. In this peace the Riders and other armed men of the garrison of Edoras were governed by an officer of the rank of marshal . . . When Théoden became, as it seemed, prematurely old, this situation continued, and there was no effective central command: a state of affairs encouraged by his counsellor Gríma. The King, becoming decrepit and seldom leaving his house, fell into the habit of issuing orders to Háma, Captain of his Household, to Elfhelm, and even to the Marshals of the Mark, by the mouth of Gríma Wormtongue.[4]

Théoden was seventy when Gandalf arrived at Edoras after his escape from Isengard. There was evil at work and when he left he took with him Shadowfax the Meara. The Mearas of Rohan were descendants of Felaróf, the horse of Eorl, whom Eorl rode without bit or bridle and who understood all that men said. Felaróf, or Mansbane, killed Eorl's father Léod. It was he who tamed the horse, subjecting the killer of his father to his will. The symbol is a strong one. The son of a slain father, who was a King, exacts his vengeance, not by slaying the killer, but by turning the instrument of death to the furtherance of the exploits of King and people. Certainly, only Eorl could ride Felaróf. The horse and his descendants were long-lived, as long as the normal life of men. The Mearas became the horses of the Kings of Rohan and none other could ride them. They were sacrosanct to the monarch. We can assume that Théoden rode Shadowfax, although it is not recorded that he did so. But upon the return of the horse on 23 February TA 3019 he would allow no one to ride him.

This is significant. The ability of the King to mount and ride this unique type of horse in a culture that is so very horse-oriented must be symbolic of his ability to rule. That Théoden cannot ride the horse is as significant as the emasculation of the wounded Fisher King. He cannot fulfil his sacred and symbolic role of mounting and riding the horse that only Kings can ride, and thus, the horse runs wild – a symbol of the untamed chaos into which his Kingdom will fall. As the shadow lengthened, Théoden's inability to rule became more apparent. Responsibility for the protection of the realm fell upon Théodred and Éomer, but they were not blessed with the sacrament of coronation.

Gandalf's return with Aragorn, Legolas and Gimli was not welcomed by Théoden. It was Gandalf who had taken the Sacred Horse. Yet Théoden's dismay at Gandalf's return is as much a result of his own downfall and the sickness surrounding both him and his Kingdom as the removal of Shadowfax by Gandalf. Had the King been a strong and healthy ruler, it is doubtful that he would have surrendered the steed with the words 'take a horse and go' and it is doubtful that the Sacred Horse would have let another, even Gandalf, ride him. Théoden was not sorry to see Shadowfax return unaccompanied by Gandalf, nor did he mourn Gandalf's death as reported by Éomer. But in the Golden Hall it is Gríma who has assumed the role of spokesman for the King. Théoden had fallen under the spell of Saruman conveyed by Gríma and had been ailing for a long time. His land had sickened in the sense that it was assailed and he no longer led the Muster to war as had been his wont. The defence of the realm was left to deputies who had to fight the machinations of Gríma without appearing disloyal, renegade or mutinous. The death of his only son, Théodred, at the Battle of the Fords of Isen was for Théoden the final straw. His impotency, coupled with despair, led him to a position where the land would fall, not without a fight, but fall nevertheless without the vital King to lead his people. Thus we have the parallel with the Fisher King.

The Healing of the King is accompanied by portents in the elements.

> But the wind had shifted to the north, and already the storm that had come out of the East was receding, rolling away southward to the sea. Suddenly through a rent in the clouds behind them a shaft of sun stabbed down. The falling showers gleamed like silver, and far away the river glittered like shimmering glass . . . Now tall and straight [the King] stood, and his eyes were blue as he looked into the opening sky.[5]

The recovery of the King is heralded in nature and is welcomed by his subjects. Háma and Éomer see his recovery as a new day after the night of Théoden's incapacity. A new enthusiasm infects both King and subjects and as Théoden takes the sword of Éomer, a symbol of kingly power, he cries aloud the call to the arms of Rohan. His guards leap to attention. Théoden now takes command of the situation and the Palace of Meduseld becomes a hive of activity as the King prepares to march to save his land. His recovery heralds a turnaround in the fortunes of Rohan. The victory at Helm's Deep is followed by Saruman's downfall at Isengard. The Healed King is strong enough to resist even the Voice of Saruman. From the Muster at

Dunharrow Théoden rides to his destiny at Pelennor, having saved his Kingdom, and extends his power against the evil of Mordor, felling the Captain of Harad and even challenging the Lord of the Nazgûl. It is Tolkien's justice that he must die, having fallen foul of evil and despair, and his death is glorious and the subject of song and verse. His previous incapacity is reflected in the line, 'Out of doubt, out of dark to the day's rising.' His rejuvenation and its importance to the land and its people is echoed in the line, 'Hope he rekindled, and in hope ended.'

Yet if we view Théoden as the Fisher King who recovers, we can also see in Denethor an echo of the King of the Wood who declines and with him his rule, but who leaves an heir to follow him so that the cycle of nature may continue. Denethor was the twenty-sixth Steward of Minas Tirith. The Stewards ruled Minas Tirith in the place of the Kings after the death of the childless Eärnur in TA 2043. The Stewards were trustees for the throne until the King returned and were able to avoid the internecine wars of the Kin-Strife and the jealousies that had weakened the House of Anárion. Denethor was born in TA 2930 and was eighty-nine at the time of the Siege of Minas Tirith. He was a proud man, tall, valiant and more kingly than any man that had appeared in Gondor for many lives of men; and he was wise also, and farsighted and learned in lore. When Pippin saw him, he was reminded of Aragorn – kingly, beautiful and powerful. As Gandalf observed, 'the blood of Westernesse runs nearly true in him'.[6]

Denethor had two sons, Boromir and Faramir, by his wife Finduilas who died in TA 2988. Her death was a severe blow to the Steward who from that time withdrew into himself, and, it is said, began to use the *palantír* of Minas Anor. Thus he gained knowledge of affairs in Gondor, but was aged by his contest with Sauron. His pride and despair caused him to view others who were opposed to Sauron as allies but only if they served him alone. Denethor retreated even further into despair after learning of the death of Boromir. At the same time the assault was being mounted from Mordor. It is quite apparent that Denethor was walking the fine line between sanity and madness. He was able to order the affairs of Minas Tirith and its defences, yet his attitude towards his surviving son Faramir was curt, unforgiving and without tenderness. It was the wounding of Faramir that cast Denethor over the edge on 13 March TA 3019. As a Steward with an heir, the Stewardship would continue. But, as he thought that Faramir was dead, he could see his line coming to an end. There would be no renewal of the Stewardship and if Mordor should be defeated a King would reign, even though he was 'but of the line of Isildur'.[7]

Denethor fell into the abyss of despair. And as he did so, the tide of battle, which was running against Gondor, ran even faster. As Denethor relinquished control of the defence of the City to Gandalf the forces of Mordor broke down the Great Gate of Minas Tirith that had never been broken before. Thus the abrogation by the ruler of his power is followed by the destruction of the most powerful material symbol of his fortress. Denethor, in his despair, decided to make a sacrifice of himself, alive, and his son Faramir, believed dead. He intended to sacrifice himself to the Lord of Despair under whose thrall he had fallen. Yet, just before he burned, Denethor presaged at least some victory, but foretold ultimate ruin – 'For a little space you may triumph on the field, for a day. But against the Power that now arises there is no victory.'[8]

Thus the weakened and beset Ruler died. He did not, as the King of the Wood, die at the hand of his successor but, like the King of the Wood, died because he had lost his power, was too frail to rule, was sickened by age, time and the ravages of sorrow and despair. Although the Host of Rohan had arrived on the field and the forces of Aragorn had come from Pelargir to Harlond the death of Denethor saw the end of an era – that of the rule of the Stewards. His son Faramir survived to assume his office, and a new cycle in the affairs of Gondor commenced with the return of the King. With the departure of one ruler comes the assumption of power by another, and that other was in the form that Faramir's predecessor most feared. For despite their oath, to hold rod and rule in the name of the King until he shall return, and despite the fact that the Stewards would not become Kings, even after 10,000 years, the Stewards had become so used to the *fact* of rule that the return of the King was alien to them and beyond their comprehension or indeed their ambition. So, like the King of the Wood, Denethor was succeeded by the person he most feared – the ruler who would replace him and his line.

The symbolic decline of the goodness of nature is not so evident in the decline of Denethor as it is with Théoden. Nevertheless, as Denethor withdrew more and more from reality and forsook his duty and the strength of command that goes with it, so too did the power of Mordor on the battlefield increase until the fortuitous arrival of the renewed King Théoden and the successor of the Steward, the hero King Aragorn.

Tolkien's myth, however, is not just one of mythic symbols as far as nature is concerned. The myth is a continuing one and throughout *The Lord of the Rings* the subjects of myth become reality. In the context in which I am examining, the essences of nature come alive.

Lórien and Fangorn are linked. Both are havens harbouring things from a bygone age. The strength and power of the Eldar Galadriel and Celeborn allows Lórien to become a fortress and a place of purity, light and beauty. Galadriel derives her power from the Ring Nenya – the Ring of Water – and a Ring of elemental power. As long as she and the Ring survive (and the One Ring remains) the health and fertility of Lórien shall endure. In a sense Galadriel is the Earth Mother of the Third Age, and in a more potent sense than Lúthien. She and her Ring are to the Third Age as Melian and her Girdle were to Neldoreth in the First. It is no accident that Tolkien has coupled the fertility and continued safety of natural surroundings with the female form. By doing so he is carrying on a mythic tradition that goes back thousands of years to the Great Mother and the fertility goddesses of ancient religion. The fertility goddesses are not only the mothers of the gods. They are the Mothers of the Land and of living things. So it is with Galadriel.

In the forest of Fangorn are other creatures of myth – the Ents or Onodrim. Fangorn himself is the oldest living thing that walks under the sun on Middle-earth. The Ents may be the Shepherds of the Trees who were taught to speak by the Elves and thus became the chroniclers and censors of all living things. But more importantly for this examination they are symbolic personifications of the raw elemental power of nature and particularly that part of nature involving the things that grow in the Earth. Although the Ents are a race they reflect the essence of nature. They may talk but, as is the case with trees which grow slowly but surely, they talk slowly but surely. As a tree reflects its passage through time with bark growth, growth rings, size and stature, so the language of the Ents is an historical language. The Ent naming process is an ongoing thing, descriptive of the item and its activities. The Ents are not hasty because Nature herself is not hasty. Tolkien's personification of 'treeishness' is explained in his own words.

In all my works I take the part of trees as against all their enemies. Lothlórien is beautiful because there the trees were loved; elsewhere forests are represented as awakening to consciousness of themselves. The Old Forest was hostile to two legged creatures because of the memory of many injuries. Fangorn Forest was old and beautiful, but at the time of the story tense with hostility because it was threatened by a machine-loving enemy. Mirkwood had fallen under the domination of a Power that hated all living things but was restored to beauty and became Greenwood the Great before the end of the story.[9]

The Ents' power is enormous – almost god-like. Their power to shatter rock, their imperviousness to injury (except when continuously and grievously inflicted by axes or by fire) is elemental and of the Earth. Their physical resemblance to the trees that they love, elm, oak, birch, rowan, casts them into the category of familiar spirits of the woods or the demigods of the forests. They care for the trees, are solicitous of their welfare and aroused at the assaults of Saruman. They too have their myth which is of a tragic nature – the missing Entwives. None knew where they might be, when they went or where they may have gone. It can be that the incapability to breed and enjoy the benefits of love was one of the curses placed upon the forest familiars by Sauron who, it is suggested, destroyed the Entwives in the Brown Lands. The loss of the Entwives is symbolic of the irreplaceability of nature once it has been destroyed by the black, smoky, reeking powers of an industrial society.

Unlike the Ents, who were slow to anger and endured the onslaughts and depredations of Saruman for many years before they retaliated, the trees of the Old Forest were far more subtle, cunning and dangerous. The numbing, hypnotic atmosphere of the Old Forest drove the hobbits inexorably towards the centre of 'queerness', the Withywindle. There the powerful guiding spirit, Old Man Willow, held sway. His power was that of entrapment. His forests had suffered the onslaughts of two-legged creatures, particularly with fire in the Bonfire Glade. The Willow, like the Ents, represents the slow patience of trees and also their enormous power. Unlike the Ents, the Willow is static – he cannot move nor can he communicate directly, although Merry and Pippin are able to comprehend the Willow's intentions should the other hobbits take steps to harm him. Whereas the Ents are basically benevolent forest familiars, the Willow is malevolent. He represents the dangerous power of the forest – it can be a place of beauty and peace but it can be treacherous to those who do not treat it with respect. But at the encounter with Old Man Willow we meet the archetypal spirit of nature – Tom Bombadil.

Tolkien described Bombadil as 'the spirit of the (vanishing) Oxford and Berkshire countryside'.[10] Tolkien did not consider Bombadil important to the narrative (which is probably why he is not included in most dramatisations),[11] but his real significance is that he is the personified power of nature. Tolkien discusses Bombadil in his Letters[12] dealing with the importance of naming in the context of 'who is he' rather than what. He is Master – but only within his realm. His mastery does not in any way rely upon the gathering of material things or upon power. Nature is not like that. Like Tom, Nature will continue to *be* if left undisturbed and untampered. Tolkien describes him as 'an "allegory", or an exemplar, a particular embodying of pure (real) natural science: the spirit that desires knowledge of other things, their history and nature, *because they are "other"* and wholly independent of the enquiring mind, a spirit coeval with the rational mind, and entirely unconcerned with "doing" anything with the knowledge'.[13]

Bombadil's powers and tales that he tells indicate that he is more than just a mere parlour magician. It has been suggested by some writers[14] that he is a Maia. Although it is not clearly stated either in *The Lord of the Rings* or *The Silmarillion* the inference is clear and strong. As Tom says:

> Eldest, that's what I am. Mark my words, my friends: Tom was here before the river and the trees; Tom remembers the first raindrop and the first acorn. He made paths before the Big People, and saw the Little People arriving. He was here before the Kings and the graves and the Barrow-wights. When the Elves passed westward, Tom was here already, before the seas were bent. He knew the dark under the stars when it was fearless – before the Dark Lord came from Outside.[15]

Elrond says of Bombadil, '. . . even then [he] was older than the old. That was not then his name. Iarwain Ben-adar we called him, oldest and fatherless'.[16] Gandalf described him as his own master – withdrawn into a little land within bounds that he had set.

Bombadil's power was great. He could command the trees, the Barrow-wights and the weather. The Ring had no effect upon him. He could see Frodo even when the hobbit wore the Ring. Bombadil's power in his own realm was greater than the Maiar Mithrandir and Curunír who were respectively afraid of, and lusted for, the Ring. Also, from what Gandalf and Bombadil say, once upon a time his little realm was far more extensive than the one that he occupied in the Third Age.

Bombadil is an incarnate powerful spirit of nature, pure and innocent, without ambition or acquisitive desire. His association with Nature is strengthened by his bond with Goldberry, the River-woman's daughter. If the King of the Land represents and personifies the health and bounty of Nature, Tom carries the symbol to its ultimate conclusion – he is Nature as King. Tom is at one with his environment. None will supplant him.

His power within his realm is absolute. He is the King of the Wood who will not be replaced.

Tolkien's use of the natural idiom is varied and he uses that idiom within a number of different contexts and that after all is the essence of myth, especially in literature. It is a many layered strata with a single common base.

CHAPTER 10

A Fanfare for the Common Hobbit

Tolkien's most unique, and to many, most endearing creation
occupies a most important position in the annals of Middle-
earth. Despite the author's disavowal of allegory, inner meaning
or message in *The Lord of the Rings*, the hobbits are perhaps the
most allegorical of all his creations. Hobbits represent the
archetypal pre-Industrial Revolution English yeomen with
simple needs, simple goals, and a common-sense approach to
life. Within Tolkien's mythic framework, Frodo, Sam, Meriadoc
and Peregrine are Everyman. Everyman, in the context of
medieval literature, was a symbol for the ordinary man. His
participation in the events of his story (be it *Everyman* or *The
Pilgrim's Progress*) is a journey towards a form of self-realisation, or a conclusion that is determined by his own actions or
his reactions to events. Everyman may be a figure of parable,
teaching the audience how to avoid an unpleasant fate or
achieve a meaningful goal. He may be a figure of allegory,
explaining to his audience an essential part of man's condition.
But Everyman was rarely, if ever, a creature of ancient myth.
Mythic elements may well come into his story, and frequently
his tale could involve lessons in some moral precept that had its

foundation in Christian teaching. But rarely was he a shaper of events.

Tolkien's Everyman (the hobbit) is symbolic of the ordinary man who becomes, willy-nilly, involved in the great matters of Middle-earth. The hobbits, individually and collectively, are affected by events and at the same time shape them. They are not passive observers, blown hither and, thither by the wind of chance.

The origins of the hobbits are lost in the mists of time. They seem to have originated in 'the upper vales of Anduin, between the eaves of Greenwood the Great and the Misty Mountains'.[1] The Rohirrim, known then as the Éothéod, occupied the same area, and the hobbits occupied a part of the lore of the horse-lords.[2] Indeed their languages were similar.

> And now here before my eyes stand yet another of the folk of legend. Are not these the Halflings, that some among us call the Holbytlan? . . . Your tongue is strangely changed . . . All that is said among us is that far away, over many hills and rivers, live the halfling folk that dwell in holes in sand-dunes. But there are no legends of their deeds, for it is said that they do little, and avoid the sight of men, being able to vanish in a twinkling; and they can change their voices to resemble the piping of birds.[3]

Like the English, the hobbits of the Shire were an amalgam of breeds, the Harfoots, the Stoors and the Fallohides, and, like the various ethnic groups which make up the present Englishman, underwent migrations to reach their eventual homeland. In TA 1050 the Harfoots came to Eriador. This small, short, dark breed were creatures of the hills and highlands. One hundred years later the Fallohides, tall, slim and fair and lovers of trees and woodlands, entered Eriador. The Stoors, a bulky, mannish breed

who wore footwear and grew beards, were the only breed of
hobbits who had an affinity for water. In TA 1150 they came
over the Misty Mountains by way of the Redhorn Gate and
moved to the area between Tharbad and Dunland. In TA 1300
many hobbits moved into the Bree area, following the awakening of evil and the advent of the Witch-king of Angmar. The
Stoors, who seem to have wandered more than the other
hobbits, left the Angle and returned to the Wilderland. It was in
TA 1601 that the two Fallohides, Marcho and Blanco, obtained
leave from Argeleb II, High King of Fornost, to cross the
Baranduin (Brandywine) and enter the Shire. From this time,
Shire reckoning commenced and the hobbits, joined by the
Stoors in TA 1630, began to order their community. They survived the ravages of war with Angmar, the Dark Plague (TA
1636), the Long Winter and the Days of Dearth (TA 2758-60).
Within this setting the hobbits remained, largely keeping to
themselves and minding their own business. The simplicity of
their existence did not contemplate any technological development. Rather, their pursuits were more bucolic, of the soil, of
the hunt and of crafts. They seemed to avoid conflict and dissension with outsiders and even within their own community.

The hobbits lived an almost ideal existence but many commentators have taken their apparent simplicity and innocence
for childishness or childlikeness. Hobbits tend, in the literature
on Tolkien, to be cute or quaint and seem to bear a remarkable
similarity to garden gnomes. This error flows from two fallacies
– a failure to appreciate that *The Lord of the Rings* is, among
other things, the tale of the development and realisation of the
potential of the ordinary man and a categorisation of hobbits in
the context of *The Hobbit*. This latter fallacy stems from the
nature of Tolkien's first book in which hobbits feature. It was a
story written for children. Yet it contains a large number of the
elements of the mythology of Middle-earth. It is a quest tale in

itself. It gives us an understanding of the potential of hobbits, although it is written in an idiom more suited for children.

Bilbo the hobbit is a member of the hobbit community that Tolkien describes in the Prologue and early chapters of *The Lord of the Rings*. The hobbits follow a basic philosophy, have a tendency to be garrulous and gossipy, especially after a few pints at The Green Dragon or The Ivy Bush, use trite epithets (especially Gaffer Gamgee) and seem to be inordinately concerned with families and relationships. They had an innate conservatism and 'liked to have books filled with things that they already knew, set out fair and square with no contradictions'[4] and eschewed adventures. If there was any crime in the Shire it was more in the nature of peccadilloes, such as failure to return books and umbrellas or an inordinate attraction to another's family silver, or from incursions from the outside which may result in more work for the Shirrifs and Bounders. Thus, when Bilbo left the Shire with the Dwarves, his actions represented a substantial break from normal, accepted hobbit behaviour. 'Bilbo . . . had a good share of hobbit virtues: shrewd sense, generosity, patience and fortitude, and also a strong "spark" yet unkindled.'[5] Bilbo to himself was retiring, bookish (may one venture to say donnish) and fearfully afraid of adventures or anything out of the ordinary. Yet the 'Tookishness' within him, although fiercely suppressed, surfaces with a vengeance and leads him to Smaug's lair in the Lonely Mountain. But he goes as a burglar. He cheats at the riddle game with Gollum. Throughout, his actions are at most reprehensible, at times questionable and only rarely truly noble. But Bilbo is finding himself. He is thrust into a world that is unknown to him, full of fear, danger and difficulty; Bilbo's urge is to survive and return home. How often does he long for the safety and security of his hobbit hole. Yet instead of retreating he goes forward, even to what must be the ultimate terror and test – the conversation with Smaug. Of course, Bilbo is only a pawn in a much greater game. Gandalf's interest is to eliminate the potential menace of the firedrake. Yet Gandalf's end is not motivated by any overall strategy. The Ring is, as far as he is concerned, lost. Sauron is a dark force, the Necromancer of Dol Guldur. The threat that the forces of evil pose in no way resembles the situation that the Fellowship faces nearly seventy years later. Gandalf's action is more of a guerilla tactic; to remove one of Sauron's pieces from the board before it can do any real damage. However, Gandalf realises that the hobbits, and in particular Bilbo, are possessed of extraordinary qualities – tough as old tree roots, yet soft as butter. Indeed only hobbits are capable of voluntarily handing over the Ring, as Bilbo does before leaving Hobbiton, as Frodo offers it to Gandalf, Galadriel and Bombadil, and as Sam does when he returns the burden to Frodo in Mordor. Hobbits were difficult to daunt or kill. They could survive without the good things,

> [could] sit on the edge of ruin and discuss the pleasures of the table, or the small doings of their fathers, grandfathers, and great-grandfathers, and remoter cousins to the ninth degree.[6]

It was this potential that Gandalf saw in Bilbo and which he wished to realise with the elimination of Smaug. However, the most significant achievement of Bilbo, in terms of the overall effect upon later events, was the discovery of the Ring. Such an event was not within Gandalf's ken or intention and it is only with the benefit of hindsight and speculation into the intentions of Ilúvatar that Gandalf is able to say that 'Bilbo was *meant* to find the Ring, and *not* by its maker'.[7]

Bilbo realises these attributes that Gandalf sees within him, but like all good folk is happiest when he returns home. He has undertaken extraordinary adventures, survived extreme dangers, faced the dragon in his lair, been through the trials of trolls, orcs and spiders and has been tossed hither and yon through snow, fire, flood and tempest. And although he has faced all these trials and won through, essentially he yearns for the simple things of home. He is not unaffected by his adventures but, by the same token, neither is he dazzled by them. His understanding of the world and of his place within it is better understood but essentially remains the same – a down to earth, sensible, reasonable, prudent, merry individual. But for all that, something has changed slightly and that change is enough to rouse comment among his peers. It became rumoured that he possessed great wealth. He was a man of letters whose interests were not restricted to the Shire. He was interested in things Elvish and entertained strange visitors. Individually these things would not mean much, but in total they resulted in Bilbo being described, especially after his curious behaviour at his Party, as Mad Baggins by a conservative and obviously disapproving hobbit community. Bilbo had taken the first steps towards hobbit self-realisation, towards the universal self-realisation of the ordinary man. If Bilbo were viewed in isolation, his behaviour would be aberrant. The significance of his role, the first faltering steps forward, and, as a result, the discovery of the Ring, becomes apparent when the deeds of the four hobbits in *The Lord of the Rings* are considered. We know that in terms of an author's creation Bilbo was a 'oncer' and it was only after repeated requests that Tolkien wrote the 'hobbit sequel'. But that it was a hobbit sequel (although it developed in a way that not even the author contemplated when he started out) places Bilbo and his actions into the context of the end of the Third Age, and the role of the four hobbits of the Fellowship is a development and an extension of the tentative beginnings that Bilbo made.

To understand the hobbits' adventures as the journey of Everyman, we must realise that Tolkien saw the hobbits as human and related to Men. At Bree they were the 'little folk' as opposed to Men, the 'big folk'. They were more in touch with nature and were generally unconcerned with wealth or greed. They are made small, partly

> to exhibit the pettiness of man ... and mostly to show up, in creatures of very small physical power, the amazing and unexpected heroism of ordinary men 'at a pinch'.[8]

Although hobbits were not Utopian or, according to Tolkien, an ideal,[9] nevertheless they are a generalisation of certain basic characteristics that, although not necessarily admirable, are common to the ordinary man. A life of adventure, participating in the activities that shape and move events, the use of power, are matters generally beyond the ken of the average person. Indeed, such matters are so far out of reach that they are not even the subject of dreams and fantasies. But what happens when an ordinary man is thrust into such extraordinary circumstances that he can become a mover of events? Tolkien tells us that we have within us the potential to measure up if called upon, although we may question our abilities and worth, even upon the brink of success.

Tolkien considered himself a hobbit in matters of food and lifestyle[10] and probably a hobbit that stayed at home and had no adventures. Certainly I doubt that he considered himself a Peregrin or a Meriadoc. He was too much of a scholar to be a Sam and probably would have preferred to be Bilbo in the latter stages, translating Elvish manuscripts. Yet in a sense Tolkien the Hobbit was himself, by his art, a shaper of events because of the extraordinary success of his work.

Tolkien considered the achievements of the hobbits in *The Lord of the Rings* as the achievements of specially graced and gifted individuals.[11] Now this may suggest that the hobbits of the Fellowship were not representative hobbits. In a way they were not. Frodo's origins were shrouded in tragedy. He was adopted by Bilbo and he

> wandered by himself, and to the amazement of sensible folk he was sometimes seen far from home walking in the hills and woods under the starlight. Merry and Pippin suspected that he visited Elves at times, as Bilbo had done.[12]

He maintained the appearance of a robust hobbit (due to the Ring) and, after the age of fifty, felt a restlessness and a desire to know the world beyond the Shire. He associated with strangers. As time went by the 'oddness' of his behaviour began to set him apart from the community.

Meriadoc was a Brandybuck; one of those curious people from over the River in Buckland. It was in TA 2340 that Gorhendad Oldbuck crossed the Brandywine and built Brandy Hall in the area east of the River and next to the Old Forest. The head of the Brandybuck family (they changed their name) was the Master of the Hall and had authority in Buckland and the eastern part of the Marish. Thus Merry was not an average hobbit in terms of rank or family connection. He did, in common with most hobbits, have a degree of native intelligence that allowed him to engage in certain speculations and set in train the events that led to him and Pippin joining Frodo and Sam on the road to Rivendell.

Peregrine Took's family is also apart from the ordinary mould. Although his father was a farmer near Tuckborough at Whitwells, he was also the Thain. He was master of the Shire-moot and captain of the Shire-muster and the Hobbitry-in-arms. However, moot and muster were held only in times of emergency and although the title was but a nominal dignity, the family was accorded a special respect and had a tendency to produce 'strong characters of peculiar habits and even adventurous temperament'.[13]

Samwise Gamgee was probably the closest to the ordinary common hobbit. His father, Hamfast, was a gardener, an authority on potatoes and was fequently quoted by Sam as the fount of original sayings which in fact were trite epithets. Like his father, Sam was a gardener who had been educated to the joys of travel and the doings of the Elves by Bilbo. Sam's fascination with matters Elvish was the only thing that set him apart from ordinary hobbitry.

As *The Lord of the Rings* begins, none of these hobbits show any characteristics that would distinguish them as heroes. Although they do possess traits and backgrounds that are outside ordinary hobbits' experience, it is my opinion that they are as representative of the hobbit Everyman as one might expect. They have had no real experience of the outside world and for them to consider that they might take part in events that would shake the world would be quite outrageous. As they leave Bag End in September TA 3018 they can have no idea of what awaits them. Their immediate goal is Rivendell but that, of course, is only part of the journey of Everyman.

Everyman's journey is a form of Quest. But it is not a Quest for a defined goal. Unlike Galahad seeking the Grail, or Beren seeking the Silmaril, Everyman does not seek a particular objective. He does not consciously set out on a path which will lead to self-improvement or self-realisation. Everyman's Quest is to return to the place from whence he came, but he does not appreciate that he returns in a form different from that in which he started.

The Hobbits are sent to Rivendell. Each one displays different characteristics and as their journeys continue these characteristics are moulded, refined, strengthened or replaced. Frodo is a loner and an aesthete, a walker, a poet, a writer, one whose understanding of things around him is more acute than that of the ordinary hobbit, but not much more so. Samwise characterises devotion to duty and to his master. He works on the premise of master right or wrong. He will brook no nonsense, speak plainly and expect others to do so. He is the archetypal yeoman servant. Meriadoc represents a phase in between Frodo and Peregrin. He has not the wisdom that comes with years, yet he is no fool. He is eloquent and at most times knows his place. Peregrin is purely and simply impetuous youth. The reason they are sent to Rivendell is to carry the Ring there. They are less conspicuous and can travel more stealthily and less noticeably than others. On three occasions within the Shire they encounter Black Riders, and also meet Gildor Inglorion. Their understanding of the nature of the Riders (and the Evil that they represent) is indeed sparse, and it is not until they meet Aragorn at Bree that the true nature of the enormity of the powers that they must face is revealed to them. An interlude with Tom Bombadil gives them the experience of meeting possibly one of the oldest creatures on Middle-earth, of sharing his wisdom and, of course, his protection and powers. But at this stage there is a lack of understanding on the part of the hobbits. The stories that they are told can only be a form of fantasy, for only through experience comes understanding. Meriadoc's dream in the Barrow – 'The men of Carn Dûm came on us at night, and we were worsted'[14] – is linked to Tom's tales of the Great Barrows when 'Kings of little kingdoms fought together, and the young Sun shone like fire on the red metal of their new and greedy swords'[15] although the sun was not so young in the Third Age to which Merry referred. Nevertheless, it provides an experiential reference point, as does his encounter with the Black Rider at Bree. Apart from contact with Gandalf, whose true origin is not revealed to the hobbits until a later stage, the meeting with Bombadil is the first contact that the hobbits have with the continuing myth of Arda. They cannot appreciate or comprehend the significance of the role of Bombadil other than that he is a teacher who acquaints them with the past, albeit in rambling story form. When he is viewed in the overall scheme of things, Bombadil is the first of many strange and wonderful contacts that the hobbits have outside the Shire. He increases their understanding of the wide world outside their limited existence and experience, and enriches it.

But whereas Bombadil is but a fleeting contact, Aragorn is something else. Neither the hobbits nor the reader (nor indeed Tolkien as he wrote) appreciate who Aragorn is other than that he is a dour, dark, rather forbidding fellow who initially concerns the hobbits but wins their confidence. By allowing him to join them on the long and dangerous road to Rivendell, the hobbits put their trust in an unknown quantity. Even Butterbur, who has more contact and understanding of the world outside, but not much more, treats Aragorn with respect but wariness. But in terms of the decision to take Aragorn, the hobbits accept him at face value and Aragorn knows that this must be so. 'I had to persuade you to trust me without proofs'[16] was his motive, and, after Gandalf's letter proves Aragorn a friend, Frodo reveals that he had already made up his mind – 'I believed that you were a friend before the letter came . . . or at least I wished to'.[17] Aragorn, as good as his word, takes the party on paths seldom trodden. But not all his skill can keep the Black Riders at bay forever, and on Amon Sûl (Weathertop) the first face to face confrontation with the full dread of the Ringwraiths takes place. This is an important moment because it reveals to us the considerable strength of will that lies under the rather jolly and naïve hobbit exterior. We could expect that, faced with the terror unmasked, the hobbits would turn and flee and, given what we know of them, who could blame them. But this does not happen. Although they are terrified they all stand their ground and, what is more, fight back. Frodo, wearing the Ring, is revealed to the Witch-king but is able to draw his blade and call on the potent force of Elbereth to aid him. The hobbits are face to face with the mightiest of the Servants of Sauron. There is no Bombadil to call upon. Their fate is in their hands and after the Ringwraiths flee even Aragorn comments that Frodo is 'made of sterner stuff than I had guessed.'[18]

The journey from Amon Sûl to Rivendell allows the hobbits to grow in the face of adversity. Frodo's will is sapped by his wound inflicted by the Morgul-knife but because of his natural, but by him unrealised, inner strength, he is able to move slowly on. The concern of the other hobbits for their fellow is obvious and it does not seem that hobbits are a selfish folk. Yet even in the face of the hard road they are able to keep their spirits up, exemplified when they discover the stone trolls.

The final dash to the Ford of Bruinen is for Frodo the last test, and in his weakened condition he almost fails. The horse Asfaloth carries him across the Ford where he is able to summon up his last reserves of physical and spiritual strength and boldly he faces the Black Riders and their King alone. After his recovery even Gandalf comments on the obvious hidden reserves of strength possessed by hobbits. For the first time for the reader and for the hobbits, we are introduced to the glory and wonder of the Elvish presence in Middle-earth. The hobbits can see and participate in activities and a lifestyle and a culture that is of the Elder Days and has its origins far back in the past of Middle-earth. The proceedings at the Council of Elrond bring to Frodo and Sam, who of the company who left Hobbiton are the only ones present, an understanding of the true nature of the Ring, and the reality of the matter in which they have become involved. The trip to Rivendell was no jaunt, interspersed with the odd adventure, and the perils which they encountered were all part of an ongoing chain of events which had their origins far, far back in time. Whether they liked it or not, the hobbits had been involved in circumstances which would or could have tremendous significance in the history of Middle-earth and the result of their actions would be critical for the future of the land. By leaving the Shire and by bearing the Ring to Rivendell, Frodo and his companions had stepped out of the safe and secure haven of the Shire. Their actions, howsoever minor, could not be viewed as insignificant. Like it or not, they had become involved in the affairs of the World.

If this says anything to the ordinary man, it is that no man can operate in a vacuum. No man, as Donne said, is an island. Our actions can have complex consequences upon our relationships with each other. The choices that we make can materially affect not only ourselves, but others. The things that we do must be considered for, like it or not, we must be responsible for the consequences.

In finding the Ring, Bilbo had set in train a chain of events the final results of which he could not have realised. Yet they did happen. The Council of Elrond puts Bilbo's actions in context, as well as the other developments that have taken place up until 18 October TA 3018. The decisions that are made at the Council will determine the future development of events. When Frodo elects to take the Ring he is not only taking upon himself an onerous burden and an arduous task, he is also taking a major step in terms of his own development and that of his companions. He is moving further away from the safe, enclosed haven of the Shire with its disinterest in affairs of moment and he is choosing to involve himself further in the great matters of Middle-earth. By making the decision, he is saying, 'Yes, I am prepared to face up to whatever tests this may involve, unknown though they may be, for the greater good of all. I may not know the way, but I am prepared and am willing to seek it.'

It would have been quite understandable had he declined the

chance and returned to the Shire. But he would have been turning away from that challenge to realise the potential of the ordinary man which he and his companions represent. His choice has been thought through to a degree and knowing, as he does, the context within which his choice is made, it is all the more significant. Peregrin Took, on the other hand, chooses by impetuousness and like a stubborn child (which is entirely in character) he defies Elrond's wisdom and advice. Meriadoc's choice is because of shared hardship in the past and a desire to share in the future. As he says, 'It will be a punishment for any of us to be left behind, even in Rivendell. We have come a long way with you and been through some stiff times. We want to go on.'[19]

From Rivendell, Frodo occupies two symbolic roles and is more important in his development as Tragic Hero than as a symbol of Everyman. The focus of the development of the ordinary man is sharpened upon Merry, Pippin and Sam as Frodo's fate and destiny become more entwined with the Ring. Because of the Ring, and his task, Frodo becomes more one of the Great, aloof and introspective as the Ring begins to work its power upon him. The decision that he makes at Rivendell compels the others to follow him as his decision at Amon Hen results in a parting of the ways for the hobbits until they are united at Cormallen.

For Merry, Sam and Pippin the position has been secondary until the Breaking of the Fellowship. Merry and Pippin especially are followers who tend to subordinate themselves to the decisions of Aragorn, Gandalf and Frodo. It is not until their capture by the orcs that they are truly thrown upon their own mettle and resources. No one can be sure, least of all Merry and Pippin, what the consequences of their actions may be. Their hobbitish stamina and ability to endure what may seem to be the unendurable stands them in good stead. Pippin's youthful foolhardiness, coupled with a certain resourcefulness, allows him to risk obvious punishment by leaving the brooch as a marker on the path. He also uses the idea that they as hobbits may have the Ring to forestall Grishnákh who, although it was not intended, bears them away from the pursuit of the orcs by Éomer's *éored*. After their escape they stop and eat *lembas* seemingly disdainful of the trials and tribulations that they have endured. Such is the resilience of hobbits.

The meeting with Treebeard, the oldest living thing that walked under the sun on Middle-earth, is significant. The hobbits are representative of the youngest of the races in Middle-earth. Treebeard is the oldest and at the same time represents the vital force of nature that is so beloved by the Elves, and he is, because of this, unsullied. The hobbits' dealings with the Ents are all the more significant because they are accepted and recognised and incorporated into the Lists. They have not, as far as the Ents are concerned, reached maturity, described, as they are, as 'the Hobbit children, the laughing-folk, the little people'.[20] But despite this, as a result of their meeeting with the Ents they grow in the physical sense by drinking the Entdraughts. Their physical growing is a symbol of the further spiritual growing process that Merry and Pippin experience. Their meeting with the natural elements of Middle-earth, on their own and without guidance, represents a further step in their progress and their understanding of the world. Despite the difficulties that they suffer and the experiences that contribute to their development, they are not so dazzled as to forget their essential hobbitishness. Consequently, we see them revert to Shire behaviour when, at the ruined gates of Orthanc they are found enjoying food, drink and pipeweed. Yet, as Gimli says, 'I would swear that you have both grown somewhat'.[21]

Although they have grown, Pippin has not shaken off youthful impetuousness and for the last time disobeys orders when he looks into the *palantír*. By doing this he comes face to face

with Evil and undergoes the form of trial that such a confrontation involves. Indeed, all the hobbits face such a trial; Sam in
facing and battling Shelob; Merry in wounding the Lord of the
Nazgûl; Frodo by claiming the Ring. Such a trial is necessary
for Everyman. Without coming face to face with Evil his progress is nothing. Evil is his potential other self. To succeed he
must face it, battle it, overcome it or choose against it. Pippin's
will is not wrenched from him by the Dark Lord. As a result of
his experience he will have a greater understanding and awareness of Evil in the future.

To understand leadership and to be an effective leader one
must know the meaning of service. It is therefore no accident
that both Merry and Pippin pledge themselves to leaders of the
peoples of Middle-earth – Merry to Théoden and Pippin to
Denethor. Their fealty is not requested, demanded nor com-
pelled but, in the nature of duty, is given willingly and freely
without fear or thought of reward. The service that is offered is
service out of love. For Pippin the service is even more valuable
in that his pride was somewhat stung by the scorn of Denethor.
For Merry, the offer follows the suggestion of Théoden that
Merry become his esquire. For both hobbits their formal period
of service is short, but the reality of their service continues.
With a stubbornness that we have come to recognise they
persist in their duty, Merry by riding with Dernhelm/Éowyn to
Gondor, and Pippin to continue in his efforts to save the
Steward of Gondor and his heir from the despair of madness
and from the pyre. Both hobbits lose their overlord. Because of
Pippin's actions, Faramir is saved. In attempting to save his lord,
Merry confronts the Nazgûl and, with the blade of Westernesse,
is able to wound him enabling Éowyn to dispatch the Witch-
king as his head bows.

At this stage, the affairs of Merry and Pippin become more
ordered and subject to the direction of Gandalf and Aragorn.

For them, the realisation of their potential and the culmination of their adventures occurs when they return to the Shire. Even after all that they have been through they are able to maintain contact with their own Shire reality after the Field of Pelennor, for the true man may reach to touch the stars, yet keep his feet firmly upon the ground.

Sam has been in service all along. As Frodo's gardener and as helper, servant and companion he doggedly attends to the practical needs and wants of the travellers and their pack animals. He is excessively cautious and possessed of a rather innate conservatism. His desires and goals are limited – to look after his master and to see the Elves. Even so, his involvement with the Elves is not with their culture or their language or their wisdom or lore. Sam looks upon Elves as higher beings of wonder. His interest has been awakened by Bilbo's tales and to see an Elf is his main personal goal. Sam's horizons are limited. He does not seek greater things or even greatness itself. He knows his place and he intends to stay there. He represents, if anything, that curious aspect of the English class system, where everyone has his place, and woe betide anyone who wishes to change his place. Sam is unambitious for himself. But he has such dogged determination in the rightness and wrongness of things that he has no fear of expressing what he feels to whomsoever will listen, and on occasions his opinions and his tongue get the better of his discretion, especially with Aragorn at Bree and with Faramir at Henneth Annûn. Only when he has spoken his truth and had his say does he realise, belatedly, that he has stepped out of line, and that it is not seemly for one of his place to speak in such a way to people who occupy a position of greater responsibility than he.

In terms of characteristion and attitude, Sam is one of the most finely worked of the dramatis personae of *The Lord of the Rings* – the other is Gollum. Tolkien says of Sam that he 'can be very "trying".[22] He is a more representative hobbit than his fellow travellers

> and he has consequently a stronger ingredient of that quality which even some hobbits found at times hard to bear: a vulgarity – by which I do not mean a mere 'down-to-earthiness' – a mental myopia which is proud of itself, a smugness (in varying degrees) and cocksureness, and a readiness to measure and sum up all things from a limited experience, largely enshrined in sententious traditional 'wisdom' . . .
>
> Sam was cocksure, and deep down a little conceited; but his conceit had been transformed by his devotion to Frodo. He did not think of himself as heroic or even brave, or in any way admirable – except in his service and loyalty to his master. That had an ingredient (probably inevitable) of pride and possessiveness: it is difficult to exclude it from the devotion of those who perform such service. In any case it prevented him from fully understanding the master that he loved, and from following him in his gradual education to the nobility of service to the unlovable and of perception of damaged good in the corrupt.[23]

Sam, in terms of development, remains static until his personal cusp at the Pass of Cirith Ungol. Prior to this his actions have been as a follower and a helper. He had demonstrated abilities of common sense and practicality and of making do with what is available.[24] At times he acts as a buffer between Frodo and Gollum, and at times a despairing third party to Frodo's tolerance of Gollum. At the Pass, by deserting Frodo to wreak his vengeance upon Gollum and to release his pent-up hostility towards the pitiful but mean creature, he allows Frodo to be wounded by Shelob and unwittingly allows Frodo's capture by the Orcs. His blind courage in facing Shelob is motivated by the tragedy that has befallen his master – the same sort of motivation that drives Merry to wound the Lord of the Nazgûl. This is his conflict with the raw power of evil, especially when we consider that Shelob is the last child of Ungoliant and has a heritage that extends as far back in time as the First Age to her lair in the Mountains of Terror. Sam becomes a heroic figure, and although his wounding of Shelob is not mortal, it is sufficient to disable her severely and sever her further involvement with the matters of the Ring.

> No such anguish had Shelob ever known, or dreamed of knowing, in all her long world of wickedness. Not the doughtiest soldier of old Gondor, nor the most savage Orc entrapped, had ever thus endured her, or set blade to her beloved flesh.'[25]

The other important action of Sam Alone is that he takes the burden of the Ring and the obligation to carry on the Quest. Like Frodo at Rivendell he does not know 'the way' or what it may involve. Yet he understands the concept of duty freely assumed. His reaction to the Ring and its effect upon him is commensurate with his size – that is with his size of character. Sam is no hero. He does not have the size of character of Aragorn nor even of Frodo. His use of the Ring is limited by the level of his desires. Thus the Ring works upon him as

> Samwise the Strong, Hero of the Age . . . and at his command the vale of Gorgoroth became a garden of flowers and trees and brought forth fruit. He had only to put on the Ring and claim it for his own, and all this could be.
>
> In that hour of trial it was the love of his master that helped most to hold him firm; but also deep down in him lived still

unconquered his plain hobbit-sense: he knew in the core of his heart that he was not large enough to bear such a burden, even if such visions were not a mere cheat to betray him. The one small garden of a free gardener was all his need and due, not a garden swollen to a realm.[26]

As things came to pass, Sam *did* have more than one garden after he renewed the Shire.

Sam demonstrates his amazing strength in that, having taken the Ring, *he gives it up*. Although he is 'reluctant to give up the Ring and burden his master with it again',[27] nevertheless his surrendering of the burden is not accompanied by the sense of unwillingness suffered by Bilbo or Frodo. Of course, they had held the Ring longer than Sam, but the nature of the Ring was such that no one would willingly give it up. Only hobbits, it seems, have the strength to let it go. The other significant fact is that although he has borne the Ring, Sam does not feel any desire to repossess it. His realisation of his own capabilities and limits came to him when he wore the Ring. If he was not aware of them before, they came to him at that time. Although, compared with Aragorn or Boromir, he is unambitious, he has the potential to take the burden or a duty when required, yet be unaffected by it. For Sam, to realise himself in this way is vital. His strength is essential if he is going to assist Frodo to Sammath Naur. Without him the Quest would fail, and if he were obsessed with regaining the Ring he would go the same way as Gollum. Whether or not Sam actually realises *all* these things, once he releases the Ring, he thinks no more of it. He will not take it up again, nor does he desire to. In this respect he mirrors the nobility of Faramir who would not take the thing if it were lying on the roadside. Sam's love and sense of duty to his master override the base and raw lusts that the Ring engenders, and although the ultimate fate of the Ring is decided by Frodo and

Gollum together, it is Samwise the Strong who makes it possible for Frodo to reach the Crack of Doom.

The reunification of the hobbits and the celebrations following the fall of Sauron, the Crowning of the King, and the Wedding of Arwen and Elessar, although eucatastrophic in the overall tale, are glittering *entr'actes* for the hobbits. It is the return to the Shire, to their homeland, that is most significant for them. Their adventuring has been a preparation for what they must face. They can no longer rely on wizards and Rangers, although technically the Shire is a fief of the King. As Gandalf says:

> You must settle its affairs yourselves; that is what you have been trained for. Do you not yet understand? My time is over: it is no longer my task to set things to right, nor to help folk to do so. And as for you, my dear friends, you will need no help. You are grown up now. Grown indeed very high; among the great you are, and I have no longer any fear at all for any of you.[28]

In fact, Everyman, now experienced beyond the bounds of his own immediate home, is ready to return and save his home from whatever cruel fate has befallen it. The hobbits are to bring back to the community the experience, knowledge and collective wisdom that they have acquired upon their quest. When they return to the Shire, they find it changed; not even the Shire can remain in a vacuum, although it has done so in their minds. But the change has not been natural progress, which would be acceptable, or for the better, which would be delightful. It has been for the worse, and after all that the hobbits have been through such a change is inimicable. The Shire has been transformed into a police state; rules abound, enforcers are abroad. The delightful hobbitish pleasures have been proscribed.

The grown hobbits immediately defy the system and by their force of character are able to subdue those less strong-willed of their fellows. Merry, by sounding the Horn of the Mark, brings in an attribute external to the Shire, as has Saruman in the form of a blight. The world has come to the Shire in the form of the forces of Evil and Good. In microcosm, the Great Game of Middle-earth is played out in the archetypal representation of idealistic England. The Battle of Bywater, although fierce, is a walkover for the hobbits, although a distressing result of it is that the blood of hobbits stains the ground of their native land. The true nature of the growth of the hobbits is revealed when Frodo expels Saruman.

> You have grown, Halfling . . . Yes, you have grown very much. You are wise, and cruel. You have robbed my revenge of sweetness, and now I must go hence in bitterness, in debt to your mercy.[29]

After the passing of Saruman, the rebuilding begins. The hobbits are welcomed as heroes, although there is a reluctance to embrace their increased stature. The Gaffer finds the wearing of ironmongery an unnecessary affectation and out of keeping with the mores of hobbit fashion, preferring a 'weskit' as more in keeping with the Shire's sartorial norms. Merry and Pippin are called 'Lordlings', a diminutive for two hobbits who have had a part in shaking the world. For themselves they are unchanged unless they are more fair-spoken, jovial and full of merriment than before. They are not rejected, and, with the exception of Sam, treated more with caution. Frodo has little honour in his own country and at a later stage Merry and Pippin returned to Gondor where they had high rank. Frodo has less and less to do with the affairs of the Shire and finally departs for the Undying Lands. Sam, the Common Hobbit, remains. His influence upon the Shire is great. His wisdom as a man of the soil has increased and is symbolised by his use of

Galadriel's gift which is used, not for himself, but for the benefit of all and the most potent symbol of his experience in the World is the magnificence of the Mallorn Tree.

Although Frodo, Merry and Pippin represent those aspects of hobbit character which are rough-hewed when they leave the Shire, they are trimmed and shaped by their experiences. Each of them represents a part of the human character which becomes more sophisticated. But it is Sam who is the real Everyman. He leaves as an unambitious servant, and returns as an altruistic but modest hero, but a servant still, but now his service is wider – not to one, but all his fellow men. Is this the Sam who was so harshly disposed to Gollum? The realisation that Gollum too had a part to play allows Sam to see things not only in black and white, but also in the many shades of grey. We may find Sam trying, but who are we to condemn him, for we ourselves may be as trying to those around us whilst at the same time attempting to be staunch and sensible and often succeeding. When he returns to the Shire he is changed, older, quieter, less free with his rustic views and his bar-room wisdom. He remains subordinate and loyal to Frodo. Only when Frodo passes over the Sea is Sam truly alone, the developed man who has realised his potential and now, free from the constraints of the past and his duty to his master, can go forward. When he says 'I'm back' he is not only speaking a fact – that he has returned from his excursion with Frodo – but he is also speaking symbolically. Everyman, the Common Hobbit, is home in the bosom of his family and his community. His service to one man has finished. His service to the community has begun and Sam becomes Mayor of the Shire for seven terms. His vision of himself as a gardener has been partly realised. But he did not expect, nor anticipate, that he would become a leader and servant of the community and we are aware that the honour will not go to his head. He will remain Sam, but an older, wiser, better, more spiritually enriched Sam. For he *is* the Common Hobbit; he *is* Everyman. The other aspects of the human character, represented by the other hobbits, have altered too, as has the Shire which, although in a Golden Age, has lost its innocence. Upon his return from the Havens, Sam has realised his potential – it is journey's end.

And we too are Everyman. The achievements of the few realise our collective potential as human beings – they exemplify and reflect our dreams and enrich our existence. In the end, Sam's departure for the Havens and the Undying Lands – the heavenly realm of Valinor – holds out hope and reward for all well-lived lives.

NOTES

References in the text fall into three major categories:

1 Books by J. R. R. Tolkien or edited by Christopher Tolkien.
2 Books about J. R. R. Tolkien and his works.
3 General references especially to sources covering mythology.

The books by Tolkien are *The Lord of the Rings*, *The Silmarillion*, *Unfinished Tales* and the essay 'On Fairy-Stories'. Because of the proliferation of editions of *The Lord of the Rings* and the variations in pagination, all references have been made to the book number (as stated by Tolkien in the contents) and the chapter number. I have also abbreviated references to Tolkien's works in the following way:

The Lord of the Rings –	LOTR (book number, chapter number).
The Silmarillion –	Sil. (Page number) All references are to the hardback edition published in 1977.
Unfinished Tales –	UT (page number) All references are to the hardback edition published in 1980.

1 The books about Tolkien and his works are listed below and (where necessary) the abbreviations are noted following them. Not all these books have been the subject of specific reference in the text, and comprise a bibliography that was used in the preparation of the manuscript.

Carpenter, Humphrey, *J. R. R. Tolkien, a biography*. London: George Allen & Unwin, 1977. (*Biography*)

Carpenter, Humphrey, *The Inklings*. London: George Allen & Unwin, 1978.

Carpenter, Humphrey, *The Letters of J. R. R. Tolkien*. London: George Allen & Unwin, 1981. (*Letters*)

Carter, Lin, *Tolkien: A Look Behind The Lord of the Rings*. New York: Ballantine Books, 1969.

Foster, Robert, *The Complete Guide to Middle-earth*. London: George Allen & Unwin, 1978.

Helms, Randel, *Tolkien's World*. London: Thames and Hudson, 1974.

Helms, Randel, *Tolkien and the Silmarils*. London: Thames and Hudson, 1981.

Isaacs, Neil D., and Zimbardo, Rose A., *Tolkien – New Critical Perspectives*. University Press of Kentucky, 1981.

Kocher, Paul H., *Master of Middle-earth – The Achievement of J. R. R. Tolkien*. London: Thames and Hudson, 1973.

Kocher, Paul H., *A Reader's Guide to The Simarillion*. London: Thames and Hudson, 1980.

Lobdell, Jared (ed.), *A Tolkien Compass*. New York: Ballantine Books, 1980.

Lobdell, Jared, *England and Always – Tolkien's World of the Rings*. Grand Rapids, Mich: William B. Eerdmans Publishing Company, 1981.

Manlove, C. N., *Modern Fantasy –Five Studies*. Cambridge: Cambridge University Press, 1975.

Nitzsche, Jane Chance, *Tolkien's Art – A Mythology for England*. London: Macmillan, 1979.

Noel, Ruth S., *The Mythology of Tolkien's Middle Earth*. London: Thames and Hudson, 1977.

O'Neill, Timothy R., *The Individuated Hobbit*. London: Thames and Hudson, 1980.

Ready, William, *The Tolkien Relation*. New York: Warner Books, 1969 (formerly *Understanding Tolkien and The Lord of the Rings*).

Tyler, J. E. A., *The Tolkien Companion*. London: Macmillan, 1976.

2 For those who are interested in further background reading, the following may be consulted:

Allan, Jim, A *Speculation on The Silmarillion*. London: The Tolkien Society, 1976.

Allan, Jim, *An Introduction to Elvish*. Frome, Somerset: Bran's Head Books, 1978.

Becker, Alida (ed.), *The Tolkien Scrapbook*. Philadelphia, Pa: Running Press, 1978.

Carter, Lin (ed.), *The Young Magicians*. New York: Ballantine Books, 1969.

Carter, Lin, *Imaginary Worlds – The Art of Fantasy*. New York: Ballantine Books, 1973.

Crabbe, Katharyn F., *J. R. R. Tolkien*. New York: Frederick Ungar Publications, 1981.

3 The general references to sources for mythology are set out below. Although they are arranged alphabetically, I must pay particular tribute to two authors whose works were of immeasurable assistance in examining the complex (and at times frustrating) fields of mythology and tragedy. They are:

Lesky, Albin, *Greek Tragedy*. London: Ernest Benn, 1978. (Lesky)

Ruthven, K. K., *Myth – The Critical Idiom*. London: Methuen, 1976. (Ruthven)

Generally:

Campbell, Joseph, *The Hem with a Thousand Faces*. Princeton University Press, 1969.

Crow, W.B., *The Arcana of Symbolism*. Wellingborough, Northants: The Aquarian Press, 1970.

Cunningham, Adrian (ed.), *The Theory of Myth*. London: Sheed & Ward, 1973.

Dunne, John S., *The City of the Gods*. London: Sheldon Press, 1975.

Eliade, Mircea, *Myth and Reality*. London: George Allen & Unwin, 1964. (*Eliade 1*)

Eliade, Mircea, *Yearning for Paradise in the Primitive Tradition* (see Murray below). (*Eliade 2*)

Eliade, Mircea, *Myths, Dreams and Mysteries*. London: Fontana, 1968. (*Eliade 3*)

Ellmann, R., and Feidelson, C. (eds), *The Modern Tradition*. New
York: Oxford University Press, 1965.

Graves, Robert, *The Greek Myths*. Harmondsworth, Middx: Penguin
Books, 1962. (*Graves 1*)

Graves, Robert, *The Larousse Encyclopaedia of Mythology*
(Foreword). (*Graves 2*)

Graves, Robert, *The White Goddess*. London: Faber, 1952.

Leeming, David, *Mythology*. New York: Newsweek Books, 1970.

Levi-Strauss, Claude, *Myth and Meaning*. London: Routledge and
Kegan Paul, 1978.

Murray, Henry (ed.), *Recurrent Themes in Myth and Mythmaking*.
New York: George Braziller, 1960.

Shapiro, Max S., and Hendriks, Rhoda A., *Mythologies of the World*.
New York: Doubleday, 1979.

Preface

1 For an analysis of the versions of stories that occur within Greek
Classical mythology see Robert Graves *The Greek Myths*

Foreword

1 Lost Tales I, p. 17.
2 Ibid., p. 24.

Chapter I

1 Graves 1, Vol. 1, p. 12.
2 Ibid., p. 13.
3 Turner, Victor, 'Myth and Symbol', in *International Encyclopaedia
of Social Sciences*, Vol. 10. London: Macmillan, 1968, p. 576.
4 Eliade 1, pp. 5-6.
5 Weisinger, Herbert, 'An Examination of the Myth and Ritual
Approach to Shakespeare', in Murray, Henry A., *Recurrent
Themes in Myth and Mythmaking*, p. 135.
6 Ibid., pp. 135-6.
7 Ruthven, p. 1.
8 Pindar, *Olympians*, I: 28; *Nemeans*, VII: 23.
9 Thucydides, *History*, I: 21, p. 1.
10 Creed, J., 'Uses of Classical Mythology', in Cunningham, A., *The
Theory of Myth*, p. 7 et seq.

11 Strenski, I., 'Mircea Eliade – Some Theoretical Problems', in
    Cunningham, A., *The Theory of Myth*, p. 68.

Chapter 2

1 Leeming, *Mythology*, 1970.
2 This discussion has drawn heavily upon the following: Campbell,
   J., *The Hero With a Thousand Faces*; Leeming, *Mythology*;
   Kluckhohn, C., in Murray, Henry A., *Recurrent Themes in Myth
   and Mythmaking*, pp. 46-61; Weisinger, H., in Murray, Henry A.,
   Recurrent Themes in Myth and Mythmaking, pp. 132-41.
3 Eliot, T. S., *'Ulysses, Order and Myth'*, reprinted in Ellmann, R.,
   and Feidelson, C., *The Modern Tradition*, pp. 679-81, and cited in
   Ruthven, pp. 76-7.
4 Ibid.

Chapter 3

1 Letters, p. 144.
2 LOTR II, 2.
3 LOTR II, 7.
4 LOTR VI, 5.
5 Sil., p. 15.
6 Sil., p. 16.
7 Sil., p. 17.
8 Letters, p. 235n.
9 Sil., p. 20.
10 Sil., p. 17.
11 And, of course, it is the secret fire, the creative spirit, of which
    Gandalf is the servant.
12 UT, p. 401; Sil., pp. 30-1.
13 LOTR I, 7.
14 LOTR II, 2; Foster, p. 388.
15 Sil., p. 29.
16 See Chapter 5.
17 Letters, p. 235.
18 Sil., p. 35.
19 Sil., p. 37.
20 Sil., p. 48.
21 Sil., p. 100.

22 Letters, p. 186.

23 Kocher, *A Reader's Guide,* p. 35.

24 Letters, p. 284.

25 LOTR IV, 4.

26 LOTR IV, 5.

27 Letters, p. 197.

28 Sil., p. 262.

29 Ibid.

30 Letters, p. 176.

31 Letters, p. 236.

32 Sil., pp. 15-16.

33 Sil., p. 301. A similar comment is recorded in LOTR II, 2: 'Into Anduin the Great it fell; and long ago, while Sauron slept, it was rolled down the River to the Sea. There let it lie until the End.'

34 Sil., p. 48.

35 Sil., p. 279.

36 LOTR VI, 5.

37 Sil., p. 44.

38 LOTR VI, 4.

39 Sil., p. 254.

40 UT, p. 395.

41 Helms, *Tolkien and the Silmarils,* p. 25.

42 Kocher, *op. cit.,* p. 3.

43 Sil., p. 187.

44 Sil., p. 265.

45 Foster, p. 254.

46 Biography, p. 93.

47 Ibid.

48 Kocher, *op. cit.,* p. 42.

49 Letters, pp. 286-7.

50 Biography, p. 93.

51 Sil, p. 63.

52 Sil., p. 88.

53 Sil., p. 42.

54 Letters, p. 286.

55 Sil., p. 64.

56 Letters, p. 286; as to a 'Fall' see Letters, p. 203.

57 Foster, p. 117.

58 Letters, p. 202.
59 Ibid.
60 Letters, p. 237.
61 UT, p. 391.
62 Sil., pp. 281-2; LOTR VI, 9.
63 Letters, p. 411.
64 Letters, p. 213.
65 Letters, p. 347.
66 Sil., p. 278.
67 Sil., p. 279.

Chapter 4
1 Tom Shippey, *The Road to Middle-earth.*
2 O'Neill, T.R., *The Individuated Hobbit.*
3 LOTR III, 4.
4 LOTR, Appendices.
5 UT, p. 240.
6 UT, p. 189.
7 Letters, p. 242.
8 *The Hobbit,* chapter 8.
9 Ibid., chapter 10.
10 Ibid.
11 Letters, pp. 185-6.
12 Letters, p. 188.
13 Letters, p. 216.
14 LOTR II, 6.
15 LOTR IV, 8.
16 Ibid.
17 LOTR III, 5.
18 Ibid.
19 LOTR III, 8.
20 LOTR, Appendix A.
21 UT, p. 277.
22 Ibid.
23 UT, p. 403.
24 UT, p. 404.
25 LOTR III, 11.
26 LOTR VI, 5.

27 Sil., p. 295; UT, p. 275.
28 LOTR IV, 5.
29 Sil., pp. 295-6.
30 LOTR III, 6.
31 LOTR III, 2.
32 LOTR IV, 5.
33 UT, p. 228.
34 LOTR III, 8.
35 Letters, p. 152.
36 Letters, p. 153.
37 See *The Mabinogion*; *The Nibelungenlied*.
38 UT, p. 199.
39 Sil., p. 271.
40 Sil., p. 280.
41 Sil., p. 293.
42 LOTR I, 2.

Chapter 5

1 Letters, p. 197.
2 W. H. Auden, 'At the End of the Quest, Victory' reprinted in Becker, A., *The Tolkien Scrapbook*.
3 Letters, p. 242.
4 Kocher, *Reader's Guide*, p. 249.
5 Helms, *Tolkien and the Silmarils*.
6 LOTR II, 2.
7 Sil., p. 17.
8 Ibid.
9 Sil., p. 18.
10 Sil., pp. 65-6.
11 Sil., p. 85.
12 LOTR III, 11.
13 Sil., pp. 254-5, 260.
14 Sil., p. 32.
15 Letters, pp. 243-4.
16 LOTR V, 9.
17 Letters, pp. 152-4.
18 LOTR I, 2.
19 LOTR II, 2.

20 Ibid.
21 LOTR IV, 5.
22 LOTR IV, 1.
23 LOTR VI, 3.
24 Ibid.
25 Letters, p. 160.
26 In 'On Fairy-Stories' Tolkien describes the imperative as 'thou shalt not or else thou shall depart beyond into endless regret'.
27 Letters, p. 195.

Chapter 6

1 Lesky, p. 2.
2 Lesky, p. 8.
3 *Hamlet*, 1:5.
4 *Macbeth*, 111:4.
5 *Macbeth*, V: 5.
6 Lesky, p. 45.
7 Letters, p. 150.
8 UT, pp. 58-9.
9 UT, p. 60.
10 UT, p. 64.
11 Ibid.
12 Sil., p. 208.
13 Ibid.
14 Sil., p. 210.
15 Sil., p. 211.
16 Sil., p. 223.
17 Sil., p. 224.
18 LOTR II, 2.
19 LOTR VI, 3.
20 Ibid.
21 Letters, p. 328.

Chapter 7

1 Sil., p. 241.
2 LOTR II, 6.
3 The original Elessar was made by Enerdhil, the jewel-smith of Gondolin, and was worn by Eärendil. *Unfinished Tales* (pp. 248–52)

does not make it clear that this was the stone that Aragorn wore. One version of the tale is that Olórin brought the Elessar as a token from Yavanna. The other is that it was made by Celebrimbor, and was given to Galadriel. That the Elessar was destined for the Returning King, links Aragorn with his ancestor Eärendil. A third, and highly speculative, view could be that the Elessar came to Elrond, son of Eärendil, from his father, especially having regard to the fact that it appears to have passed from Galadriel's House to that of Elrond frequently.

4   LOTR II, 9.
5   LOTR III, 2.
6   LOTR III, 11.
7   LOTR V, 2.
8   Ibid.

Chapter 8

1   Sil., p. 102.
2   Sil., p. 105.
3   Sil., p. 148.
4   Sil., p. 194.
5   Sil., pp. 248-9.
6   LOTR II, 2.
7   LOTR IV, 8.
8   Biography, pp 64, 71.
9   LOTR III, 5.
10 Helms, *Tolkien and the Silmarils*, p. 38.
11 Letters, p. 148n.
12 John I: 1-14.
13 Sil., p. 37.
14 Sil., p. 69.
15 Sil., p. 76.

Chapter 9

1   James Frazer, *The Golden Bough*. London: Macmillan, 1960 (abridged edition), p. 13.
2   Richard Cavendish, *King Arthur and the Grail*. London: Weidenfeld and Nicolson, 1978, p. 128.
3   Ibid. pp. 140-1.

4   UT, p. 367.
5   LOTR III, 6.
6   LOTR V, 1.
7   LOTR V, 7.
8   Ibid.
9   Letters, pp. 419-20.
10 Letters, p. 26.
11 Letters, p. 178.
12 Letters, p. 192.
13 Ibid.
14 Foster; David Day, *A Tolkien Bestiary.*
15 LOTR I, 7.
16 LOTR II, 2.

Chapter 10

1   LOTR, Prologue.
2   LOTR Appendix A.
3   LOTR III, 8.
4   LOTR, Prologue.
5   Letters, p. 365.
6   LOTR III, 8.
7   LOTR I, 2.
8   Letters, p. 158.
9   Letters, p. 197.
10 Letters, p. 288.
11 Letters, p. 365.
12 LOTR I, 2.
13 LOTR, Prologue.
14 LOTR I, 8.
15 LOTR I, 7.
16 LOTR I, 10.
17 Ibid.
18 LOTR I, 12.
19 LOTR II, 3.
20 LOTR III, 10.
21 LOTR III, 9.
22 Letters, p. 329.
23 Ibid.

24 Such as herbs and rabbit.
25 LOTR IV, 10.
26 LOTR VI, 1.
27 Ibid.
28 LOTR VI, 7.
29 LOTR VI, 8.

INDEX